CHOCOLATE ECLAIRVOYANT

CHOCOLATE ECLAIRVOYANT

AUNTIE CLEM'S BAKERY
BOOK TWENTY-SIX

P.D. WORKMAN

PD WORKMAN

ISBN: 9781774688830 (KDP Paperback)
ISBN: 9781774688847 (KDP Hardcover)
ISBN: 9781774688861 (Lulu Paperback)
ISBN: 9781774688854 (Large Print)
ISBN: 9781774688878 (Digital)
ISBN: 9781774688885 (Auto-narrated audiobook)

ALSO BY P.D. WORKMAN

MYSTERY/SUSPENSE:

Auntie Clem's Bakery

Culinary & Pet Cozy Mysteries

Gluten-Free Murder

Dairy-Free Death

Allergen-Free Assignation

Witch-Free Halloween (Halloween Short)

Canine-Free Christmas Caper (Christmas Short)

Stirring Up Murder

Brewing Death

Coup de Glace

Sour Cherry Turnover

Apple-achian Treasure

Vegan Baked Alaska

Muffins Masks Murder

Tai Chi and Chai Tea

Santa Shortbread

Cold as Ice Cream

Changing Fortune Cookies

Hot on the Trail Mix

Fateful Plateful

Cut Out Cookie

On the Slab Pie

Wedding Cake Crush

A Waffle Death

Murder Meringue Pie

A Fowl Play on Christmas Day (Christmas crossover story)

Cinn-Full Secrets

Muffin to Lose

Custard Cream Conspiracy

Mock Apple Alibi

Chocolate Eclairvoyant (Coming Soon)

Quiche Me Goodbye (Coming Soon)

Recipes from Auntie Clem's Bakery

Parks Pat Mysteries

Police Procedural Set in Canada

Out with the Sunset

Long Climb to the Top

Dark Water Under the Bridge

Immersed in the View

Skimming Over the Lake

Hazard of the Hills

Knows the Hills

Spanning the Creek

Sanctuary in the Stream

Echoes of the Engine

Bench with a View

Beneath the Icy Depths

Grounded in the Wind

Reservoir of Secrets

Peril in the Blooms

AND MORE AT PDWORKMAN.COM

To the mama bears, papa bears, and all of the protectors.

CHAPTER 1

*H*arold watched Erin take the tray of eclairs out of the oven. The tops were golden brown and they had puffed out perfectly. Erin handled the tray gently, hoping they wouldn't collapse the instant she put them down or they started to cool. She was hopeful that she had the balance of ingredients right this time and that they would hold their shape so she could fill and glaze them without making a big mess.

The results were always delicious, even if they didn't look good, but she wanted them to look good. She wanted the gluten-free eclairs to be practically indistinguishable from the traditional eclairs made by the pastry chefs in French patisseries for generations.

She knew how it should work in theory, the way that the moisture content of the choux should make the pastries puff up. And the first few attempts had puffed, but they had not stayed that way for long.

"Do you think it will work?" Harold asked eagerly. "They look great!"

"Fingers crossed," Erin told him. She hoped that if she cooled them slowly, they would have the chance to "set" before the pastry cooled too much and they would maintain their shape.

"At least we know they'll taste good!" Vic, Erin's young baking assistant contributed, as she placed spoonfuls of cookie dough on a baking sheet on the adjacent counter in the kitchen of Auntie Clem's Bakery.

"Yeah," Harold agreed. "I almost hope they don't work because the failures taste so good."

"You're not going to be able to keep up with the failures," Erin said. "Even if you share them with your family and fill your freezer!"

"I can try," Harold declared, thrusting out his stomach and patting it. He had the long, lanky frame of an adolescent, and being a celiac, he was on the skinny side to begin with. At least with Erin moving into Bald Eagle Falls and opening Auntie Clem's Bakery, a bakery devoted exclusively to gluten-free baking, he now had a wide variety of delicious baked goods to choose from.

Before Auntie Clem's, there hadn't been many gluten-free options for celiacs in the county. A few prepackaged breads and cookies on the grocery store shelves. One or two stores in the city that brought in a wider variety of goods at shockingly high prices. Or else what mothers could make at home. Modern moms were busy with a lot of outside commitments. They couldn't all spend time slaving over the oven, trying to learn the baffling array of new ingredients and techniques necessary to master gluten-free baking. Especially if their kids also had to be dairy-free or had other allergens, which, luckily, Harold did not.

"How did the custard taste?" Erin asked, going over to the fridge to ensure it was ready for her once the eclairs had completely cooled.

Harold grinned. "What makes you think I tasted it?"

Erin and Vic both laughed. "Because you always taste it," Erin chuckled. She pushed a few locks of dark hair that had escaped her bobby pins back into place and washed her hands. Her hair was too short to keep pulled back into a sleek ponytail like Vic's fine blond hair, and she suspected that even if it were long enough, it would still refuse to stay corralled by the elastic.

At the jingle of bells from the front of the bakery, Erin and Vic both left the kitchen to enter the storefront area and serve their next customer. Vic stood behind the till and Erin behind the display case, ready for the next sale.

But instead of a customer, it was Frank Grayson, delivering the day's mail.

"Oh, hi, Frank," Erin greeted, giving him a warm smile. "How's it going?"

"A real pretty day out there," Frank told her, using his forearm to wipe a bead of sweat that trickled down from his temple. "Perfect day for a picnic."

He handed over a thick wad of mail, wrapped neatly with a couple of rubber bands.

"Couple new catalogs in there," he observed, knowing how Erin loved to pore over the baking supplies and equipment catalogs to see what she could pick up for a good price, drooling over the more expensive equipment she could not afford, and fantasizing about how it could transform the bakery.

"Thank you!"

"Y'all have a nice day," he told them, and turned to continue to the next store on his route, the Book Nook. He allowed a group of women to enter the bakery, nodding and holding the door open like a gentleman before going on.

Erin nodded to the group, including Mrs. Peach, her next-door neighbor, and Betty Thompson, two seniors who used walkers. Edna, a woman who worked at the library with Betty, was with them, as well as a couple of younger women Erin didn't know well but who occasionally came for the ladies' tea on Sunday.

"We are going to take a few minutes," Betty warned. Erin knew it was true. Betty always took a long time to look over the offerings in the display case, ask her questions about the ingredients or how they were prepared, and finally decide what to buy.

The other women might make their choices faster, but they would wait for Betty to figure out what she wanted first. There was a sort of "order of seniority" that the customers followed. Erin didn't always follow what gave one person priority over another, she just went with the flow.

Erin took the rubber bands off of the mail and shuffled through it quickly, handing a couple of note cards over to Vic. There had been a lot more mail since word of Willie's death had gotten out. A lot of condolence cards, flower deliveries, casseroles, and myriad other sympathies expressed with small-town charm. For once, people seemed to have put aside their judgments about Vic being transgender and were just treating her as they would any other woman.

What was left was primarily bills, flyers, and catalogs. Erin turned to take them to her office to review later. Vic flapped one of the cards at her. "This one is addressed to you."

Erin took it back and looked at it. She had just assumed all the personal notes and cards would be for Vic and hadn't looked at the addressee name. But her name was neatly written on the envelope.

"Oh, sorry. I didn't even notice." Curious, she slid her thumb under the corner of the flap to tear it open.

She unfolded the crisp stationery and looked at the sentences penned inside with a frown.

"What does it say?" Vic asked, reading something in Erin's expression.

Erin read the words aloud slowly as if saying them precisely would make them make sense.

A recipe long forgotten stirs trouble anew— Vengeance and blood will soon ensue. Tread carefully, I see danger brew!

CHAPTER 2

"W hat?" Vic's eyes were wide with alarm.

Erin looked back down at the neat loops of the handwritten note.

"What is this?" she demanded.

"I don't know. That's really weird," Vic said, shaking her head. "Where did it come from?"

Erin turned the envelope over, but there was no return address. She looked for a postmark, but of course, everything was machine-processed now, and the barcode meant nothing to her.

"I don't know. Maybe Frank knows."

"Who would send such a thing?" Mrs. Peach asked.

It wasn't until then that Erin realized she had read the letter aloud in front of customers. She had been so stunned by the contents of the letter that she had not even thought about them. She had just fastened on to the little verse and read it to Vic without regard to the other people within earshot.

"Oh!" She folded the letter along the original fold lines. "I'm sure it's just a prank. Someone having a bit of fun."

"That didn't sound like a joke," Betty argued. "It sounded like a threat."

"No, not a threat," Edna disagreed. "It said 'I see,' like it is a prediction or vision. That isn't a threat."

"No one can see the future," Mrs. Peach pointed out. "Someone is trying to make trouble."

"Or it is a prank," Erin repeated. "Sometimes people just make things up, try to get people excited."

"They obviously want to stir things up," Vic agreed. "I mean… it says so right in the verse."

Erin looked back down at it, giving a little laugh. "I guess it does," she agreed. "I don't think this is anything to worry about. Just someone playing a game."

"It's not very funny," Betty said. "It's in very poor taste."

"Yes," Erin agreed. She tucked it into her apron pocket. "And I'm sorry I read it out. I wasn't thinking. Did you decide what you wanted to buy?" She directed her gaze to the food inside the display case, hoping to distract everyone from the letter. "Those chocolate chunk cookies are fresh from the oven."

Betty was still scowling about the letter and did not look at the chocolate chunk cookies. Mrs. Peach tried to help.

"Oh, those look very good," she agreed. "Now, what about these? Butterscotch bars? I don't think I've had those before."

"They are delicious," Erin obliged. "Melt in your mouth. I highly recommend them. They have a shortbread crust, and if there's one thing about gluten-free flours, they make great shortbread."

"They sound wonderful," Mrs. Peach agreed. "Do you want some of those, Betty?"

"I want to know who sent that letter. Sending a letter like that is a dangerous thing!"

"Dangerous?" Erin echoed.

"You could incite a panic. People are very impressionable."

Erin thought that "dangerous" was probably a stretch. It might concern some people, but they would quickly see that it was just a made-up prediction.

"What if it really is a vision?" Edna asked. "You can't deny that there are fortune-tellers who can catch glimpses of the future."

"It is not a vision," Betty told her sharply. She was determined to shut down this suggestion. "There is no such thing as clairvoyance."

Edna drew herself up to her full height, which, due to her age, was not great. She stood as tall as her permanently hunched spine would allow, making herself as imposing and authoritative as she could.

"'There shall not be found among you anyone who... practices divination or tells fortunes,'" she quoted. "Why would that warning be in the Bible if there was no such thing as clairvoyance?"

"It means no one should claim to have clairvoyance," Betty shot back. "Not that seeing the future is a real thing."

"That's not what it says," Edna disagreed. "There *is* real clairvoyance, and we are warned against practicing it or having people among us to practice it."

"I don't think we need to worry that a grievance over an old recipe is going to cause bloodshed," Erin said lightly, putting as much humor into her voice as she could. Never mind the recipe book that had recently caused them so much trouble. Or the muffins that had brought death into her sphere more than once. "Now, what can I get you ladies?"

Edna, Betty, and Mrs. Peach eyed each other, but no one stepped forward to continue the argument. Erin nodded, hoping that would be the end of it. She was kicking herself for having read the note aloud without thinking. After all that had happened in Bald Eagle Falls, she should have known better.

"Those butterscotch bars are mighty tasty," Vic prodded.

"I don't know," Betty said, unwilling to give up the conversation yet. "I think we need to be concerned about this threat. Maybe you should call the police, dear."

Erin smiled. "I will take it up with Officer Piper. I'm sure he'll have some good advice on it."

Betty's scowl softened slightly. "He is a fine young man."

"Yes, he is," Erin agreed. "And I'll be sure to tell him you said so."

Betty giggled at that, sounding more like a teen girl than the mature woman she was.

"Everybody loves Officer Handsome," Vic teased.

"Well, he's my Officer Handsome, so everyone else had better just look and not touch."

Vic and Betty chuckled about this. Erin felt that the tension had broken and things would be okay now. The ladies would forget about the letter and its strange prediction, and her faux pas in reading it aloud in front of the customers would be forgiven.

Sometimes, Erin thought she was doing a pretty good job navigating the Bald Eagle Falls social environment. She was getting better at predicting what things would be acceptable or unacceptable to the church ladies. What things were just "not done" in the South. What people expected from her.

And sometimes, she felt like she was still out of her depth, flailing around and trying to stay afloat while people pelted her with more unhelpful rules rather than helping her find her way safely back to shore.

Betty made her selections, and Erin breathed a sigh of relief as she paid for her order and headed for the door. Edna and Mrs. Peach placed their orders without any further comment on the letter's predictions. Once they were on their way with their baking, Erin felt like she was safely ashore again.

She smiled tentatively at the women still waiting to be served. Both were regulars, but not usually inclined to visit or say anything other than make a few comments on the weather or Erin's latest new creations in the display case.

"What can I do for you today?" Erin asked Tara Waldon.

Tara was older than Erin, but not as old as Edna and Mrs. Peach. Erin suspected she was around sixty. She had long dark hair and a penchant for bold, bright colors. She looked into the display case, a frown on her face. She glanced at Vic at the cash register, and spoke to Erin in a low voice.

"I really don't think it is appropriate for you to joke around and act so silly, especially about your boyfriend, when *she* has just lost hers."

Erin caught her breath and tried to figure out what to say to this. As far as the rest of Bald Eagle Falls was concerned, Vic's partner, Willie Andrews, who had recently taken up leadership of a local crime family, the Dyson clan, had been assassinated by factions within the clan.

What they didn't know was that the so-called assassination had just been a sham, set up by Willie and a few loyal friends, as a way for Willie to get out of the clan. Willie would remain dead in the eyes of the Bald Eagle Falls residents until Willie felt that Nelson Dyson's leadership of the syndicate was secure and he could afford for it to be known that he had actually left the clan.

So, for the time being, Erin and her best friend and employee had to continue the act that Willie was dead and Vic was deep in mourning.

"Oh…" Erin swallowed. "I'm sorry, Vic. I didn't mean to… make you feel bad."

"You are a nice girl. You should be more careful," Tara told her firmly. "Be more sensitive to her feelings."

Erin nodded her agreement. Vic tried to find a way to move Tara past the topic. "I was joking around too," she said, "It wasn't Erin being insensitive. Sometimes… you just have to laugh. You need something to pull you out of your funk. When my maw-maw died, we went home and put on the silliest, most slapstick movie we could find. It was just the only way to move on."

Tara shook her head, but didn't tell Vic that there was something wrong with her if she was able to laugh about things after her romantic partner was killed. But Erin had the distinct feeling she was thinking it.

"Everyone mourns differently," Vic declared. "I just… want to go on as normal. Sitting around at home isn't going to do anything for me. I need to work. To keep my hands and mind busy with other things. I don't want to just sit at home thinking about Willie all the time."

Especially since Willie was hiding out at Vic's place, and if Vic spent all day there, they got on each other's nerves. It was easier to just follow their regular routine and leave Willie to entertain himself as he had while he'd been going through chelation therapy.

Tara sniffed and turned her attention to the display case. "Well, I do think you are not being very sensitive to your friend's needs," she told Erin. "She shouldn't have to feel like she has to come to work and put on a brave face for everyone."

Erin opened her mouth to object, then changed her mind. She nodded solemnly. "Yes, you're right," she agreed. "We'll need to sit down and have a talk about this. I hadn't thought about it that way."

Tara looked at her for a moment longer, then nodded. "Good," she pronounced. "Now, then... I think I will go with a loaf of multigrain, six dinner rolls, and a pizza shell. And maybe... a half dozen of the butterscotch bars."

"Great." Erin gathered the items and put them into boxes or bags. "And thank you for your advice."

When both women had been served and left the bakery, Erin turned to Vic, shaking her head.

"Am I ever glad that you are *not* mourning Willie. I don't know if I could handle it."

"You did pretty good while we both thought he was dead."

But Erin had been a wreck before Willie had shown up, revealing that he was, in fact, still alive. She couldn't stop crying, set off by seeing her best friend in such pain. She had wanted to hold her, to make her feel better when there was nothing she could do to take away the pain or make it better.

"Don't worry about Tara," Vic said. "Mary Lou said she used to do family dispute mediation. So she is always meddling in other people's relationships, thinking she needs to fix them."

"Really? That would be a tough job."

Vic nodded. "No kidding. I like helping other people out, but couples or family counseling... I don't think I could handle that."

"Was that true about when your maw-maw died?"

Vic nodded. "Yeah, sure. Sometimes, the only way to stop crying is by laughing. She wouldn't have wanted us sitting around weeping over her. She would have been drinking, cracking jokes, and getting the grandkids together for a game of poker."

Erin laughed. "She must have been some woman."

"She was!" Vic agreed. "And I want to grow up to be just like her."

CHAPTER 3

*S*peaking of Officer Handsome," Vic said, "don't look now, but here he comes."

Erin looked out the front window and saw Terry walking down the other side of Main Street with K9, his German Shepherd. When they reached the end of the block, he would cross the street and come down the other side, stopping in at the bakery for a refill of his water bottle and a gluten-free doggie biscuit for K9.

Erin eagerly anticipated Terry Piper's visits while she was working. Some weeks, it seemed like she hardly ever saw him because his work schedule did not align with her bakery schedule. She was getting home from the bakery just when he was getting ready for an evening shift.

She looked at the clock on the wall. "We should get those loaves in the oven before the supper rush."

Vic raised her brows at Erin. Erin ignored the knowing look and took the mail she had set to the side to her tiny office in the back. Harold already had the loaves in the oven, as Erin had expected.

The warm kitchen was filled with the yeasty smell of the baking bread and the buttery aroma of the freshly-baked eclairs.

"Look at your pastries," he told Erin, motioning to the oblong eclairs, which he had transferred from the trays to the wire racks to finish cooling. "They are holding their shape."

Erin broke into a grin. "That's awesome. They look really good, don't they? What time did you put them on the cooling racks? We'll need to make sure we don't move them too soon in the future."

He checked the time and worked it out, and Erin updated the detailed notes she had been keeping on the eclair project progress.

"They are going to be so good!" Harold enthused. "Are they going to be chocolate? Are you using a chocolate fondant topping?"

"Yes. We'll start with the traditional flavors and then branch out into some more adventurous ones when we've got the classics down pat."

"Like what?"

"Maybe invert them and have a chocolate filling and vanilla topping. Maybe coffee, cinnamon, or strawberry fillings. There are a lot of possibilities, once you've got the shell working."

"I guess this means I don't get any to take home today," Harold said mournfully.

"I'm sure you have enough of the failures in your freezer to keep you going for a few weeks."

"I could still fit a few more in."

"You can help us taste test the successes, but you won't be able to take them all home."

Harold grinned and shrugged his narrow shoulders. "Okay."

Erin shook her head and returned to the front of the bakery. Her timing was good, and Terry was just coming in the door with K9.

"Ah, there she is," Vic commented. "Everything okay in the kitchen?"

"The eclairs worked!"

"Mercy. Those are going to be delicious." Vic put her hand over her stomach. "I'm really going to have to be careful!"

Vic was quite a bit taller than Erin and didn't have to worry as much about putting on weight. Erin felt like every dessert she consumed showed on her waist because she was so short.

"Eclairs?" Terry repeated.

Erin looked at him. She had been talking about the eclairs for days now. He sounded like he hadn't heard a word of it. As if this were the first time anyone had mentioned anything to do with eclairs.

"Yes, the new recipe I have been working on," Erin told him sternly. "You know. The ones I have been talking about."

"Oh, yeah. Sorry, I thought you said something else. Glad to hear they are coming together. Who doesn't love an eclair?"

Good recovery. Erin shook her head. He had better watch out, or he was really going to put his foot in his mouth one of these days. She remembered when he used to hang on every word she said. Now, he was too easily distracted by the game on TV or what was happening at work. She was no longer a mystery to him. Or he didn't think he had to work to get her, now that they were living together.

"Were you going to tell him about the letter?" Vic asked.

"Well… not now. I was going to save that for later."

"What letter?" Terry asked curiously.

"Just a weird letter I got today. Somebody playing a prank. It's nothing. It just upset some of the ladies. I shouldn't have read it while anyone was here."

He leaned on the counter, frowning at Erin. "Maybe you should give me the details. I don't understand what kind of letter you are talking about. Weird? Prank? Upsetting?"

"It's just…" Erin tried to think of how to describe it, but there was no point in delaying and trying to talk around it. She might as well just show it to him.

Erin pulled it from her apron pocket and unfolded it. She held it out in front of Terry. He stepped closer to look at it. He frowned.

"Well, that is a weird letter," he admitted. "Is it supposed to be a threat? A poem? Or just a prank, like you said?"

"I think it is just a prank. But some of the ladies who were here this afternoon thought that… it was a threat or witchcraft. I guess wild predictions now fall under fortune-telling."

"Well, I can see how mentions of blood and violence would be upsetting, though not why fortune telling would be more upsetting. I guess… people come at things from their own perspective. And for some people, that is always a religious stance."

"Do *you* think people can predict the future? And that if they can, it's witchcraft and you should… I don't know, what do they do with modern witches?"

She had a sudden recollection of a recent call from Reg. Though Reg Rawlins, a foster sister of Erin's, tried to keep her conversations with Erin fairly low-key, she often went off on a tangent to make commentaries on paranormal concepts or people around her that she claimed were witches. Erin only knew one witch, and she wasn't the type who thought she could perform magic spells. But Reg's current fortune-telling scam and paranoia led her to believe some bizarre stuff and apparently attracted some like-minded individuals.

"People see and hear what they want to," Reg told Erin during their last call. "If they don't believe in something, they won't be persuaded by anything that happens around them. They'll think it is just a scam or a trick."

That's because it is just a scam, Erin wanted to tell Reg. But she didn't want to hurt Reg or make her too mad to call back again. As different as the two of them were, Erin didn't want a permanent rift between them.

Reg had performed some pretty nifty tricks when she and Erin had been younger. Erin knew her scams could be very convincing. But their foster parents had worked hard to disabuse Erin of the idea that Reg really was magic or hearing spirits. They explained to her about Reg's diagnosed mental illness and how it could affect her perceptions of the world around her. It wasn't that Reg was lying or trying to fool her. She just wasn't well. Her brain didn't work the same way as Erin's.

"Some people are skilled prognosticators," Terry said slowly. "I don't think that makes them magic, just good at predicting the future. And this letter doesn't fall into that category. This is more like what a sideshow fortune-teller does. Making broad, vague predictions and allowing people to interpret them to fit their circumstances."

"Yeah." Erin turned the paper around to reread the words

herself. "I mean, a recipe... obviously, this is a bakery, and we're bound to come across an old or forgotten one at some point. And everybody is going to experience danger at some point, no matter how hard you try to avoid it."

Terry nodded his agreement. "And vengeance and blood... those are still pretty general. A lot of people want to get back at someone for something they did in the past. Everyone has had a disagreement or has had someone cross them somehow." He shrugged. "That's all she's doing."

"So you don't think it's anything to worry about, right?" Erin asked. "I can just toss this out."

"I don't see a problem tossing it. There is no threat. Predicting blood and threatening it are not the same thing."

"Good." Erin folded it and put it back into her apron pocket. She looked at Vic. "It's just a prank. Someone trying to get people upset for no good reason. There's no need to be concerned about it."

"No, because nothing bad ever happens in Bald Eagle Falls," Vic returned. "It isn't like we've never *seen* blood and vengeance here."

Erin hoped that, for once, they had seen the end of violence in Bald Eagle Falls. Or at least with Erin's or Vic's involvement in it. The clans would be able to find stability now, and the violence that had accompanied the friction between the two factions would fade from their lives. The clans might still be running illegal operations, but it wouldn't impinge on the lives of Erin, Vic, or the others in their circle of friends. They could live their lives baking cookies and eclairs and not be concerned.

Terry looked at his watch. "I'd better be getting on my way," he told them. "I'll see you tonight."

"You're off for supper, right?"

"Yes... but I've got a bit of paperwork to process. I don't know, you might want to plan on supper without me tonight, and we'll have something nice tomorrow. Tonight, we'll just... have some time after that. Before bed."

Erin sighed. "Okay. You're going to order something at the police department, then?"

"Yes, I'll have something brought in so that I can push through and get the paperwork done. Then I won't have it on my mind tonight."

Erin nodded. "See you later, then."

He leaned in to give her a peck on the cheek, then took his partner back outside to continue the investigation.

CHAPTER 4

*E*rin drove Vic home, as usual. It was the logical thing to do when Vic lived in the loft apartment over Erin's garage. They had space of their own when they needed it, and closeness when they wanted that. Even spending all day together at work, they often spent time in the evening or on weekends or holidays. They just really enjoyed their time together.

"Don't make anything," Vic told Erin as they got out of the yellow VW bug. "I'm going to bring something over."

"You're going to bring something over? What?"

"I haven't decided yet. What are you in the mood for?"

Erin shook her head. "Doesn't matter. Anything I don't have to make."

"Perfect. I'll bring you something, then. You'll be surprised and delighted."

Erin smiled, preparing herself to be surprised and delighted. After letting herself in through the back door, Erin walked to the front to check for deliveries or messages.

Ever since Willie's supposed death, she had been receiving packages for Vic. They didn't want anyone going to the loft where they might accidentally encounter Willie, so Erin and Vic had told people to please send all deliveries or offerings to Erin.

"We don't want anyone tripping on those rickety stairs," Erin said, though the stairs were perfectly level and solid, not at all rickety. "And half the time, deliveries end up going to my front door anyway, because people don't understand there is another residence on the same lot."

"Besides, I don't want to have to deal with getting it all sorted out or having to make my place presentable for people," Vic added, with a quivering lip. "Erin can take care of that for me."

Erin picked up a potted African violet that had been left on her step and pulled a sticky note off the door. She placed them on the table where Vic would see them when she arrived.

"Oh, ain't that purty," Vic commented when she saw the little purple violet. "Who sent that?" She opened the small envelope clipped onto a plastic stick pushed into the dirt. "Oh, my Aunt Vi." She shook her head. "Bless her heart, the woman hasn't had a kind word to say to me since I came out as a woman. Very anti."

"Well, maybe she's over it," Erin said with a shrug. "She didn't have to send you anything."

Vic nodded. She looked at the sticky note. "And a dinner from Susan Brown, the owner of the family restaurant. Just give them a call whatever night I want it. Isn't that sweet?"

"Are you sure you don't want to do that tonight?" Erin asked, nodding to the covered dish Vic had brought over from the loft.

"Lands, no." Vic removed the lid from the casserole, revealing a macaroni casserole. "Baked mac and cheese. Don't know when the last time I had one of these was, but it used to be one of my favorites. You know, whenever Ma was cooking for a funeral."

"Okay, throw it in the oven. I'm going to have a quick shower while it warms."

Vic agreed.

Orange Blossom, Erin's big orange cat wandered into the kitchen and gave a long, languorous stretch, quivering from his nose to his tail, followed by a wide-mouthed yawn before sniffing the air to determine whether Vic's dish contained tuna fish or anything else he might like.

"Sorry, no tuna today," Vic apologized. "Just macaroni."

Blossom sniffed the air again before turning to Erin with a loud, piteous meow. The poor creature had obviously been starving all day. Erin reached down and scratched his ears.

"Oh, you poor thing."

Blossom yowled and rubbed against Erin's hand, his front paws lifting from the floor. He dropped back to all fours and meowed again, loudly and insistently.

"You poor, poor thing," Erin teased. She petted his head and stroked his back. Blossom pulled away from her and licked down the fur on his back with swift, decisive movements. He glared at Erin.

"You don't want nice pets?"

He rubbed against her leg and wound around her insistently, his demands getting louder.

Vic and Erin laughed. Erin went to the pantry and opened a new can of cat treats.

"Look at this; you even get a nice fresh package! Isn't that worth waiting for?"

He meowed impatiently while she removed the foil seal and took a couple of treats out. She slid them across the floor and Orange Blossom galloped after them, skittering on the floor. After Orange Blossom demonstrated his prowess a few more times, Erin put some wet and dry food in his dishes, got out a carrot and some other veggies for Marshmallow, the rabbit, and headed again toward the bathroom for a shower.

"Hold down the fort," she told Vic. "And don't let them tell you they're still starving."

"Oh, I know," Vic agreed. "Nilla is the same way. It doesn't matter whether Willie has just fed that little varmint five minutes earlier; he'll still bark and whine like he hasn't had anything for a week."

Erin knew very well that while she was in the shower, Vic would still sneak the animals another treat as she waited for the casserole to bake.

When Erin stepped back out of the bathroom, the air was filled with the rich, savory smell of the macaroni casserole. The animals were happy, Orange Blossom washing in a patch of sunlight in the living room and Marshmallow approaching Erin for a few ear scratches.

"That smells wonderful," Erin told Vic.

"Don't it just." Vic tapped out a message on her phone and opened the oven to take out the casserole.

"We should probably have some vegetables to go with that," Erin suggested. "Just straight dairy and carbs will not do this figure any good." She slid her thumb behind her waistband, wincing at how tight it was.

"I threw together a salad," Vic nodded to the counter where a green salad was waiting, "and nuked some peas in the microwave." She wrinkled her nose. "Don't know why we have to ruin a perfectly good meal with vegetables, but…"

Erin grinned. Even though Vic didn't need to watch what she ate quite as closely as Erin did, she was usually pretty careful to eat balanced meals.

She opened the cupboard to get out the plates.

"For three," Vic advised.

"Willie is coming over?"

"That man is going stir crazy. I'm going to take him out to one of his mines and leave him there for a week. He'll be much happier out in the wilderness than being cooped up in my apartment all the time."

Erin looked at her and didn't bother to point out that Vic still hadn't gotten herself a driver's license. Terry had gotten after her for driving a couple of times before, and she was normally happy to just be Erin's or Willie's passenger, but she had been known to borrow a vehicle and take off on her own on occasion.

"I know, I know," Vic held up her hands in surrender and rolled her eyes. "Don't let Terry know."

"Just tell me beforehand, and I can drive him somewhere."

"Drive who?"

CHAPTER 5

*E*rin looked up as Willie came in the door. He gave her a friendly smile.

"You're not looking half bad for a dead man," Erin told him. He was of average height, a little heavyset, and while Erin had known him, his skin had always been stained dark from his mining and processing activities. But since he had been forced to admit how he was being poisoned by the heavy metals he was exposed to and had to mend his ways, using more modern processing methods and protective gear, his skin had lightened several shades.

His dark stubble was more visible than ever, now that it contrasted with his lighter skin. He still looked like a homeless guy in his ball cap and blue jeans, but not so grubby. She had been afraid of him the first time she had met him. Now she knew he was a good guy, a protective watchdog for her and Vic, and would do anything to protect them. Including pretending to be dead.

"I feel like I'm doing nothing but sitting around watching soaps all day. Need to get out and do something."

"Well, until you're ready for everyone to know you're not really dead, you'd better keep your head down. You want me to drop you off somewhere? Vic said something about dropping you down a mineshaft."

Willie looked at Vic as she carried the hot casserole dish to the table. Vic shook her head.

"I didn't say down a mineshaft. Just... abandoning you somewhere."

She set the dish down on a hot pad and gave a little shriek as Willie grabbed her and kissed her. Vic pushed herself away from him after a minute, laughing, her cheeks flushed a bright red.

"You're a beast," she teased.

"Yes, and tired of being cooped up in a cage all day. Being abandoned out in the wilderness doesn't sound half bad."

He had always been a solitary person, so it wasn't the fact that he was alone in Vic's apartment that was making him crazy. It was the fact that he needed to be doing something. He had fixed everything he could in Vic's apartment in the first few days, and aside from doing a complete renovation, there wasn't much left for him to occupy himself. Erin couldn't see any problem with dropping him off on one of his isolated properties in the backwoods. No one would see him to report to the Dyson clan that he wasn't really dead.

"Well, you decide where you want to go and pack your bags, and I'll drop you off in the middle of the night," Erin promised.

"Better not be the middle of the night. You need your sleep. But next time you have an afternoon off, or if you want to drop me off before bed some night, it might just save our relationship."

Willie smiled at Vic, who took it all in good humor. She probably wouldn't mind a little space to herself, either. They were both independent, and Willie hadn't moved in full-time before his "death." But he couldn't turn on lights at his house or be seen coming and going by his neighbors when he was supposed to be dead.

Erin hadn't seen or heard any big blow-ups between them like they'd had before and during Willie's chelation therapy for heavy metal poisoning. She'd been worried for a while there about things getting physical. Willie had not been himself.

But he was back to his old self now, laid back and pleasant most of the time, though she was sure he and Vic still butted heads over some things and got on each other's nerves living too close together.

The three of them worked together to set the table and sat down to eat. The macaroni casserole was creamy and topped with crispy, savory breadcrumbs. The rich scent of melted cheese filled the air, and Erin wished she could eat the whole dish. But she limited herself to one small serving and rounded out the meal with the salad and peas.

They had just barely sat down when there was a scratching at the back door, and Vic got up to let in Nilla, the little white dog she had adopted after the death of his owner. He ran in and immediately approached Orange Blossom, earning himself a hiss and a swipe at his nose. Undeterred, Nilla ran over to Marshmallow. All Marshmallow did was thump his back legs on the floor, not kicking Nilla in the face. Nilla ran to the front door, barking and wagging his tail—and the rest of his body—excitedly.

"You just came inside," Vic told him in exasperation. "If you want to play outside, you go out back."

But the lock on the door turned, and Terry opened the door. Nilla rushed up to greet K9 and jump up on Terry's legs. Terry growled and pushed him back. "Down, Nilla. Sit."

Nilla growled and backed up. He barked his objections at Terry, who stomped one foot to back him up more. Nilla tended not to like men other than Willie. Even though he knew Terry and was used to him, they were not great friends.

Terry pointed to the back door. "Go play outside," he told K9.

K9 eagerly dashed for the back door, and Nilla followed. Vic let the two dogs out into the backyard and stood at the door for a moment, watching them. She turned back to the table.

"I thought you weren't going to make it for dinner!" Erin told Terry. She smiled to let him know she was pleased, not disappointed, by his unexpected arrival.

"I managed to get things cleared up faster than I expected, so I took the chance you would still be eating or there would be leftovers." He sniffed the air and nodded approvingly at the table. "I have to say I am not disappointed to give up fast food for one night."

"Oh, you have to try this casserole," Erin told him, "I've never tasted anything so good."

Vic put another plate and cutlery on the table at Terry's chair. It made for a cozy table, but Erin didn't mind.

"It's to die for," Willie quipped.

"Oh, that's terrible," Vic giggled, slapping him lightly on the arm.

She and Terry sat down in their places and resumed the meal.

"So," Willie wiped his mouth with the back of his hand. "Any chatter? Is everything still quiet?"

"Haven't picked up any rumors of you being alive. You're safe for the time being. Although, I thought you were going to stay inside at Vic's to avoid anyone seeing you."

Willie shrugged. "I think I'm pretty safe going back and forth between the garage and the house, as long as I check to make sure there isn't anyone out in their yards or over here for a visit. Vic said it was safe."

Terry nodded as he shoveled several bites of casserole into his mouth. He burned a lot of calories on patrol and chasing down calls. "You still need to be careful."

"I am. We were just talking about me staying at one of the mines for a few days. Give us both a bit of space."

Terry raised a brow. "Might be a good idea," he said with a nod. "Gets you out of the way and somewhere you don't have to worry about being careful not to be spotted. Vic can come and go and not worry about a friend showing up at the door and creating an awkward situation."

Vic nodded. "People are starting to back off a little, but there are still a lot who figure I need someone with me all the time. Don't people who are grieving ever want to be alone?"

"I think it's because there hasn't been a funeral," Erin contributed. "People generally go back to normal after the funeral, but since you haven't had any kind of memorial, they are still waiting."

Vic rubbed her forehead. "Well, I'm not having a funeral. I've told everyone that I'm waiting for answers back from Willie's extended family and that the police haven't released the body yet. But sooner or later, people are going to figure out that I'm stalling."

"People probably won't stop sending their love until you've had some kind of service," Terry advised, agreeing with Erin.

"But I can't! Not when I know he's not dead. It's bad enough that I'm accepting everyone's flowers and meals. I don't think they'd ever forgive me if I put on a sham funeral. Besides, funerals are *really* expensive. I had no idea." She shook her head in amazement.

Willie frowned, lines appearing between his brows. He ate a couple more bites before inquiring. "How do you know that? Have you actually been looking into it?"

"Well… I did, sort of. Just to see what the prices were like. I wasn't planning on having one. But they charge by the hour for all the attendants that come and frown solemnly at everyone. And I'd need to take out a mortgage to buy a casket."

"You can't take out a mortgage on a property you don't own," Erin pointed out.

"Well, yeah, exactly. I don't know how I would get the money otherwise. Start pulling bank jobs, maybe. I'm sure Pa could set me up with some people, but the clan would never give me that kind of money, no matter how big the job was."

While Willie had been caught up with the Dyson clan, Vic had grown up in the Jackson clan, their rivals. It was all very Romeo-and-Juliet. Or would have been, if Romeo had been twice Juliet's age and they lived together for a while before Juliet realized he had once been part of the Dyson clan.

Both had renounced their families, but that hadn't prevented the clan from pulling Willie back into things and forcing him to accept the leadership of the Dyson clan—before he had escaped by making it look as though he had been killed.

The doorbell rang and Erin looked at Vic, rolling her eyes. They all knew it wasn't going to be for Erin. But she was the homeowner, so she would be the one to answer the door and tell them that Vic was not available right now. She stood up and went to the door, looking back over her shoulder to the kitchen to make sure Willie had removed himself from the line of sight of the front door before opening it.

"A couple of arrangements for Vic," Fiona McKinley advised, offering Erin two new condolence arrangements. One was dominated by gorgeous white lilies.

"Oh, these are lovely," she told Fiona, dipping her nose down as if to smell the lilies, but she didn't inhale, finding the scent overpowering even at a distance. "I'll pass them on."

"How is Miss Victoria? Everyone asks; it would be good if I had something to tell them."

"She's doing as well as can be expected," Erin said carefully. "She's trying to go on with life the best she can right now. Under the circumstances."

She tried not to disclose anything or to say anything that people would throw back in her face when they found out that Willie was actually alive. She hadn't told Fiona anything that was untrue. Fiona just didn't know the actual circumstances Vic was trying to deal with.

"Well, give her our love. Everyone is thinking of her. If there is anything she needs, you'll be sure to tell us, won't you?"

"Yes, of course," Erin agreed.

She waited for Fiona to withdraw, but she stayed there, hesitating, looking as though there were something else she wanted to say. Erin shook her head uncertainly. Fiona had already said everything that could be expected.

"I heard… that you got a strange note at the bakery today," Fiona offered awkwardly. She smoothed her long, dark hair as if it were untidy, but it was not. She looked very sleek and professional, always a walking, talking advertisement for her efficient and well-run shop.

"Oh. Yes, I did. I don't think it was anything serious, though. Just a prank."

"Someone said that it was a prophecy of death and destruction."

"Well... I wouldn't have put it that way, exactly. It wasn't exactly a *prophecy*."

"Oh?" Fiona looked disappointed. "That's what I heard. It sounded like... something you got from a fortune cookie or an oracle."

"Well, maybe, yes," Erin agreed. "Very vague and open to interpretation. You know how these things are. They want you to make something of coincidences. But it isn't..." Erin searched helplessly for the right word, "prophetic."

"What did it say?" Fiona asked. "Do you still have it? Could I see it?"

"Uh, no." Erin put her hand on the door and pushed it a quarter inch toward Fiona. "I'm sorry, I was in the middle of dinner..."

"Oh." Fiona's upbringing took over and she immediately remembered herself. "Of course, I'm so sorry to interrupt your meal. I just thought I would get those to you on my way home."

Fiona knew there wasn't any point in paying someone to deliver the arrangements to Erin during the day, when she wasn't even there.

"It's no problem," Erin assured her.

Fiona nodded and withdrew, allowing Erin to close the door. She considered turning off the front light, but she didn't want any of the ladies tripping out there if they brought over a dish, plant, or expression of condolence for Vic. So she left it on and returned to the table. She showed the arrangements to Vic and then put them on the counter before sneezing loudly.

CHAPTER 6

*W*illie had been camping out at one of his mines for a few days, and Erin had also dropped Vic off there the night before so that she could spend a night with him when she wasn't on shift at the bakery in the morning. Then, the plan was to move him to another location and bring Vic back home. Erin didn't know how long they would need to cycle through locations to keep Willie happy and not reveal to anyone that he wasn't really dead.

She hoped it wouldn't be months. If it were going to be long, maybe they could find Willie an old, nondescript truck and a good disguise so that he could get himself from one location to another without anyone being the wiser and just make supply drops every week or two so that he didn't have to return to town for anything.

It was all very complicated. Erin had never considered how inconvenient it would be to be dead.

The extra running around, keeping the secret, and managing visitors and their casseroles and flowers for Vic was wearing on her. She probably should have gotten Charley to cover her Saturday morning shift, but she had thought it would get easier and the condolences fewer.

"You look plumb tuckered out," Bella observed as she put her wavy blond hair up and pinned it securely in place before putting on a cap. "You're doing too much."

Erin rubbed her temples and forehead, massaging the sore, knotted muscles. "I know. I just keep thinking it will get easier. But I've got tomorrow off. I'll catch up on my sleep tomorrow."

"Tomorrow, you're going to be planning out your week and the promotions and running the errands you didn't get done during the week," Bella pointed out, demonstrating to Erin that either she was too predictable or Bella too observant.

Erin's cheeks warmed and she grimaced at the young woman. "I'll be careful," she promised. "I won't do too much."

"I've heard that one before. You're supposed to be giving yourself the weekends off."

"I know, but Vic needed some time, and…"

"You should have scheduled Charley or Cheyenne."

"You're right. I should have."

"Why don't you get some office work done between the busy times? Then you won't have so much to do tomorrow and can relax more."

Even though Bella was just a teenager, she planned to be a business owner when she got older. She had a good head for business and knew the kinds of decisions that were needed to make them profitable, and her suggestions were usually sound.

Erin looked toward the front of the bakery, but she knew that Saturday mornings were slow compared to the rest of the week. People like to sleep in and slow down, not starting their days until several hours later than usual.

"Go on," Bella urged. "Everything is in the ovens. I'll set up the display case and we'll get the second batches in before we open. Harold and I can handle things until the lunch rush."

"Well, okay," Erin agreed. "I'll get some computer work done."

Bella watched her until she was sitting in front of her computer to ensure she wasn't distracted by another job on the way there. She gave Erin a cheeky grin and a thumbs-up, then returned to her work.

Erin did not like most of the computer work, so it usually got put off until the last minute, making it even more stressful to get it done. She would much rather be baking than doing administrative tasks. Maybe she should hire a business manager next rather than another part-time employee. But she became immersed in her work and didn't resurface until she heard Bella calling her name.

"Oh, yes?" Erin glanced at the time on the status line and looked at Bella, framed in the doorway. "Sorry, I didn't realize how late it was. Are you clocking out?"

"Not yet. There's… I don't know whether to say it is a problem."

"What's going on?" Erin stood up and tried to reengage with her environment. She had been completely immersed in her work.

"Charley got here, but she has something for you…"

"What?" Erin headed toward the front of the bakery. Charley wasn't in the kitchen, so she was out front. Erin stepped out behind the counter and looked at Charley to see what she wanted. A few customers were waiting to be served, but everyone seemed to be frozen, focused on Charley instead of the baking.

"What's up, Charley?"

"Well, I don't think it's really anything important," Charley said tentatively. "I just… I came in the front, and there was an envelope on the sidewalk." She held it up for Erin to see. "It has your name on it. I thought you had dropped it…"

Erin looked at the envelope. A small note card or personal letter. The writing on the front was vaguely familiar. She took it from Charley. The envelope was still sealed, so it wasn't something Erin had previously seen and opened. And she hadn't dropped it on the way back from the mailbox because Frank, the postman, delivered all of her mail directly to Auntie Clem's.

So who had dropped it on the sidewalk?

"It's for you," Charley pointed out, waiting for Erin to open it.

"Yeah, I know, but… where did it come from?"

"The sidewalk," Charley repeated, taking the question literally.

"But who sent it? And why was it on the sidewalk? Was it mailed?" Erin turned it over, but there was no sign of a postmark or barcode. Not the mail system, then. Had someone been intending to deliver it to her by hand and had dropped it? But then, why hadn't they returned for it?

"Oh," the penny dropped, and Charley suddenly got it. "You don't think this is another letter from your secret admirer, do you?"

"My secret admirer?" Erin repeated, thinking of a past case.

"Your... secret fortune teller," Charley corrected herself with a chuckle. "Do you think it's another prediction? Or an explanation of the first one? I haven't heard about any sudden deaths that could be considered fulfillment of the first prediction."

"It didn't say anything about a sudden death," Erin corrected quickly. She smiled at the customers standing by, waiting for her to open the new letter and find out. "I'll just put this away for later." She tucked it into the pocket of her apron. "What would you like, Clara?"

Clara stared at her, openly curious. Her brassy red hair was pulled back away from her face, and her jewelry was more understated than it usually was when Erin saw her at the police department offices, where she acted as the receptionist and primary administrative support.

"You aren't going to open it now?" she prompted. "Don't you want to know whether it is another threat?"

"The other one was not a threat," Erin returned. "It was just a joke. Someone playing around."

"Then why are you afraid to open it?"

"I'm not. I just want to leave it for later and do my job now. There are customers to be served, so let's get that taken care of."

Erin looked at Clara expectantly, and when she didn't say what she wanted to order, looked at the next customer in line.

"You need to open the letter," Clara said firmly, as if she couldn't believe Erin wouldn't want to jump on that right away. "If it is another threat, you need to report it to the police. They need to act on it right away if you want to catch this guy."

Erin took a deep breath and let it out in a long sigh. "You shouldn't let yourself get wound up by something like this. It really isn't all you are making it out to be. Someone wanted to get a reaction from people, and you're just reacting exactly how they want.

If you ignore it and don't make a big deal of it, they'll stop doing it."

"What makes you think they just want attention?" Clara challenged.

"Well… it's obvious. Why *would* you write a letter like that? To stop a bad thing from happening? To let someone know that you saw it happening in the future? What do they expect a baker to do about this violence that is supposedly going to happen? If you wanted to stop someone, you would tell the police. Why tell me? I don't even believe in clairvoyance or visions or whatever you want to call it."

Clara considered this, frowning, her lip sticking out in a pout. "There must be some reason they chose you."

Erin nodded. "Because people come here to chat. Especially at the ladies' tea tomorrow. And whoever wrote this letter wants her predictions to be front and center. She wants to hear and see people going crazy over it. She wants drama and excitement."

"She? You've decided it is a woman? What makes you think that?"

Erin shrugged. "Looks like a woman's handwriting to me. I don't know any men who write that way."

"What way?" Clara leaned forward, looking at the pocket Erin had stuffed the letter into. "Can I see?"

"You're not going to leave until you get a look at that letter?"

Clara gave a slow smile. "Well… I don't know. I might leave eventually."

"I could call the police and ask them to remove you."

"And then you'd have to show Terry—Officer Piper—the note, wouldn't you? And he'd take it in as evidence, and I would get to see it then."

It didn't seem right somehow. But Erin didn't want to have to show it to Terry or deal with the police about it. She didn't think it was criminal or even a threat. As she had told everyone who cared to ask, it was just a silly prank. Someone trying to get a rise out of Erin and her customers. And they were going to give her just what she wanted.

Frustrated, Erin pulled the envelope out of her pocket. She didn't want to give the letter-writer what she wanted, but she didn't want to waste any time on it, either.

"Look, it's nothing," she announced. "You'll see."

She tore open the flap and pulled the single sheet of folded paper out of it. She unfolded it, trying to handle it by the edges as much as possible.

When the bakery opens its doors, beware those who seek more than pastries and s'mores.

Erin gave an exaggerated shrug and shook her head. "Tell me this is a threat," she challenged, holding it so that Clara could see it. She read it aloud to the other bakery patrons.

"Ooh, spooky," Bella said with a dramatic shudder.

Erin glared at her.

"Well, it is!" Bella said defensively. "S'mores make me think about camping and telling ghost stories around the fire. And someone who comes into the bakery looking for more than just treats? It makes you wonder, doesn't it? What exactly did they come here for?"

"To read some silly letters," Erin declared, refolding the letter and putting it back in her pocket.

Bella giggled. "Spooky letters," she corrected. "Who doesn't like a little paranormal prediction?"

She hadn't been quite so amused when Reg had made her think that her dead grandmother's ghost was trying to communicate with her. In fact, Erin remembered her being pretty shaken up about it. But Erin kept her mouth shut. Bringing up that old matter in front of listening ears was probably not a good idea.

"No more," Erin said. "It's not Halloween. Let's get these customers their baking so they can get home and make their dinners."

She retreated to the kitchen, not wanting to hear any more of the comments about the letters.

Though, of course, there was no magical barrier in the doorway that would prevent her from hearing what was going on in front.

CHAPTER 7

*E*rin got to work on muffin batters for the next day. She liked to let them soak overnight so that the finished product would be smoother and less grainy. She didn't usually start them until later in the day, but she was counting on the mixers making enough noise to block further conversation of paranormal predictions from the front of the bakery from reaching her hearing in the kitchen.

She wasn't paying much attention to anything or anyone else, but after a few minutes of clattering around the kitchen, making as much noise as possible, she noticed Harold's demeanor and stopped what she was doing.

Harold's face was pale and he was watching her closely, as if afraid that she might explode like a ticking bomb.

"Harold." Erin switched off the mixer in front of her and picked up a spatula to scrape down the sides of the bowl. "What is it? You look like you've seen a—" she caught herself, "seen a mouse."

"Nothing." Harold shook his head. "I just wondered what you were so upset about, that's all. If they're just silly notes…"

"I'm just irritated that everyone is making such a big deal of them. I mean… we've dealt with a lot of stuff around here. A lot of things that really *were* scary or dangerous. So why overreact to a few little rhymes about nothing? Why should someone sending anonymous notes be of any concern to anyone?"

Harold nodded. He licked his lips. "It isn't anything," he agreed. "I guess they're just looking for something to talk about."

"I'm sure this will overwhelm all the other gossip at the ladies' tea tomorrow."

"Are you going to be there? At the ladies' tea?"

"No, I'm taking it off, as I've been instructed." Erin rubbed her aching forehead with the back of her hand. "I know I need the rest. So I'm going to do my best to get it."

Harold nodded. "Yeah, you should. We don't want you to be sick again."

Erin had spent a couple of weeks sick with a concussion when Harold had initially started, missing his first days on the job. She was sorry she had missed his first few days, but Vic and the others had made sure that everything went smoothly, and Harold was good at following the checklists and written directions in the recipe and procedure binders Erin had painstakingly created. Some people —*ahem, Charley!*—did not like to follow the proper procedures, figuring she knew better ways. She had ruined more than one batch of baking by not sticking to the instructions.

"Don't worry about the letters," Erin told Harold.

He might tell her that it wasn't anything, but Erin got the feeling that something about the letters was bothering him. But he was a teenager, trying to look and sound like an adult. For some reason, he didn't want to be pinned down and admit that he was worried about the poetic predictions.

"No, I know," Harold agreed. "I don't believe in psychics."

Erin nodded her agreement. "Tell you what," she said, "why don't we fill some eclairs for the ladies' tea tomorrow?"

Harold looked surprised. They didn't usually make anything special for the ladies' tea; instead, they used cookies and treats from the freezer to give the women a variety of sweets to go with their tea. It was mostly about having a place to socialize after the church services, not about having anything special to eat. They enjoyed the treats, but Erin didn't see the need to go all-out for an event she did as a favor to the ladies, especially when she had to have a staff member there and the ladies paid by donation rather than for each thing they ate and drank.

"You want to do eclairs for tomorrow?"

"Why not? We've got the time, and if they get a taste tomorrow, they'll buy them on Monday, right?"

"Sure," Harold agreed. "They won't be able to resist once they get a taste."

"And they're fun to make," Erin told him. "Are you up for it?"

"Yes," Harold agreed enthusiastically.

"Good. I have the pastries in the freezer. We will slice them open, fill them with vanilla custard, and top them with a chocolate fondant. I have a new fondant recipe I want to try out. I just need to print it off."

She ducked into her tiny office to find the file on her computer and send it to the printer. The printer jammed, as it seemed to be doing a lot lately, and it took Erin a few tries to get it running smoothly again. The printing was a little streaky. It probably did need a new ink cartridge. It had been giving Erin warnings for weeks, but she knew that it always gave her a warning when there was still plenty of ink left, and she refused to change it until she saw evidence that it was actually running out of ink.

"Uh—Miss Erin!"

The tone of Harold's voice made Erin forget the recipe in her hand, and she hurried out the door to find out what was wrong.

Harold was running water into one of the sinks, looking worried. Erin frowned and went over to see if the drain was clogged or something had broken.

"I'm sorry," Harold told her, looking stricken. Erin looked into the sink. Harold held his hand under the stream of water, and at first, she didn't understand what was going on. Then he pulled it back, and she saw the blood fill a gash in his hand and start streaming into the bottom of the sink.

"Oh, my goodness." Erin grabbed a towel from the stack of

clean linens and wrapped it quickly around Harold's hand, pulling it tight. "Here, hold this down with your thumb. What happened?"

"I'm sorry!"

"It's okay. We'll get you over to the doctor to have it looked at. Might need a few stitches. What were you doing? How did you cut it?"

"I was trying to cut one of the frozen eclairs in half, like you said, but…"

"You're supposed to let them thaw for a few minutes before cutting them," Erin told him, shaking her head. She hadn't yet written out the proper procedures for the eclairs. She should not have given Harold something to do that was not explicitly described in the procedure manual. "If you try to cut into something that is frozen, and especially if you are trying to cut it while holding it in your hand…"

"You might get cut?" Harold finished, swaying a little.

"Hey, stay focused," Erin told him. "I don't want you fainting on me. Bella!" she raised her voice to call Bella from the front. "Bella!"

Bella stuck her head in the door, confused by Erin's shouting. "What's up?"

"You're going to need to close up. I don't want to leave you working by yourself. I need to take Harold to the doctor."

"What's wrong?" Bella looked at Harold's towel-wrapped hand. "What happened?"

"I cut myself," Harold explained.

Bella looked at the floor, where Erin had not seen Harold had spilled a few drops of blood before making it to the sink. He had stepped in one of the drops, leaving a red skid and footprint behind.

"Oh, blood," Bella said. "Just like in the letter!"

"*Not* just like in the letter," Erin insisted. "It said 'vengeance and blood,' not a kitchen accident."

"It said it was because of a recipe," Bella reminded her.

"'A recipe long forgotten,'" Erin quoted. "This isn't an old recipe long forgotten; it is a brand-new recipe that I created myself."

"Well, maybe it was created before, and you didn't know you were actually re-creating it. And whoever was the original creator didn't like—"

"Bella," Erin cut her off. "Did you hear what I said? I need you to close. Now. I don't want you here by yourself. It's in our policies and procedures that no underage employee will ever be left alone."

Erin had run the bakery by herself for the first few months, and even as an adult, it wasn't easy to do it on her own without someone else working in the kitchen. And, of course, there were safety issues and other risks with just a minor working there while she took Harold to have his hand looked at.

"Why don't I just call someone?" Bella suggested. "Charley or Cheyenne…?"

"I'm leaving now, and I'm not leaving you working alone while you wait for one of them to arrive. Enjoy the early release. You have the rest of the day to do what you want."

Bella reluctantly returned to the front to serve the last couple of customers and lock the front door. She turned the sign to Closed.

"What about the closing procedures?" Bella asked worriedly, as Erin shooed her out the back door.

"We don't have time. I'll come back later and finish. For now, we just make sure the ovens are off and the burglar alarm set."

All three of them double-checked the positions of the oven knobs, and Bella and Harold watched Erin arm the burglar alarm and pull the door shut.

CHAPTER 8

I'm sorry," Harold apologized, holding the towel wrapped around his injured hand. "That was really stupid."

"Things happen. I hope your mom doesn't get too upset with me."

He shook his head. "She won't get mad at you for something I did. I do stupid stuff at home, too."

Erin chuckled. "We all do stupid stuff. It happens. We're human."

"But you always say not to cut toward yourself. I knew that. And I've heard it from Scouts and Uncle Nelson, too. I always thought you had to be right stupid to cut toward yourself and to accidentally injure yourself with a knife. Now look at me!"

"I don't think it is too serious. The doctor will take care of it and you'll be fine."

"I know. But I made you close early, so you lose that income for the rest of the day. You should dock my pay for making you lose money."

"It will work out. They'll come in on Monday instead."

"But what if people needed something for Sunday dinner, and now they can't get it because the bakery is closed?"

"Then they'll have to pick up some rolls or cookies from the grocery store before it closes. It will be okay."

"Everyone will hate me because I ruined their Sunday dinners."

Erin shook her head. She pulled up outside the medical clinic and parked. There were only a few cars in the lot. Not a busy time. They would be in and out quickly.

"Let's get you looked after."

She took Harold into the clinic. After introducing him to the young lady on reception, she withdrew to look at the magazines on the side table so that Harold could answer any private information himself. Thirty seconds later, he was sitting beside her. He showed her the form the woman had given him to fill out.

"Why do I have to do all this stuff when my hand is hurt? Heart disease? Liver disease? Cataracts? How am I supposed to know all of this family medical history?"

"Do you know what your grandparents or great-grandparents died of? Do either of your parents take any medications?"

"I don't know." He shook his head. "It's not like we talk about all that stuff."

"Well, check off any you know and tell them they'll have to talk to your mom about the rest. Or call or text her and ask her what to check off."

Harold grimaced. "I have to call her? I don't want her to know what I did."

"You're going to have to call her anyway. She'll need to pick you up to take you home. And it isn't like she won't notice your bandaged hand. She'll have to be told what happened."

"She's always telling me that I need to be more careful. I'm so clumsy. I'm always running into things or breaking stuff. And I'm not good at sports."

"I've seen you play basketball. You're not that bad."

"Playing with my friends. Not playing on a team."

"Well, I'm not sure I could get a basket even shooting with my friends. You're not that clumsy. You haven't had any problems at the bakery."

Harold checked off a few boxes on the admission form.

"Yeah," he admitted. "I'm pretty good at following checklists; that makes it easy. If I'm not following instructions, though, I can goof up…"

He looked at the towel wrapped around his hand and winced. "That was so stupid."

"Well, we'll just need to ensure you always have a checklist or instruction sheet to follow. That's okay. I like putting them together."

They didn't have to wait long before a nurse called Harold's name. He looked at Erin. "Are you going to come in with me?"

"If you want me to. Is your mom coming? Do you want to wait for her?"

"I just want someone to… keep me company. She's coming, but I don't know what time it will be when she gets here."

"Okay." Erin stood up and followed Harold and the nurse into the small waiting room.

The nurse took Harold's clipboard and glanced over his answers before putting it aside. "So, what do we have here?" She took his hand and carefully unwrapped the towel. It wasn't a deep cut and did not spurt blood when the makeshift bandage was removed. But blood did well up from the cut. Nurse Kelly dabbed at the cut a few times, examining it closely.

"Yes, that's a nice cut, isn't it?" she observed. "But it doesn't look too bad. Just the flesh. We'll have Dr. Mike stitch it up and you'll be as good as new. You don't have any allergies?"

"Just celiac disease."

"You haven't ever reacted to any medications? Freezing at the dentist?"

"No. I just get a headache after."

"Sure," she nodded. "Good. We'll get you numbed up here and Dr. Mike will be just a few minutes."

Erin watched Harold's face as Nurse Kelly irrigated the wound and prepared the needle. He was pale and looked away. He obviously didn't like needles, but was determined not to make a big deal of it, to look strong in front of Erin. When he glanced at her, she just nodded, careful not to treat him like a kid.

Harold bit his lip as Nurse Kelly jabbed him in the hand and injected the anesthetic into several locations around the cut.

"That will just take a few minutes," Nurse Kelly assured him. "You'll be nice and numb for the stitches." She pressed gauze over the still-bleeding gash. "Just hold that in place until he gets here." She looked at Erin. "Give me a shout if there are any problems."

Erin nodded. When Nurse Kelly left, Harold let out a long sigh, looking down at the injury. "Will I still be able to work? I won't have to take time off, will I?"

"I doubt it. As long as it doesn't hurt too much for you to do your job."

"Good. I feel terrible about it. I don't want to make it worse by not being able to come in."

"Everybody makes mistakes," Erin assured him again. "I've made plenty. And got hurt, too. It's part of being human. We're not robots."

"Sometimes I wish I was. Everything would be so much easier."

Erin wasn't sure how much she would enjoy life as a robot. She might be more efficient, but she wouldn't get the same joy out of doing her job or delighting her customers. And robots were not immune to breakdowns or bugs.

In a few minutes, the Dr. Mike came in. He was a young man with short blond hair. Erin had seen him around town, but didn't know him well.

"Hi, Harold," he greeted. "How is that coming along? Is it all numb?" He took Harold's hand and removed the gauze to look at it. He prodded the edges around the wound. "Can you feel that?"

Harold shook his head. "No, it is all numb."

"Good. We'll get started then. Have you had stitches before?"

"When I was little. I don't remember it."

"Some people like to watch, but most feel better if they don't. If you feel faint or nauseated, you might want to look at Miss Erin and talk to her about something else."

Harold nodded and looked at Erin, apparently deciding that he was not being a wimp if the doctor suggested this course of action. "Sorry I bled on your floor."

Erin laughed. "Yes, how rude is that? Don't worry about it, Harold. It's tile. It cleans up easily."

And it wasn't like he was the first person to bleed on the floor. Erin tried to stay focused on Harold's face and not be distracted by memories of Mr. Inglethorpe lying on her kitchen floor. She smiled so Harold wouldn't think she was angry about it. "Blood is easier to clean up than corn syrup."

"That stuff is *really* sticky."

"Yeah. Do you know I dropped a bottle of corn syrup on the floor back when I first opened the bakery? It wasn't even full, but what a mess, and it seemed like I was finding sticky spots for months. You wouldn't think it would splatter easily, being so thick and sticky, but it goes everywhere when a bottle explodes like that."

"Explodes?"

"Well… there were no explosives involved, but it just splattered everywhere. And that corn syrup… I don't know if I ever got it all cleaned up before the building burned down."

"That was the old location?"

Erin nodded. "Yeah. Across the street."

Harold looked down at his hand and the doctor suturing it for a moment. Then he looked away again, back at Erin.

"You don't think it was like Bella said, a fulfillment of the prediction in that letter?"

"No. Not at all. People have accidents all the time. I could predict that; it doesn't make me clairvoyant." She smiled. "It isn't like the letter said, 'Harold will cut himself when preparing eclairs.' Now, if it said that, I would be surprised. But only if you hadn't heard the prediction. And you weren't the one who had predicted in the first place."

Harold's brow furrowed. "Why would I predict that I was going to get cut? And wouldn't I be more careful not to if I knew that?"

"Sometimes people want attention, so they make things happen."

"That's crazy. I wouldn't hurt myself on purpose."

He looked away from her for an instant, then back. "I get hurt enough without hurting myself on purpose."

His words raised the hairs on the back of Erin's neck. She flashed a look at the doctor, but he didn't appear to be listening.

"You get hurt a lot?"

Harold scowled and shook his head. "I didn't mean that. Just that I get hurt sometimes. Have accidents. And I don't like it. Why would I want to hurt myself more?"

"Some people like the attention. They like the way it feels when someone is taking care of them."

"Well, I don't. I mean, I want to get it fixed, and I don't want it to hurt, but I don't *want* to have to get stitches."

Dr. Mike finished the neat row of stitches and examined them. "There you go. You probably won't even have a scar. The receptionist will give you aftercare instructions. Keep it clean, and don't do anything that will tear the stitches out, and it will heal in no time."

"Thanks." Harold looked down at the stitches and seemed relieved that it was finished.

Dr. Mike put a piece of gauze over the cut and taped it securely in place. "Call me if you have any concerns. If it gets hot or hurts more, or looks swollen or discolored. Or if you have any questions about care. How's your mom?"

"She should be here soon to pick me up."

"Good. Take it easy for a while. Be careful with knives. And hot pans. You're going to be a bit clumsier with that injury. You'll need to be more careful than usual."

Harold nodded. "Okay, thanks."

CHAPTER 9

*A*fter Harold got his aftercare instructions from the receptionist, he went to the front window to see if his mother was there. He looked nervously over his shoulder at Erin.

"She'll be here before long. You don't have to stay here with me."

"I think I'll stick around for a while, just to be sure."

"She said she's on her way."

Erin nodded. "I hope she wasn't too upset about you getting hurt. I don't want her to think I run an unsafe kitchen."

"No… I'll tell her it was just because I was being stupid. She won't be surprised."

Erin put her hand on his shoulder. "Don't put yourself down, Harold. You're a smart kid, and I don't think you have any more accidents than anyone else. This was the first time anything has happened at the bakery."

"Yeah, but I do stuff at home and school too. There aren't a lot of distractions at the bakery, but when I get all hyped up or confused and there is a lot of stuff going on…"

"Give yourself a break."

He gave her a half smile, as if he didn't know what to think of this advice, and turned back toward the window.

"Remember when I went fishing with Uncle Nelson?"

"Well, sure, it wasn't very long ago."

"I've been other times too. I remember I went once when I was little. My brothers were old enough to go, so I was allowed to tag along. Mom said they could keep an eye on me and help me so I wouldn't be any trouble for Uncle Nelson."

Erin nodded her understanding. "So this is something he does regularly, taking all the nephews or cousins out on a fishing trip?"

"Yeah. He says he likes to stay in touch with us all. But that trip I went on when I was just little...? I got a fishhook in my foot."

"Ouch!" Erin winced at the thought. "I'll bet that hurt! They're barbed, so they can do real damage when you pull them out."

"You're not supposed to just yank 'em out," Harold agreed. "So I went and found Uncle Nelson and showed it to him. There are different ways to take them out, depending how deep they are. He couldn't use any of the pull-out methods because it had curved around so far, he had to push it all the way through, then got his cutters and cut the barbed end off and pulled it out."

Erin grimaced, trying not to picture it. "How old were you?"

"I was about six. Uncle Nelson said I did everything right, not trying to pull it out myself and going to him for help. He said I was really brave for sitting still while he pushed it through and cut it off. I hardly even cried."

"Ouch, I think I would cry!"

"I was afraid that if I cried, he would just leave it in my foot until I went home, and I didn't want my mom to know. After the fishhook was out, we soaked my foot in cold water for a long time, and then he put some stuff on it and bandaged it up. I didn't have to have stitches then."

"What about a tetanus shot?"

"He said he didn't think I needed one."

Erin gazed out the window. "Did you ever tell your mom?"

He grinned and shook his head. "No! She would just have told me it was my own fault, and I guess it was."

"What about your brothers, who were supposed to be watching you?"

"They didn't tell her either."

"No, I mean, where were they while all of this was going on? How did you get a fishhook in your foot when they were supposed to be taking care of you?"

"Oh. I guess they weren't watching very carefully. I was trying to fish on my own. They were probably off drinking or something."

"And just left a six-year-old to fend for himself?"

He shrugged. "I thought I was grown up."

"Well, I guess you were."

Harold stood a little taller at that remark. "I guess I was," he agreed. "Oh, there she is."

He headed for the door, but then stopped when he saw his mother getting out of the van that had stopped in front of the clinic. He waited uncertainly by the door until she entered.

"I'm all done," Harold told her, displaying his bandaged hand.

Mrs. Melville looked sourly at Erin. "What happened?"

"Harold just slipped while he was cutting. It was a superficial wound," Erin assured the woman, though her heart was pounding hard, and she felt like she'd been hauled up before the principal at school to account for her actions. "He'll be able to go back to school and work right away. Hopefully, it won't cause him too much pain. The doctor stitched it up, and I'm sure it will heal quickly..."

"Aren't your knives sharp enough?"

"Yes. It was just a freak accident..."

Mrs. Melville looked at Harold. "Is that so?"

Erin swallowed. "I'm sorry it happened at the bakery. Harold is an excellent worker, and we haven't had any accidents like this before."

"I've heard about plenty of strange business being associated with your bakery. Deaths, even. I had my reservations about Harold going to work there, but he assured me it would be a safe workplace."

"It is," Harold insisted. "It was just a stupid mistake. It was me."

"You said you would be careful."

"I am careful. This is the first time something has happened."

"Is it? Or is it just the first time you've had to tell me?"

Erin had to suppress a laugh at that, reflecting on how reluctant he had been to tell her and had hoped to hide the injury from her.

Mrs. Melville sensed a reaction from Erin and turned to look at her. Erin managed to keep a solemn expression.

"Boys," Mrs. Melville said with a dismissive shake of her head. "They have to try everything once. You can't tell them anything."

"And you've had how many?"

"Harold is the third. Believe me, it is a miracle that they have all survived."

"I can't imagine," Erin told her in an admiring voice.

This seemed to mollify Mrs. Melville's ire over Harold being injured in the bakery. She patted Harold on the shoulder as she turned to exit. "Thank Miss Erin for looking after you, and apologize for taking her time."

Harold nodded. "Thank you, Miss Erin. I already told her I was sorry. I told her she didn't have to stay with me."

"She knows what it is like to be a mother. She knew not to leave you alone until I could get here."

"Yes'm," Harold agreed.

"He'll be back at work on Monday," Mrs. Melville assured Erin. Erin followed them outside to get to her own car and gave them a little wave.

"See you later, Harold. Heal quick!"

He nodded and climbed into the van. They peeled off before Erin was even in the seat of the VW.

CHAPTER 10

*E*rin checked the time before heading back to the bakery. She didn't think she needed to eat before finishing the closing procedure at Auntie Clem's, or that it would take her very long to complete everything on the list.

It was strange going to the bakery alone, especially so late in the day, and to find the bakery deserted. Erin remembered to disarm the burglar alarm so she wouldn't end up with the police outside her door, and locked the heavy back door behind her.

The closing procedure was second nature to her, but she was used to running through it with Vic or one of the other employees, not with doing it alone. She took out the written checklist so she wouldn't forget any steps. Before anything else, she needed to mop up the blood smears on the floor.

She could only imagine what the letter-writer would think if she were to see Erin mopping up blood in the kitchen. Would it be proof, as Bella had suggested, that the writer was clairvoyant and had seen Harold's accident in the bakery's future? But none of the rest of the prediction was true. There was no vengeance, no forgotten recipe.

What had the second letter said? Erin found it still in the pocket of her apron.

When the bakery opens its doors, beware those who seek more than pastries and s'mores.

Could it possibly be more vague? Watch out for what? People who were hungry for more than dessert? Someone who had a motive other than to buy the baking? Like the letter-writer herself? What was the point? Just to get attention? To make people think that the bakery was dangerous?

Erin knew from experience that the warnings were more likely to attract people to Auntie Clem's than to scare them away. The threat—or actual existence—of something macabre always seemed to pull people in. The Morning Sunshine muffins were still bringing people in from all over the country after the well-publicized death of Gerald Montgomery due to his strawberry allergy.

The eclairs that Harold had removed from the freezer were now completely thawed. Erin quickly sliced each one horizontally as they sat on the counter, not picking them up to slice toward her palm, as Harold had. The custard was already made in the fridge and the traditional poured fondant would be pretty quick to pull together.

She generally offered a selection of *amuse-bouches* for the ladies' tea, one or two-bite desserts that could be sampled without spoiling everyone's appetite for Sunday dinner. The eclairs were much too big to fit that classification. And once they were filled, they would be very sweet and rich. Erin experimented with dividing them into four slices before filling and frosting them, as cutting them later in the process would likely squish out all the custard.

Her phone rang.

Erin ignored it the first time. She was in a flow state, everything falling into place, her mind completely occupied with what she was doing. She was not ready to deal with anything happening outside the bakery.

The phone rang again. Erin groaned and worked for a few more seconds before putting her tools of the trade aside and grabbing her phone.

"Hello?"

"Erin?" It was Terry's voice. "Are you okay?"

Erin looked around her. The eclairs were nearly done, and then she could finish closing, and be home to make dinner. By then, Terry might be getting off work and be able to join her. She could take a few of the eclair bites home to sample for their dessert. One of the perks of working in a bakery.

"Yes, everything is fine. I'm just finishing up here, and I should be home in an hour or so."

"What is taking so long?"

"Uh…" Erin looked at the clock on the wall. "Oh, I had no idea it was so late. I'm sorry."

"How do you not know what time it is? Did you send everyone home? When I drove by the bakery, the Closed sign was up."

"Yes. Oh, long story. Harold cut himself, and I had to take him over to the doctor to have it looked at. So I had to close. But without running through the usual closing procedure. So I came back to finish up and…"

"Lost track of time. What did you get so engrossed in? I didn't think your closing procedure was that enthralling."

Erin laughed. "No, it isn't. But you know I've been working on these eclairs and decided to fill some for the ladies' tea tomorrow…"

"I thought you kept the ladies' tea preparations to a minimum."

"Well. Usually. I'm just really excited about these eclairs. I'll bring some home with me…" Erin offered.

"If eclairs are on offer, I'm not going to turn them down," Terry admitted. "But you should leave soon. Are you nearly done?"

"Almost. I'm sorry. I'll be as quick as I can."

CHAPTER 11

*T*erry opened the back door for Erin, which made it easier for her to carry in the platter of eclairs for dessert. She set them down on the counter and shared an embrace with Terry, who smelled of soap and was dressed in his t-shirt and cargo pants rather than his uniform.

She was really late getting home.

"Have you eaten?" she asked.

"Made myself a sandwich. I could still eat if you want to have something together. But I bet you're exhausted after such a long day at the bakery." He looked at his watch. "Over twelve hours."

"I know. Plus, sitting at the doctor's office."

"How is young Harold?"

"He's okay. Just a cut on his hand." Erin indicated the location on her own palm. "He'll be back at school and without missing any time."

"Good. We don't want any more rumors of bad luck at Auntie Clem's."

Erin cast a glance at him.

"What?" Terry demanded.

"Did Clara tell you already?"

"Did Clara tell me what?"

Erin scratched the back of her head, wishing she hadn't brought it up. But she couldn't very well keep quiet about it now.

"That we got another letter."

"Another letter." Terry looked blank at first, then nodded. "The prognostication."

Erin laughed. "Yes, exactly. The puzzling poetic prognostication."

"What did this one say? And how did you get mail delivery today?"

"It didn't come in the mail. It was on the sidewalk outside the bakery with my name on it."

"And Clara was there?"

"At Auntie Clem's, yes. She wouldn't let me get away with opening it later. Insisted that I open it right away or she would call you and you would make me."

Terry chuckled. "That's not quite how it works." He opened the fridge to look through the leftovers and ingredients.

"I just didn't want everyone to be focusing on the letters. They're just so... dramatic. I don't know. I want to say 'fake.'"

Terry nodded. "Fake works. They aren't real... fortunes or prophecies. Just something to get people's attention."

"Do you believe in *real* prophecies?"

Terry turned to look at her, lips pursed. "In modern times? No. Ancient prophecies, like in Biblical times... maybe. I don't really know what I believe about that."

"You think there might be real prophecies in the Bible. Like God actually talking to people to tell them what was going to happen."

"Maybe." He pulled a few bowls out of the fridge. "I think that some events might warrant prophecies. The birth of a Savior. The end of the world. Maybe a couple of things in between."

Erin found it hard to believe that Terry could believe in such things. He was a smart, thoughtful person, and she did not equate that with someone who could believe in fables. She knew he was a man of faith, at least on holy days, but that was more like faith in the inherent goodness of the universe than a literal belief in the stories in the Bible.

And Terry, like many of the others in Bald Eagle Falls, had a hard time believing that Erin could *not* believe in any of those things. She'd had a number of them say that she must at least believe in Christianity, even if she hadn't picked a particular sect to affiliate herself with. They didn't quite believe that she didn't believe in any of that stuff.

"What do you know about the Melvilles?" she asked, deliberately changing the subject.

"Not a lot," Terry admitted. "They haven't done anything to bring themselves to the attention of the police department. They've just recently moved back to Bald Eagle Falls from Nashville, but I think they have roots here." He raised his brows. "Not many people move to Bald Eagle Falls unless they have some roots here. It isn't exactly a hot tourist destination."

"I'm just curious if you know anything about his mom."

"I know little about her other than the fact that she didn't want us talking to Harold when we were dealing with the Christmas thefts."

"She seems a little..." Erin tried to think of a word that would express what she wanted without making a big deal of it. "She's quite... strict? Critical?"

Terry gave a small shrug. "So are a lot of women in these parts."

"Yes," Erin agreed, thinking of Mary Lou, Angela Plaint, Mrs. Foster, and other women she had come to know in Bald Eagle Falls since she had moved there. She knew several women who seemed to be extra strict with their children, raising them with rigid religious or moral standards. But did that ensure the children kept to the standards they had been raised with? Or did they rebel or stray from those teachings just as quickly as Erin or the runaways she had met in the foster care system?

"How does it work... with families that are in the clans?" she asked Terry. She started setting the table. "I mean, Vic was raised Christian and goes to church in the city. She's probably almost as devoted as the women who attend church here and then come to the ladies' tea. Her parents are religious, but they are members of the Jackson clan. Organized crime. They must be aware of crimes being committed even if they don't participate. And her Pa and brothers were obviously involved. So... how do they reconcile that?"

"Cognitive dissonance," Terry said, "believing in two conflicting sets of information at the same time. Believing that they are righteous and obeying God's laws, while at the same time knowing that they are stealing, murdering, and committing all kinds of other breaches of God's law."

"How do they do that?"

"I don't know." Terry shook his head as he cut open some rolls to make sandwiches. "I think it is different for different people. Some believe that they have a special dispensation to do what they do. That God told them to, that it is for the greater good. Some believe that as long as they do some kind of penance or ritual afterward, they will be absolved. Some never admit that they are aware that what they are doing conflicts with what they say they believe."

Erin looked into the living room and saw Orange Blossom curled up on the couch, Marshmallow and K9 stretched out together on the floor. Terry had obviously fed them and taken care of any need while Erin had been missing in action, immersed in her work at the bakery.

"What are you thinking?" Terry prompted. "Is there something going on with Harold that you are concerned about?"

"I don't know. There are... things I am concerned about. But they may be nothing. They're just... things that raise red flags for me, but they are probably not anything."

"Do you feel safe with Harold working there? If you don't feel safe with him, there are things we can do."

"No, no," Erin protested. "Harold is a lovely boy. I don't ever feel threatened by him. I worry *for* him. Whether he is being treated right. How much clan stuff he is exposed to. I worry about his education and whether he has friends. How he feels about himself..."

"Oh, I see," Terry nodded, smiling. "You've adopted him."

Erin shook her head. "I don't have any desire to raise a teenager. I just want to make sure he is okay."

"Do you want to talk about any of those red flags? I won't share them with anyone else."

"No. Not yet. I'll just… keep an eye on him myself." She met Terry's concerned glance. "It isn't like he comes to work with bruises or burns. Or that I've seen anyone in his family hurt or threaten him."

"But you've lived in a lot of different families and learned some of the nuances."

"I guess so, yeah. I probably see a lot of things that aren't really there just because of the way I grew up. Kids who grow up in regular families don't have to worry about the same things as kids growing up in foster care or other… situations. I'm sure everything is probably fine with Harold."

CHAPTER 12

*E*rin started getting phone calls almost the instant people began to leave Auntie Clem's after the ladies' tea.

"I want to order eclairs for the PTA meeting at the school," Fiona told her. "They were so wonderful."

"Great," Erin approved. "Just email me how many you need and what date and time, and I'll make sure I have them ready for you."

"I will. I was so sorry to hear about Harold getting hurt. How is he doing, do you know?"

"Well, I haven't heard from him today, but he was okay last I saw him yesterday. It was just a minor injury, really. The doctor said that he would be fine. He will be back at school and work."

"That's good to hear. I guess the letter was right after all."

"The letter? No, it wasn't anything to do with the letter. It was just an accident."

"But the letter predicted it, didn't it? It said there would be blood in the bakery, and there *was*."

"That isn't what the letter said."

"It said it was because of a recipe, didn't it? And it was. You were testing a new recipe, and Harold ended up cutting himself..."

"One has nothing to do with the other," Erin said firmly.

"What else do you think is going to happen? Something else at the bakery? The second letter was a warning about something that was going to happen in the bakery. People with evil intentions."

"Not necessarily. Something about people who come for something other than s'mores," Erin said casually, even though she knew the exact words perfectly well, "but I don't sell s'mores, so everyone comes there for something other than s'mores, don't they?"

"No, it was a threat," Fiona protested.

"It wasn't a threat. It's just a silly prank," Erin assured her.

Melissa was the next to call, bubbling over with the latest gossip, most of which related to the letters and the bakery, all with her own special spin.

"The police are looking into it," she told Erin as if Erin didn't live with one of the members of the police department. "They want to know who is sending these letters and how they know everything that is going to happen," Melissa gushed.

"No one knows anything that is going to happen," Erin assured her. "Anyone could make vague predictions about things that will happen around town and then interpret events that took place as being fulfillment of the predictions. I could say... that you'll have a hard time going to sleep. And then when you do actually have problems going to sleep, you're going to think it is a fulfillment of the prediction. Or I could say that we're going to have a rash of thefts, and then after the next couple of thefts occur—that would have occurred anyway—then I say it's proof that I saw the future. And I guess I did. I knew that there would be thefts in the future. Just like I know there will be clan activities, people running out of gas, and... people sending casseroles to Vic because of what happened to Willie. I don't have to be a prophet to make those predictions. I don't have to be clairvoyant."

"That's not what happened," Melissa insisted. "It was a real psychic prediction. Someone among us," she drew the words out, "has powers beyond the ordinary."

"Melissa, I thought you didn't believe in things like witchcraft and paranormal stuff."

"Oh, no," Melissa assured her. "Those things are real. There are all kinds of evils in the world."

"Well, Terry doesn't believe that they are real psychic predictions, and the police department wouldn't be investigating anything if they thought they were real psychic predictions. You don't break any laws by making psychic predictions. If they are investigating, It is because they have decided the letters are threats."

"They are warnings," Melissa said, "not threats."

"Then there isn't anything for the police department to investigate, and you should stop circulating that rumor."

"It isn't a rumor," Melissa huffed. "I know what is going on in the police department."

"And they have a psychic investigations department now?"

"They don't have anything of the sort!"

"Oh, there's the door," Erin lied, deciding to shut the conversation down. It clearly wasn't going anywhere. "Don't worry about calling me back. If there are any developments, Terry can let me know."

She ended the call and rolled her eyes. It sounded like things might have gotten slightly out of hand at the ladies' tea. The word of Harold's injury had gotten out, and the thought that there had been blood in the bakery after the initial letter had stirred everyone up.

She let the next few calls go to voicemail. But then Vic's name showed up on the caller ID. Erin swiped to accept the call.

"Hi, Vic."

"How's it going, Erin? What's this I hear about Harold getting hurt?"

"It was only minor. He slipped with a knife. Got a few stitches, and he'll be as good as new. How did you hear about it already? I thought you and Willie were going to be unreachable today."

"Well, that was the idea," Vic agreed. "And I should have turned my phone off. But I didn't. I figured I would just ignore any calls. And we would be out of service half the time because of the caves, so we would have plenty of peace and quiet."

"And then you started getting calls after the ladies' tea," Erin predicted.

Vic laughed. "You must be psychic."

Erin chuckled. "There seems to be a lot of that going around."

"What is this? I leave town, and everything goes to heck? I guess you've probably had calls from everyone, too."

"Well, yes and no. I didn't talk to very many of them. This has obviously got everyone stirred up for no good reason. Once I figured out that everyone was going to call me to gossip about these ridiculous predictions, I decided to just let them go through to voicemail. I can weed out those who want to order eclairs and ignore the rest of the nonsense."

"I heard about the eclairs. Sounds like they were a smash hit. But who am I talking to? Of course you knew they were going to be a hit. Right from the start, you knew they would be."

"Once I could get them right," Erin agreed.

"And this batch was right."

"This batch was right," Erin agreed. "I've got the recipe and the timing figured out. So we can start filling orders. They'll probably be served at every public event for the next three months."

"That's awesome. Well, I'll be in tomorrow and we'll figure out the production schedule to make sure that we've got enough of them and can fill and frost them before the meetings."

"I have something else in mind, too," Erin told her, the idea starting to form in her head.

"What?"

"You'll see tomorrow. I want to work out the details."

"You can't do that to me!" Vic told her. "Come on, you need to tell me your idea."

"If everyone wants to talk about the letters… then we'll make sure they have something to talk about."

"You are a genius at marketing," Vic told her admiringly.

Erin had learned quickly that there was no point in trying to fight gossip or tradition in Bald Eagle Falls. Instead, she could use the small-town grapevine to her own advantage. Sales at Auntie

Clem's Bakery were always the best after a murder or other tragic event. Everyone drew together to discuss tragedy and rumors. Why try to swim against the flow?

CHAPTER 13

*E*rin stood on the customer side of the counter and looked critically at the signs. She had also cleared off the community bulletin board on the wall closest to the display case to extend the theme.

She met Vic's eyes and nodded. "Okay. Let's do this."

Erin walked to the front door, flipped the sign over to Open, and turned the bolt to unlock the door. She opened the door to greet her morning customers with a welcoming smile. She had been right to expect the group of early morning customers to be larger than usual.

The ladies walked in, murmuring and whispering to each other. They all stopped a few feet back from the display case.

The first sign was *Pastries* and stood behind a platter of full-size, fully decorated chocolate eclairs. The next sign was *S'mores*, and stood behind a shallow box filled with packages of gluten-free graham crackers, chocolate squares, and large marshmallows. The third sign read *More* and an arrow pointed down at the display case.

There was a collective gasp from the group, followed by giggles.

"And the letters!" exclaimed Cindy Prost, Bella's mother, as she walked over to the bulletin board to examine the original letters in plastic sleeves pinned up in the place of honor. She read the second letter aloud.

When the bakery opens its doors, beware those who seek more than pastries and s'mores.

Erin took her place behind the counter, arms folded, and looked at the ladies.

"So what will it be?" she asked. "Pastries, s'mores, or…" She let the pause hang in the air for a few long seconds, "more?" she finished ominously.

More laughter and giggles. Mary Lou was the first in line. She smiled at Erin. "More," she said dryly.

Erin smiled. "What would you like?"

Mary Lou smoothed her wrinkle-free pantsuit over her hips, considering the options.

When she had placed her order and moved to the till to pay for it, Cindy was still standing at the bulletin board looking at the letters. Erin supposed she should be grateful that Cindy wasn't making negative comments as usual and motioned to Tara, standing next in line. "What can I get you?"

"Well, I'm going to need to get a half dozen of the eclairs. And then, maybe, something more…"

"Everybody is going to want something more today," Erin said with a little laugh. "Of course, people usually come for more than just pastries or s'mores." She wanted to emphasize the silliness of the verse. It didn't mean anything. It wasn't ominous. It was just a little rhyme someone had composed to get people talking.

"I don't think you should make light of it," Tara said, her lips thinning as she frowned. "You don't know *who* could come into this bakery with some… violent plan."

"In the bakery?" Erin shook her head. "No one is planning anything violent in Auntie Clem's. People come here to buy their baking, not to do anything to hurt anyone."

"You don't know what is in people's minds. You can't deny that things *have* happened here in the past."

"And in other places in Bald Eagle Falls. And I'm sure the same is true of every other town and neighborhood in the state. It doesn't just center on Auntie Clem's. We don't have 'bad karma' or something like that."

"You shouldn't make fun of it," Tara insisted. The other ladies quieted, listening to Tara and growing more solemn. "This is not a joke. You should be paying attention. Preparing yourself. Thinking about what is going to happen. Because something *will* happen, you know."

Erin rolled her eyes and shook her head. "What else would you like?" she asked, refusing to engage any further on the matter.

"Do you know what this is?" Cindy suddenly asked in a loud voice. She reached out and tapped the center of one of the letters.

Erin looked at her, unsure what she was trying to draw attention to. "What?" she asked cautiously, pretty sure she would not like the answer.

"There is a watermark on these pages."

Erin had registered the watermark only in passing. It was good quality notepaper. Folded neatly into thirds so that it fit perfectly into the matching envelopes. She thought it was fairly old stock. Something someone had found in a grandmother's desk and decided to put to use.

"Yes, there is a watermark," she agreed.

"Not just any watermark," Cindy said slowly and deliberately. "It is the Melville coat of arms."

Erin swallowed. "What?"

Cindy turned to her, showing her teeth in a shark-like smile. "The Melville coat of arms. Where is young Harold today?"

Erin shook her head. "He's at school. He won't be in until this afternoon."

"You might wanna have a word with him about these letters he has been passing off as psychic predictions. They are obviously just a ploy to get more people into the bakery. A marketing ploy. Maybe one that you're a part of, seeing how you seem to have leaned into this pretty hard."

The other customers exchanged wide-eyed looks with each other.

Erin shook her head. "That's ridiculous," she told Cindy. "Anyone who has been in here knows that I've been trying to get people to ignore the letters. I have said over and over that they are just someone's idea of a prank and don't mean anything."

"Is that what you were thinking when you were mopping up blood on Saturday?"

Erin swallowed, trying to keep down the nausea that threatened. She saw not just the few drops of blood that Harold had dripped and walked through, but the large pool of blood that had surrounded Mr. Inglethorpe when Erin had discovered him.

There was no way that Harold had written those letters. And no way he had cut himself to fulfill the prediction of blood in the first letter.

"Cindy," Erin looked Cindy Prost directly in the eyes and held her gaze. "Do you have any complaints about the way I handle my employees who are students? Do you think I take advantage of them in some way?"

Cindy looked away, but looked back again in an instant, unable to find anything else to look at. "Bella has been very happy here."

"Did I leave her here alone yesterday to handle the bakery herself and to mop up blood all alone when I took Harold to the doctor?"

"No."

"Would I let anyone bully her because she is just a teenager? Or for any reason?"

"No," Cindy shook her head, her expression grim. "Of course not."

"Then what makes you think I will let you bully Harold or cast aspersions at him?"

"I didn't—all I did was say that these letters are written on Melville stationery. And they are. It's a fact."

"And you asked where Harold was and said he was mixed up in this prank."

"Well, I don't know that he *isn't*—"

"We don't go throwing accusations at teenagers around here without pretty solid proof that they've done something wrong. I've protected Bella from people jumping to conclusions and making accusations, haven't I? Do you think I wouldn't do the same for Harold?"

Cindy muttered something and shook her head, looking down at the floor.

The bakery was quiet enough to hear a pin drop. Erin didn't know that she'd ever heard it that quiet at Auntie Clem's other than when she was there by herself, and sometimes not even then.

"I don't care whose stationery it is. Who knows where the writer got it from? And I'll say what I've been saying all along—it's just a prank. Someone looking for attention. It's not witchcraft. It's not a prophecy. It's just silly words on the page."

She released Cindy from her gaze and looked at the other customers. They stood around, looking surprised and embarrassed. Of course, everyone had been enjoying the gossip surrounding the letters and speculation on who had written them and what they meant, so they all felt guilty for buying into the hype and giving the letter writer exactly what she wanted.

Cindy dropped her hand to her side and stepped back from the bulletin board. Erin didn't look at her, waiting to see whether she was going to stay and have to talk to Erin to place her order or whether she would slink out and make do with bakery goods purchased off the shelf at the grocery store this week.

Tara stepped forward to place her order. She wore a sunny yellow jacket and looked at Erin with lowered brows, contrary to her usual pleasant disposition. It was the second occasion in a row that she had disapproved of Erin's reaction to something. Erin's stomach tied in a tight knot. She was a people pleaser by nature and hated to think that Tara might not like her or might decide to stop coming to Auntie Clem's for her baking.

"You're very loyal to your employees," Tara observed. She did not use a disapproving tone, and Erin searched her face, trying to figure out whether she was pleased or displeased with this. Despite her frown, Tara did not seem upset with Erin this time, but perhaps was just concerned with the confrontation with Cindy. It wasn't pleasant to have to deal with an argument first thing in the morning, especially when she expected the atmosphere in Auntie Clem's to be cheerful and pleasant. Erin herself found confrontations first thing in the morning particularly vexing. She didn't want to stay in a bad mood all day, but it would take some work to get back on track.

"I try to be a good boss," Erin told Tara with a nod of agreement. "And I have some really good workers. Both Harold and Bella are amazing. So diligent, quick learners, eager to try new recipes and take on new responsibilities." She kept her voice loud enough that Cindy would hear Erin praising Bella to a third party. Whatever Erin's feelings about Cindy, she must have done something right to raise such a great kid. And Erin knew how loving "Aunt Cindy" was to Adrienne's kids. Her whole demeanor changed around them. It was too bad she hadn't had more children of her own.

"Well, you might face challenges in defending Harold against all of the gossip," Tara said. "Sometimes the best thing to do is keep quiet and not make a big deal of it. You know the story of how the wind blows the feathers away. You can never catch all of the feathers."

Erin opened her mouth to ask what story Tara was talking about, then decided to let it go. She didn't want to take half an hour to deal with each customer. She needed to get everyone through. So instead of trying to argue with Tara or figure out what story she was talking about, she just nodded sagely.

"Thank you for your advice," she said. "Now... what can I get you today?"

CHAPTER 14

*P*hew!" Vic exclaimed, once all the customers had been served and they were alone again. "That was unexpected." With her hands on her hips, she looked at the signs Erin had set up for the Pastries, S'mores, and More. "I still like it," she decided. "Deciding to go with the flow and 'leaning into' the drama around the letters is much better than constantly trying to butt your head against it."

Erin sighed and nodded. "I hope so. It just seemed like... why fight it? Like with Gerald Montgomery's death and the Morning Sunshine muffins. If people are going to come here to buy them because they want to eat the last thing he ate, then why not make the best of it? Make it a special, selfie-worthy experience instead of refusing to ever make those things ever again?"

"Well, that's certainly been a profitable choice," Vic agreed. "You are the master at taking advantage of the situation."

Erin frowned. "Taking advantage sounds negative... like I'm doing something that might hurt someone else."

"I didn't mean that. I just meant... taking the opportunity when you've got it. Making the best of a situation."

Erin nodded slowly. She let out another sigh, feeling like she hadn't been able to breathe properly since Cindy had first announced that the watermark on the stationery was the Melville coat of arms. The next problem she faced was how to bring it up with Harold. She didn't want it to sound like an accusation. But she wanted to know if there was any connection between him and the letter writer.

The bells on the front door rang as Erin was turning to go back into the kitchen. She turned back around, pasting a smile on her face for the next customer, and she saw that it was Terry, K9 standing alert at his side.

"Oh, Terry. How is your day going?" She pushed a stray lock of hair back from her face with the back of her wrist. No matter how many bobby pins she used or how well her hair seemed to be secured at the beginning of the day, it was always starting to escape by noon.

"Well, I'm just fine," Terry ventured. "I'm wondering how you are?"

She looked at him, wondering how much he already knew. Terry stood looking at the signs, then moved over to the letters on the bulletin board. "Very clever. You seem to always be able to spin current events in a way that will benefit the bakery."

Which Erin thought was just another way of saying what Vic had. That Erin was good at "taking advantage" of any situation.

"Did you hear?" she asked Terry as he looked at the letters. "About the…"

"About the watermark? Yes. It's not easy to make out. I'm surprised Cindy was able to see it."

Erin frowned, watching Terry. "Do you think she's right? About it being the Melville coat of arms? Maybe it's something else, and she's just making it up. Or mistaken."

Terry took out his phone, turned it on, and held his phone screen up beside the stationery. On the screen, Erin could see a red shield with white crescent moons positioned sideways, arms reaching up.

Terry nodded and put the phone back away. "Looks pretty similar to me. But since there is no color in a watermark, it could be another coat of arms. The Melville coat of arms is white crescents on a red field, but with a watermark, it could just as easily be white crescents on a blue field."

"Or any color."

"Exactly. I guess I will need to have a talk with Harold."

"Why?"

Terry raised his brows. "Well, he's the logical person to talk to about letters being sent to Auntie Clem's Bakery. He is the one with access to both the stationery and the bakery."

"But he didn't need access to the bakery. The letters weren't left on my desk. They were delivered to Auntie Clem's. From outside. Harold didn't need to be here."

"You don't think that it is awfully coincidental that Harold works at the bakery and the letters include his family's coat of arms? You know I don't like coincidences."

"You don't know that it was Harold who wrote the letters."

"No. That's why I would like to talk to him. When does he get in? Does he work here today?"

"You can't talk to him here."

"Why not?"

"I won't allow it. You can call his mom and talk to him at home if she allows it."

"There's no point in me driving all the way out there. Not when he is right here in town most of the day."

"I won't let you question him at the bakery. He has work to do here. I don't want him to be distracted from his work so he has another accident. And I don't want him to think this is somewhere he could be ambushed, somewhere that isn't safe for him. I want him to be happy to come here, not dreading it."

"You know I'll be careful. I won't upset him."

"No."

He looked at her, head cocked slightly. "How can you tell me no?"

Erin folded her arms and shook her head. "Just like this. No. Talk to his mom about it. But not here."

She knew why he was reluctant to talk to Mrs. Melville about getting an interview with Harold. After the Christmas present thefts, Terry had questioned Harold and been shut down by Mrs. Melville. She had not been pleased that he had even attempted to talk to Harold. She was bound to react the same way if Terry tried to speak to him about the letters and the watermarked paper.

CHAPTER 15

*E*rin was half-expecting to get a call from Harold telling her that he couldn't come in for his usual shift, but had to go straight home after his last class. Or he might say that his hand hurt too much to work for a few days. But he showed up at the appointed time, knocking on the back door and slouching into the kitchen with his backpack, pale and weary.

"Hey," Erin greeted softly. "How are you doing, Harold?"

He looked at her, studying her face with concern. "I'm just here for my shift," he said. He put his backpack down in her office and grabbed an apron from his peg.

"I know. That's great. I just wondered how you were. It might have been a pretty rough day for you, with your sore hand and… things."

"Yeah, it kind of sucked. But I've been waiting all day to get back here where I can relax and just… make some muffins."

Erin drifted over to one of the counters and started to pull together the next tray of white rolls for the ladies who would be shopping before dinner. Harold mirrored her movements, going to his workstation to start on the recipe she had left for him.

Erin said nothing, letting him relax and get into his happy place. Asking him a bunch of questions as soon as he got there

would not do her any good. He had told her what he needed—
time to just be alone with his muffins—and she could wait until
he'd had a chance to relax. She wondered how long it had taken for
word to get to him that he was now the prime suspect in the case of
the psychic letters. On top of having a sore hand.

She glanced over at him. He was wrestling to get a comfortable
hold on the bowl he was supposed to be mixing by hand. Luckily,
he didn't have to hold the spoon in his injured hand, but he was
struggling to hold the bowl still while he did so.

"You can use the mixer," Erin told him. "I know you were told
to always mix the muffins and quick breads by hand to keep them
from getting too tough, but you've done it for long enough to know
what the consistency of the batter should be and how much is too
much."

Harold looked at her, one brow raised skeptically. "Are you
sure?"

"Yeah. Put it on the lowest setting, let the mixer go for a few
seconds, scrape down the sides, and mix just until incorporated,
just like when you do it by hand."

"Okay." Harold set about following her instructions.

Erin was not concerned about him overmixing like a newbie.

"A bit stiff and sore today?"

Harold nodded. "Yeah. It's not bad. I've had a lot worse, but it's
annoying when I want to do something like this, and I just can't
hold it the way I normally would."

Erin made a sympathetic noise. "I'm glad you didn't hurt it any
worse. At least you didn't have to miss any time."

Harold watched the batter like a hawk, letting the mixer work
for no longer than a couple of seconds at a time. He removed the
mixing bowl, ran the spatula through it and, with a satisfied smile,
started spooning it into the muffin cups.

"Yeah, me too. The guys think I'm crazy to want to come to
work. They were all saying oh, now I can take some time off and
just slack off for a while. But that's not what I want to do!"

Erin remembered how difficult it had been for her to not be

able to work while she'd had a concussion. She had really wanted to just jump back in, but her brain had not cooperated.

And Willie was experiencing the same thing, going stir-crazy because he had to keep his head down and not let anyone see him until everything was settled with the clan.

"Some of us just like to keep ourselves busy. I always had to work to be able to put food on the table from one day to the next, before starting Auntie Clem's. I got used to that. I can't just sit around doing nothing. Even when I'm home after work, I need to test new recipes, work on Clementine's genealogy, or work on a new marketing plan or my week plan. Not just watch TV."

Harold nodded his agreement.

They continued to work together in silence. Erin pondered when she might find the right moment to discuss the letters with Harold when he unexpectedly turned to her and brought it up himself.

"You know I didn't write those letters."

"I never thought you did," Erin agreed. "That's what I told them when they suggested it."

"Yeah," he acknowledged in a low voice, apparently having also heard that part. "It's just crazy to think that I would! Like, what, I wanted everybody to think that I am clairvoyant? Why? Because they would admire me for it or something?"

"I don't think that anyone is really *thinking* about it," Erin admitted. "I think they're just jumping to conclusions without any thought."

"I didn't write them."

Erin had seen Harold's handwriting in the past, and it was nothing like the feminine script on the letters. Like anyone his age, Harold preferred to tap or record notes on his phone and only wrote by hand when he was required to fill out a paper form. He was worse than Erin was at writing labels or prices for the baking in the display case. They both tried to imitate Vic's round, perfect letters without success.

"I didn't think you did," she told him again.

"Ain't no reason for no one to think that," he muttered.

83

"I guess they think it is your family's stationery. Something about the watermark."

"It's not mine. I don't have any paper like that."

"Does your mom or dad?"

"I don't know. Not that I've ever seen. Who even has notepaper anymore? No one sends handwritten letters. Not my parents, anyway."

"Not many people do," Erin agreed. It would have to be someone older than she was. Maybe someone older than Mrs. Melville. "So you don't think the paper has anything to do with your family?"

"No. The Melville coat of arms? What is that? I've never even heard of that before. That's like... I don't know. Something they would use in England in the dark ages, right? Knights and rich families."

Erin nodded, unsure of how common such a thing was or when it would be used.

"How would Cindy Prost even know what the Melville coat of arms looks like?" Harold demanded. "She had to have just made that up. If my family doesn't know what the Melville coat of arms looks like, how does she?"

Another good point. But Erin had a feeling no one was going to listen to logical arguments in Harold's defense.

CHAPTER 16

One of the problems with Willie being dead was that Erin didn't have someone to call upon to do her handyman work. Those things that Terry didn't have the knowledge or skills for or didn't have the time to tackle. Erin had been able to just happen to mention those little jobs to Vic or to Willie himself, and sometime in the next few days, Willie would find the time to pop over and snake out her drains or deal with a lamp that had shorted out or replace a part on the Volkswagen.

She hadn't realized how many of these little jobs he helped her with until they started to pile up in his absence.

Eventually, she had asked Mary Lou and a couple of the other women for the names of the men they usually hired to do minor repair or home maintenance jobs that they didn't have the tools or experience to do themselves. Jasper Thompson's name had come up a few times, so she had eventually called him to see if he would tackle a few jobs around her house. Old houses needed a certain amount of maintenance. It was her house, and Terry had plenty of work to keep him busy. He didn't need to be bothered with all of her small jobs.

"Thank you again, Mr. Thompson," she told him when she

opened the door for him and watched carefully to ensure that Orange Blossom didn't bolt for the door while he was carrying several toolboxes into the house.

"Jazz," he told her. "Nobody calls me Mr. Thompson. It's Jazz!" He held out his hands, palms forward and fingers played in a choreographed move Erin recognized as "jazz hands."

It was the sort of thing she would have expected from a young actor or dancer, not a retiree like Jasper Thompson. He was obviously still in good health and capable. She just didn't see him as the dramatic dancer type. He had on an old ball cap, with tufts of white hair sticking out the bottom. His face was well wrinkled with age and sun, but the lines mapping his face all pointed up.

"Jazz," she said with a laugh. "Okay. And I'm Erin. I really appreciate you coming by to take care of some of these things."

"Of course. Young lady like you ain't expected to do everything herself. Of course, females are just as capable as anyone else to do jobs around the house, but your time is spent running the bakery. You can't do that *and* do all of these little things too. I've been doing them since I was a little tyke. You don't have the time to train up on all of these things."

Erin nodded. She agreed with everything he said, yet it made her feel guilty for not tackling it all herself rather than making her feel better about hiring him.

"I made a list," she told him, "so you can just go through and get done what you can, and I don't have to hang over you or interrupt you. Is that good? You don't mind me just giving you a list and leaving you to yourself?"

"Not at all, not at all," he assured her. "I'm perfectly fine getting around on my own. Did a few jobs for your Aunt Clementine when she was still alive. It's like coming home." he glanced down at the list. "Some of these are probably jobs I did twenty years ago that need to be patched up."

"Oh, really? I didn't know you did anything for Clementine. Isn't that funny? Well, I guess I'll leave it to you."

Erin looked at her watch and hoped he wouldn't be there when

Terry got off shift. She didn't want to make him feel guilty for not doing more around the house.

Jazz had been there for a couple of hours, working on various items on Erin's list, when the doorbell rang. Erin looked out the peephole and was surprised to find her youngest employee standing on her doorstep. She opened the door.

"Harold. Hi, what are you doing here?"

Her first thought was that he had run away from home and was hoping to be able to stay with her. What would she do if he asked her for help? She couldn't very well take him in. Though she had done just that when she had discovered Vic living in the basement of the bakery at night. Harold was a little younger than Vic had been, but the circumstances were not that different.

But as it turned out, Mrs. Melville had not kicked Harold out, he hadn't run away, and he wasn't looking for someone to take him in. He presented Erin with a covered dish.

"Mom asked me to bring this in," he explained. "For Miss Victoria."

"Oh," Erin took the warm dish from him. "Well, thank you. Thank your mom for me. That was a very nice thing to do."

"She says she misjudged you and wanted to make it up to you. It's not exactly the same thing, giving the casserole to Miss Victoria, but…" he shrugged. "You two are always together; I'm sure you're sharing a lot of the meals."

Erin gave him a nod and a wink. "Can't put much past you, can we?"

They had, of course. He didn't know that Willie wasn't actually dead and was also eating his share of the donated casseroles.

Harold nodded and stepped back, preparing to leave.

"Tell your mom thanks for me," Erin repeated.

"I will."

She shut the door after him and was startled when Jazz spoke from behind her.

"Good kid, that Harold," he said. "Long time since I've seen him."

"You know him?" Erin asked in surprise, turning to Jazz. He stood near the kitchen doorway with a large roll of duct tape in his hand. "I thought they just recently moved here from Nashville."

"Sure," he agreed. "They were living in Nashville for a while, then came back to Bald Eagle Falls."

"They're from here? They aren't newcomers, then?" She remembered Harold talking about being an outsider, being different and viewed with suspicion around the time of the Christmas thefts.

"Harold was probably six or so when they moved away. For a kid, that's a long time."

Erin nodded her agreement. "Yeah. He wouldn't have grown up with the other kids or had a chance to build those friendships. He would be an interloper as a teenager, even if he had been born here."

Jazz made a noise of agreement. "Coming back here when you're grown up is different."

Erin knew that he was talking about her, not just Harold. She had not been born in Bald Eagle Falls, but her parents were from there. They had only been visiting Clementine or staying with her for a while when her parents had been killed and she had been shunted into foster care. Maybe her father had been looking for work; Erin didn't know. They hadn't shared that information with a kid, or if they had, it hadn't made any impression on her. It wasn't until Clementine's death that Erin had returned to Bald Eagle Falls as an adult, deciding to make the most of the legacy from Clementine to try to open the bakery she had long dreamed of.

"Yeah," she agreed. "It's got to be hard as a teenager. I know what it is like trying to make new friends at that age, trying to integrate with kids who grew up together."

The story of her childhood. Maybe that was one reason she found it easy to connect with Harold.

"You remember him when he was little? What was he like?"

"Not that different than he is now," Jazz said, stooping over one of his toolboxes to get what he needed for the next job. "Not the most well-coordinated kid. A little shy. Taller than the other kids. He was determined to learn to ride a bike, but he didn't have one and his parents wouldn't get him one. So he decided to do something about it."

Erin smiled. "What did he do?"

"He went to all of the farms within walking distance, asking everyone if they had an old kid's bike he could have. A lot of people had broken-down bikes they didn't want anymore and were happy to have him take off their hands. So his dad goes into the shed one morning and finds it filled with twenty bikes, none of which work very well."

Erin laughed, picturing it. Little Harold and a shed full of junk bikes.

"Once he heard the whole story from Harold and knew that they were not stolen, he and Harold came up with a plan of action and hired me to help Harold get one of those bikes into good working order." Jazz chuckled to himself. "We had lots of parts, so it wasn't hard to do. Harold learned all about how to take a bike apart and put it back together. He had a good mind, quick to pick things up."

"Yeah. He still does. He's been a real help at the bakery."

"People are talking about these letters... saying Harold had something to do with them, that he's trying to pull some scam."

"It's not true," Erin told him. "Couldn't be farther from the truth. You can't believe everything you hear."

Jazz nodded in agreement. "I didn't think so. I get that people don't trust his family, but that's not Harold. Harold is a good kid."

Erin blinked at this revelation. "What about his family? Why don't people trust them?"

Jazz raised his brows. "On account of his mother being a Dyson."

Erin's heart started to beat more rapidly. From Harold's stories, it had been obvious that he was a Dyson, closely enough related to Nelson to go on the fishing trips with the Dyson cousins. She had worried about how close he was to Nelson. She didn't want him to be put in harm's way because of his relationship with the man who was now, with Willie's supposed death, the leader of the Dyson clan.

"I thought everyone on the mountain was kin," she said casually. "Isn't everyone related to the Dysons somehow?"

"Sure, but not as close as Della Melville. Her father is Dwight Dyson."

Dwight was the previous figurehead of the Dyson clan, replaced when Willie had been appointed as the actual leader of the clan. He was Nelson's father. "So Nelson *is* Harold's actual uncle."

Jazz nodded. "Surely. Nelson has a whole passel of nephews and nieces. Harold is one of them."

"He wasn't sure whether Nelson was an uncle or a cousin. How could he not know that his mother and Nelson were siblings?"

"Dwight was married... I think three times. Had kids with all of them, and probably some outside the bonds of matrimony. Della and Nelson had different mothers and probably weren't both living in the house at the same time."

"Oh, okay. That makes sense. If they didn't grow up together as siblings, I can see why Harold wasn't sure what the actual relationship was. And if there are that many cousins..."

"Lots of first cousins," Jazz said, "and even more when you consider the second or third cousins floating around the county too. Unless the kids sit down together and compare family trees, they are all just cousins."

"Harold said that they call the older cousins uncle out of respect."

Jazz nodded. "Out here, where everybody is related, it's a term of respect. Makes sense that Harold wouldn't be sure how he was related to each person."

Erin thought about how they had gotten onto the topic. "So... why do the Melvilles have a bad reputation if so many people are related to the Dysons? Why does it matter that she's Dwight's daughter if there are so many of them around?"

Jazz shrugged evasively. "Some people are closer than others. Della... she's kept close to the family. Some people distance themselves from the clan, try to cut ties, to not be associated with it."

"But not Mrs. Melville."

"She's always been very close to Dwight."

Erin had tiptoed around Harold's mother before, not wanting to upset her and anxious about her attitude toward anyone who might be a threat to her son. Jazz confirmed what Erin had known instinctively. Della Melville would be a dangerous woman to cross. And if any harm or threat of harm came to Harold, look out.

CHAPTER 17

$\mathcal{I}$t had been a pretty quiet Tuesday, and Erin was relieved that the drama seemed to have blown over. She had been particularly worried about people suspecting or targeting Harold after the suggestion that he'd had something to do with the letters.

But things were almost unnaturally quiet. Maybe people had thought about who Harold was and who his mother was and had decided it was best not to get involved or do anything that might bring the ire of the Dyson clan down on them.

She was breathing more easily, back into the swing of things, making batch after batch of eclairs and thinking about some new filling and frosting combinations she wanted to try. She could experiment with several combinations and see what people liked the best.

The bells over the door jingled, and Erin smiled at Frank as he approached and held a stack of mail toward her.

But Frank did not return Erin's smile. He was slow to hand the mail to her and slow to release his hold on it when Erin tried to take it from him. Erin met his eyes, her pleasant mood evaporating.

"Frank? What is it?"

"There's another one in there."

Erin's heart sank and she felt sick.

"Another one?" she repeated. She started to flip through the envelopes Frank had handed her, knowing what she would find.

Frank didn't reply, but he didn't need to. His face was pale and his expression grave.

The predictions were written on personal-sized writing paper, so the envelopes were smaller than the business envelopes that dominated Erin's mail. It wasn't hard to pick out the letter Frank had already spotted. She pulled it out from the rest of the mail. The writing on the front of the envelope was familiar to her now. She swore under her breath, something she would have gotten after any of her employees for doing.

"What is it?" Vic asked, then realized. "Oh, no. Not another one."

"It's just a prank," Erin said lightly. But she was afraid that this one would be harder to explain away. Why did the sender have to keep sending her the letters? Why not back off once people started to get upset? Why not send them to someone else, letting Erin and the bakery off the hook?

"Are you going to open it?" Vic asked.

"No." Erin looked at Frank. "No, I don't think that's a good idea." She pressed her lips together. She didn't know what she was going to do, but she wouldn't open the letter in front of anyone. And she didn't want customers to know she had gotten another one. "Let's keep this quiet, okay? I don't want people to know that I got another one."

Frank shrugged. "I don't know if'n you'll be able to keep it quiet. I'll keep my mouth shut, but other people have seen it and might have guessed what it is."

"Dang. Okay. If people know, they know." Erin looked at Vic. "I'm going to be in my office. Can you cover the front for a few minutes for me?"

Vic nodded her agreement.

Erin left her to it and retreated through the kitchen to her closet-sized office. She sat heavily on her chair, her legs shaking and her heart thumping hard. She felt nauseated, a wave of heat and sweat going over her, making her wish she was home in bed instead of in her office looking at that innocuous little envelope.

But there was nothing to do but open it. It would just be another silly prediction, something nice and vague that could be twisted to refer to some ordinary happening in Bald Eagle Falls.

Erin took a deep breath, squared her shoulders, and looked down at the envelope. There was nothing remarkable about it. The longer she looked at it, the harder it would be to take action, so she forced herself to slide her letter opener under the flap and slice it open.

The note was written on the same stationery with the same watermark. Erin unfolded it. Would it be another baking reference? It made sense, considering the author was writing to a bakery. But she didn't know the point other than to get attention. Maybe because she knew that lots of gossip happened at Auntie Clem's. Lots of people hung out there. And there had been some incidents in the past that Erin would rather not think about. She didn't think that the writer was targeting her personally. She hoped not.

In the warmth of friend's embrace, betrayal looms with lethal grace. The truth hides behind a smile, but death wears a familiar face

Erin felt the blood drain from her face. Death? The previous notes had not been threatening. She had insisted to everyone who had talked to her about them that they were just pranks. That first one had talked about blood and vengeance. But not death.

It was easy to tie any kind of accident to a prediction that mentioned blood. Everyone got cut some time. But death was quite a bit more serious.

She had to figure this out. Was the writer escalating? Was it random? She could be pulling the rhymes out of a book somewhere. Generating them with a computer program. They might mean nothing at all.

"No," Erin murmured. "We do not have time for this. This is

silly. Some silly woman sending silly threats for no good reason. Just because she wants some attention."

CHAPTER 18

*E*ventually, with fingers that felt numb and clumsy, Erin pulled out her phone and tapped the screen to bring up Terry's name. She tapped it again to initiate a call. After a few rings, he answered, sounding distant and cheerful.

"Morning, Erin. What's up?"

Erin cleared her throat and tried to sound calm and natural. "I got another letter."

"Another letter? Oh, the poetic predictions? I didn't think you would get any more after Cindy Prost identified the watermark."

"It's the same paper again. Same envelope. Everything the same."

"Same type of general prediction? Anything more creative today?"

"Death."

"What?"

"Death, today. 'Death wears a familiar face.'"

There was silence from Terry for a moment. When he spoke again, she could tell that he was serious.

"Okay. I should come over there and have a look. Take it into evidence."

"Is that from a book or something? Shakespeare?"

"I don't know. Sounds kind of familiar. Do you think the whole thing was copied out of a book?"

"I don't know. I'll look it up. Maybe it is. I just… I don't feel good about it. It still doesn't mean anything. It's still just vague lines strung together that hardly even make sense. It's not even *good* poetry. But this one scares me." Erin swallowed. "I guess it's probably just because of Harold. How he hurt himself the other day. I can't stand to think of something more serious happening to him or one of the other employees."

"It is still just a prank," Terry said, calm and soothing. "We don't have any evidence that anyone has done anything violent or intends to. The first two letters don't even read like threats. I don't think you need to be worried that anyone is going to do anything to any of your employees."

"Okay."

"Has anyone else read or heard what the letter says?"

"No. I had the sense not to open it in front of anyone else this time."

"Good," Terry approved. "We'll just keep it to ourselves. It's best if the whole town doesn't know what it said. Easier to figure out who knows more than they should. What about Vic?"

Erin glanced toward the front of the shop where she knew Vic was working, even though there were walls between them.

"What about her?"

"Did she see what it said?"

"No. No one. Just me. Why would it matter if Vic had seen it? You know she doesn't have anything to do with this."

"I know," Terry assured her. "I just want to cover all the bases. Make sure that no one can claim they heard it from her."

Erin swallowed and nodded. "Okay."

"I'll be there in a few minutes."

"Okay. See you in a few minutes, then."

Erin ended the call. She knew he wouldn't take long. It wasn't far to any point in Bald Eagle Falls, and she didn't think he had been out of town for anything. She took a picture of the letter lying on the desk since she already had the phone in her hand.

A minute later, Vic poked her head in the door. "Is everything okay?" she asked tentatively.

Erin turned the note over so that Vic could not see the contents. Vic's eyes followed the movement; then she looked at Erin's face.

"What is it? Is it different this time?"

"I can't talk to you about it. Terry's on his way over."

"Why can't you talk to me about it? Is it something to do with me? With Willie?"

"No. Nothing like that. He just doesn't want anyone else to read it. So if anyone knows what it says... they could be a suspect."

"Oh." Vic nodded, looking relieved. Then she frowned again. "If Terry is coming to look at it, does that mean there is something for him to investigate? Is it something really bad this time?"

Erin shrugged. "He's going to have a look and see what he thinks."

"Huh." Vic clearly didn't like Erin's answer. "And you can't tell me anything about it?"

"That wouldn't be very smart. I don't want to screw up Terry's investigation."

"Okay," Vic sighed. "I'll just stay in the dark, then."

There was a noise at the front of the store, the bells ringing, and women's voices.

"You're supposed to be watching the front," Erin reminded Vic.

"I know. I just wanted to make sure you were okay."

Erin nodded. She didn't say she was okay, but Vic returned to the front to look after the customers.

Erin expected Terry to come to the bakery's back door, but there was more and more noise from the front of the store, and eventually, Erin got up to see what was going on.

Several of the women she knew from the church group and the neighborhood were engaged in conversation. They were not looking at the baking or discussing what they were going to buy next. Animosity crackled in the air.

"Look," said Lottie Sturm, her voice screechier than usual. Despite her girlish pigtails, she looked her age, an ugly scowl on her face and the afternoon sun coming in the front window lighting every wrinkle and flaw in relief. "We know who has been sending the letters. So I don't know why anybody is standing around pretending there is any investigating to be done. Somebody needs to pull Harold Melville out of class and set him straight. I don't care who he is related to; the boy needs to be put straight. Am I right?"

"Lottie," Cindy protested. She and Lottie were usually arm in arm on the same side of every issue, so it was strange to see Cindy trying to pull her friend back. "We don't know anything about it. Yes, it looks like Harold or someone in his family sent those letters, but let the police investigate it and find out."

"They are not doing anything," Lottie snapped. "They don't think that any law has been broken. They think it's just fine to mail around death threats and scare the wits out of people!"

Erin swallowed. She hadn't told anyone what was in the third letter. She didn't even know how they could already know about it. "Let's just calm down here," she suggested. Her voice was small and cracked, not the calm, authoritative tone she wanted to use. "Let's not go throwing any accusations around."

"You don't know anything about that boy or the family he is from. Admit it. You think he's just a nice young man giving you a hand in your kitchen. You don't know what a snake in the grass he is. That whole family has been—"

"Let's all keep our heads here," advised Tara, the next voice of reason. Erin could see how she had been as a mediator in family disputes. She had a very soothing voice and a firm manner. Erin could imagine how she would talk to each party, cooling them down and making everyone see reason. Helping each side to see the other's point of view. "Erin hasn't done anything wrong. She doesn't have anything to do with the letter-writer. And as much as I would like to say that it was definitely someone in the Melville family, we don't even know that. We don't even know that it is the Melville coat of arms."

"Just look at it!" Lottie insisted. "Anyone can see that it is."

"It definitely *resembles* the Melville coat of arms," Tara agreed.

"But a lot of them look similar and may only differ in color. And the watermark has no color, so we can't be sure."

"Who else in this town even has a coat of arms?"

Some of the women exchanged looks, which Erin took as evidence that there were several others in town who knew their own family crests.

"That Della Dyson has always had pretensions. Always thought she was royalty around here."

"Della Melville," Tara corrected gently. "It doesn't hurt anyone to show respect and call people by their preferred names."

"She never wanted to take her husband's name. She was born a Dyson and she'll die a Dyson. That husband of hers is lucky she didn't force him to take her name. Or at least to make her children take it." Lottie turned to Erin, her eyes afire. "Where is Harold? When does he clock in?"

"That's none of your business."

"I am a customer. I deserve the same respect as anyone else. If I want to be served by a particular employee, why can't I ask?"

"Because I said so," Erin said, folding her arms. "Just like I can ask you all to disperse if you are not buying anything."

"You can't kick us out!" Lottie insisted. She had been thrown out before, so Erin didn't know where she got that idea.

"Are you buying something?"

"I want to know what you are doing about this. Surely you're not going to let him keep working here when he is targeting your place of business with his letter-writing campaign."

Erin looked at the clock on the wall. Where was Terry? She had thought that he would be there by now.

"Lottie, if you don't want to have to explain to Terry why you are still here when I have asked you to leave, you'd better go now. You don't have much time. And if anyone else is only here to cause trouble for Harold or anyone else…"

She looked around at the rest of the customers. Tara stepped closer to the counter to show her allegiance to Erin and have a look at what was on offer in the display case today.

"Is that shoofly pie? Oh, it's been forever since I had a good shoofly pie. Not since my nana died."

Erin nodded and reached into the case for it.

There was an angry jangle of bells as Lottie flounced back out of the bakery. A low murmur followed her as everyone started whispering about the confrontation. Erin continued to help Tara, who gave her an encouraging smile.

CHAPTER 19

*T*erry arrived at a leisurely pace, K9 at his side. He stepped in the door and looked around slowly, evaluating the situation. While the cause of the confrontation was gone, he could probably still sense the atmosphere. He looked at Erin.

"Why don't you and I go to the back? Do you think Vic can handle everyone here for a few minutes? Or is there someone else in the kitchen who could come out?"

"It's just me and Vic right now."

"Well, we'll only take a few minutes."

Erin put Tara's order on the counter for Vic to pack and ring up. She looked at the other women there. "I hope everybody can be patient for a few minutes. This won't take long. Sorry, Vic."

"Oh, don't you mind me," Vic drawled, "I'll be just fine."

Erin nodded and let Terry and K9 through the hinged section of the counter so they could get through to the kitchen, and then to Erin's office.

"Sorry for coming in the front," Terry apologized. "But it looked like you were getting a regular mob going there."

"Yeah. Things were a bit sticky there for a few minutes. Lottie was ready to take a piece out of someone. She wants to know when Harold will be here so that she can confront him."

Terry shook his head. "I'll try to track her down later to have a word with her. We can't have adults stalking children."

Erin nodded her agreement. "I'm worried about the backlash against the Melvilles, when no one really knows if they had anything to do with this. Everyone seems to have just focused on Harold because he is a Melville, and Cindy says it is the Melville coat of arms on the stationery. And because he works here. But why would he try to cause trouble at the bakery when he works here? He's not a troublemaker. He's a good worker and he likes his job. Why would he try to sabotage it?"

"We never know why people do some of the things they do. But you're right; it doesn't make a lot of sense for him to want to put his job in jeopardy if he likes it. I'd like to talk to him about it."

He looked at Erin steadily, and she knew that he wanted her to facilitate the meeting with Harold. But she really couldn't. It was her job to protect her employees, and she knew that the younger employees' parents would not appreciate it at all if she were to help Terry interrogate them.

Erin didn't offer to help him talk to Harold, and Terry eventually looked away, sighing. "So, let's have a look at the newest letter." He saw it on the desk and walked to the other side to look at it right-side up.

"Did you touch the letter?"

He could already see that she had. She hadn't opened it wearing gloves.

"I tried to only touch the edges."

Terry nodded and didn't criticize her for touching it or opening it herself.

"I didn't know it was any different than the other letters, and you didn't want those ones for evidence."

"No, you're right," he agreed. He read through the verse, frowning. He looked off into space, drumming his fingertips on the desk. K9 whined at his side.

Terry looked down at the letter, motioning for K9 to be quiet. "I have to admit... I do find this one more concerning than the others. Not only because it speaks of death and the other ones didn't. But also... because things are escalating in town and the sender didn't decide to dial things back. He didn't stop sending them or wait until things quieted down again. Instead, he decided to send one while people were still upset, to add fuel to the fire."

Erin hadn't thought about that, but the thought made her shudder. She didn't like the idea of the letter writer out there, challenging the townspeople, winding them up further.

"You keep saying 'he.' But I don't think it's a man. That's not a man's handwriting."

"It could be. You and I are not handwriting experts. You're right that the writing is more feminine... but that doesn't change anything. We can't afford not to look at male suspects just because the handwriting is round. Anyone could choose to disguise their usual handwriting that way. It isn't a long passage."

Erin looked down at the writing and tried to convince herself that it could be a man's handwriting, but it just didn't make sense to her. Some people's writing was not identifiably feminine or masculine, but the clairvoyant's predictions were written in a script she didn't think could be anything but feminine. And what about the rhyming verses? That seemed more like something a woman would do too.

"So, you're going to investigate? You will take that one as a threat and see if you can figure out who sent it?"

"Yes. I'll take this one with me, and we'll see if we can get any fingerprints or track down where the paper came from. Whether the Melvilles can tell us if that is really their crest on the watermark and if this paper came from their stock."

"If it did, you don't think they would tell you that, do you?"

Terry grimaced. "Well, people sometimes surprise you. To be honest, I don't expect to be able to get anywhere with Mrs. Melville. I'm hoping I'll have better success with her husband or Harold."

"Well... good luck with that. What is her husband like? I don't think I even know what he looks like."

"I'm not sure I can tell you anything about him. He's always seemed sort of a colorless character. Mrs. Melville is the one who sticks out in the family. I don't know if you can say she wears the pants; I honestly don't know what their dynamic is like. I don't know if she's the boss or disciplinarian. You probably know more from talking to Harold."

"He doesn't mention his dad much. It's always his mom. I would say she is the boss... she's the one he doesn't want to tell—" Erin cut herself off. She didn't want to give personal information to Terry. Harold would not like her to share what he had told her in private. It wasn't like he had revealed anything big and important, but she didn't want to betray any confidences.

"He doesn't want to tell her what?"

Erin shook her head. "Nothing serious. I didn't mean to say anything. I don't want to repeat things he's said to me that he wouldn't want shared."

"He's sharing family secrets with you?"

"No, not at all. He's talked a little about his uncle and brothers. But that's about it. He's only mentioned his mother in passing, and my impression is that she is strict. Or he thinks she is strict. I had some parents in foster care that would put anyone else to shame. Kids now like to make out that their parents are tough, but most of them aren't. They're just trying to hold on and keep their kids from going off the rails. Most of them are... mushy underneath. They just want their kids to be safe and happy."

"As opposed to parents who..."

Erin thought about some of the families she had seen. Some of the dynamics between parents and children.

"Parents who are mean... who enjoy hurting... or have to be in control. I don't think Mrs. Melville is any of those things. I think she is just trying to keep her kids from getting into trouble."

Terry put on gloves to collect the letter and put it into a brown evidence envelope. He removed the gloves and put them into the garbage.

"Did anyone else touch the letter? Read it?"

"No, I told you. I just came in here and opened it, and no one else saw it or read it."

"Who touched the envelope before you?"

"Frank, the postal carrier. I don't know who might have touched it before him. Whoever sorted and gave it to him. Is that all done by machines now? People must still have to touch it somewhere along the way. Are they being mailed in Bald Eagle Falls? Do you know that?"

"We haven't investigated it yet. My instinct would be... yes. I think this is someone local. Especially since that second envelope wasn't even mailed. Just left on the sidewalk because it was a Saturday. They wanted you to get it immediately, without waiting for the postal system to deliver it on Monday."

"And you think it has something to do with the Melvilles?"

"I don't know. If the paper came from them... then there must be some connection. But I don't know for sure that it did." Terry started toward the door, K9 beside him eager to get back to business. "I'll get this to the office to see what we can find out about it," Terry promised, saluting with the envelope. "I'll... let you know if I need anything else from you."

Erin had the feeling that he had been about to tell her that he would tell her what he found out, but of course, he couldn't promise that. He shouldn't be sharing any information about an ongoing investigation with her. But bits of it might slip out. Or she might hear it through the grapevine or through the biggest leak of all, Melissa Lee.

Erin had her ways of finding things out.

CHAPTER 20

*W*hen Erin returned to the front of the bakery, she found Vic just seeing off the last customer. Vic leaned back against the counter, her back to the door as she talked with Erin, and took advantage of the lull.

"So...? What did Officer Handsome have to say about the latest letter?"

"He took it with him. He's going to investigate this one."

"Well, it's about time!"

"There wasn't anything he could do about the other ones," Erin pointed out. "They weren't threats. I didn't feel threatened by them. They were just... vague predictions. This one felt a lot more... directed and personal. And..." She didn't tell Vic that it had contained a reference to death. That would probably leak out sooner or later, anyway. Sooner, if she knew Melissa. Even Clara seemed to be personally involved in this case, and she usually stayed well out of anything the police were investigating.

Vic looked at her phone. "Harold will be getting out of school soon. I wonder if... you should pick him up."

Erin thought about Lottie and the other townspeople who were so sure that Harold or someone in the family had something to do with the letters.

"You know, that's a good idea," she admitted. "Do you want to send him a text to look for me? I'll pop over to the school."

Vic nodded. "Sure. Is there anything in the ovens that I need to keep an eye on?"

"No, they're empty right now. Harold and I will put a couple more things together before the dinner rush."

Vic opened her text app and typed out a message for Harold. Erin grabbed her handbag from her office and headed over to the school to pick Harold up.

She kept a sharp eye out for Lottie in particular. She didn't want a confrontation between the two. It was hard to know who to watch. It was the middle of the day, so people were out and about, running errands and getting their work done. She saw Tara on her way home and gave her a wave.

She didn't see Lottie, but she was sure Lottie wasn't the only one who might have a bone to pick with Harold.

Harold got release time from school to work at the bakery as part of his business course, so she was picking him up before the chaos of the dismissal bell. Most of the students still had another class or two to attend before they would be released. It wasn't hard, therefore, for Erin to find a place to stop and look for Harold, and he had no trouble spotting the bright yellow bug.

"Thanks, Miss Erin," he said as he got in. "You didn't have to pick me up."

"We're just a little worried about how some of the ladies are behaving... I didn't want anyone harassing you on your way from school to Auntie Clem's."

He nodded wearily. "Kids at school have just been..." He trailed off, shaking his head. "I wish I didn't have to go to school. I could just do home study or whatever. But Mom says I have to go and learn to stand up for myself. Show them what I'm made of."

Erin knew that she couldn't say anything bad about Harold's mother in front of him. She couldn't contradict her. That would be a good way to lose her employee and maybe end up with a vengeful Dyson gunning for her. Not a good idea. But she hated for Harold to think that the only way to deal with bullies was by getting tough and fighting them.

Harold was a kind, quiet, thoughtful boy. She knew that he hadn't been involved in sending the letters, and knew just as strongly that the way for him to succeed and become the best person he could was not by fighting with bullies.

Physical violence was not the answer. No more than Lottie's plan to confront Harold and make him answer for having sent the letters that had everyone in a tizzy.

"Things are kind of mixed up right now," she told Harold, "and this must be so hard for you." She ventured a glance at him as she drove. "But it won't last forever. Officer Piper is looking into the letters now, and the police will sort it out. And they'll ensure you're safe from anyone who thinks you need to be punished for something you didn't do. Whoever is sending those letters is responsible for their actions, not you."

She glanced at him again. Harold was staring out the window, a frown on his face.

"I don't want trouble with the police."

"I know. And you're not in trouble with the police. The police want to find out who is sending these letters. I know that isn't you."

"You don't *know* that."

"Yes, I do. You didn't write them. I've seen your handwriting. And what reason would you have to send them? You don't *want* to lose your job."

"I like my job," he agreed quickly. "You don't think I'll—you're not going to fire me, are you?"

"No, of course not. Why would I fire you for something you didn't do? I don't care what anyone says, I won't believe it."

"But what if everyone else wants you to? What if no one wants to work with me? Or the customers say they won't shop at the bakery anymore until you do?"

"I'm still not going to give in. People will come around. They can't stay away from our baking for that long." She gave him a teasing smile.

Harold wiped at his cheeks and didn't look at her. "Yeah," he agreed, voice cracking a little, "those eclairs aren't going to eat themselves."

Erin laughed. "That's right. Hey, you just gave me an idea for Halloween. What if we make the eclairs look like monsters with mouths? The white filling is the teeth, or we could do a strawberry filling for a red mouth. And then put little eyes made of rolled fondant on top and display them sideways..."

"Fondant teeth and tongues," Harold suggested with a grin, immediately catching on to the idea.

"Yes! Oh, they would be so cute. Do you think people would like them? They wouldn't refuse to buy them for their kids because they looked like devils or something?"

Sometimes, the things that Erin thought of, especially for kids, flopped because their Bible-thumping parents objected to them on religious grounds. Even though Erin had never meant to send any anti-Christian message by making Santa cookies for Christmas or ghosties for Halloween.

"No, I think they would go over really well! They would be a lot of fun. You could do a kid's decorating event some Saturday afternoon, a little workshop where they can go to the community center and put their own eyes and teeth on their eclair monsters. Or if you think it would be too messy to do with eclairs, we could just do it with cookies. They would have so much fun. When I was a kid, I always enjoyed making gingerbread men, even though we just had frosting for the faces and candy buttons."

"Great idea," Erin approved, and they talked about it all the way back to Auntie Clem's and were still bouncing suggestions back and forth when they walked into the kitchen.

Vic gave Erin an approving smile when she saw Harold animatedly involved in the discussion. She could probably guess about the bullying he was facing at school, and that he would now face from some of the adults who saw him at the bakery or on the street. She knew he needed support and distraction and that Erin was doing her best to provide it.

Rather than Auntie Clem's being a place he dreaded working

because of the letter-writer's campaign, it would be a distraction from his troubles and a safe haven.

CHAPTER 21

*N*either of them felt much like cooking or even warming up something for supper after closing Auntie Clem's. Vic suggested they take up Susan Brown's offer of a free meal at the family restaurant. For once, Vic wouldn't be hiding out in Erin's house or her loft apartment, trying to convince everyone that Willie was dead and Vic was in mourning.

"Are you sure you want to be out in public?" Erin queried. "You know that people will criticize you for going out to do anything."

"I know," Vic agreed. "And I know that there's no way I can please everyone all of the time. People will judge me and say that I am doing the wrong thing no matter what I do."

Erin nodded. "That doesn't make the criticisms sting any less."

"Well, no," Vic admitted. "And maybe I'll regret it when I'm trying to sleep tonight and can't get all the looks and comments out of my head. But then I will take a sleeping pill and go to sleep anyway."

Erin laughed. "So there."

Vic nodded firmly. "I'm going to the restaurant. Susan invited me. It was her way of helping out instead of sending over a casserole. Instead of heating something up, we just go and order what we want, and the staff will take care of us."

"It will be a nice change."

"I am getting a little tired of noodle casseroles," Vic admitted. "They're great, but they don't do my waistline any favors, and I'm getting bored with them. It's been going on for too long. The gift-giving needs to stop. Real soon."

"You might need to hold a memorial for Willie."

"I'm not going to do that when he ain't dead."

"I know. I'm just saying. You might have to bend on this a little bit."

"No way."

Country music played softly in the background, combining with clinking cutlery and the low murmur of conversation. The air was redolent with baked bread, potatoes, and steak.

Erin and Vic looked over the menus, even though they had eaten at the family restaurant enough times to have it memorized. Nothing new had been added. But they took their time in making their choices. After they had placed their orders, Susan came over to the table and drew out a third chair.

"Do you mind if I join you?"

"Sure, come over and set a spell," Vic invited. "I wanted to thank you for the offer. One *can* get a mite tired of covered dishes after a while."

"Believe me, I know," Susan agreed with a big smile. She was a tall woman, and not thin, but she wasn't intimidating like some big women. She pushed her long, curly brown hair streaked with gray back from her face and over her shoulders. "You could have just ordered over the phone, you know. I would have had it delivered to the house for you. You didn't need to come out in public and put yourself on display."

"I know," Vic agreed. "But I've been getting cabin fever. Even when you're going through something like I am," Vic was careful not to actually say that she was in mourning for her recently deceased boyfriend, "you just can't stay closeted up in the house all day long."

Susan probably knew very well that Vic was not staying home all day, but was back to working at the bakery as usual. But she didn't point this out. She reached out and patted Vic's arm. "It's such a difficult time," she sympathized. "I'll help you any way I can."

Vic nodded. "Right now, the best thing is probably *distraction*. I want to think of something else. So…" she leaned toward Susan, lowering her voice. "What's the latest gossip?"

Susan laughed. She twirled her finger around a lock of hair. "I imagine you already know all the latest details," she said. "You hear more working at the bakery than I do here."

"But I'm not allowed to speculate with the customers," Vic said, and gave Erin a significant look. "My boss is real strict about that."

"I'll bet she is." Susan leaned back in her seat. "The biggest thing is the letters, of course. And you know all about that."

"Did you hear we got a third one today?" Vic asked.

"I heard that! But no one will say what it said."

"I didn't see this one. Only Erin has seen it."

They both turned their gazes on Erin. She held up her hands. "I can't tell you anything about it. It is an active police investigation now. Terry asked me not to tell anyone what it said, so if they find someone who knows the details, they know… it is the writer or someone related to her somehow."

They both looked at her, waiting for some other detail. Some juicy bit that she could share even if she didn't tell them anything about what the letter said.

"Well, if Terry accepted that this one was something that needed to be investigated by the police, that means it was different from the others," Vic said slowly. "He said that the others were not explicit threats, just predictions, and very vague."

Erin nodded. She sipped her water.

"Does that mean that the third letter did contain a threat?" Vic asked.

Erin shrugged.

"Yes," Vic decided. "So…" She looked at Susan. "Who do your sources say it is? And don't just say Harold Melville because…" she shook her head. "That just doesn't make any sense. We know it's not Harold."

"I don't know about eliminating Harold," Susan said, "but he's not the only person in that family. People are just blaming him because he works at Auntie Clem's."

"You think it is someone else in his family? Della?"

"She certainly has grudges with enough people in Bald Eagle Falls. She could be aiming them at someone who works at Auntie Clem's. Not Erin," she said generously, giving Erin a quick smile. "Erin might just be getting the predictions because she has helped the police solve cases in the past. The target could be... someone else, and she just wants Erin to be able to link the threats with the actual actions..."

"Who else at Auntie Clem's could she have a grudge against?" Erin asked, frowning. As far as she knew, Mrs. Melville didn't have a problem with anyone working there. Would she have let Harold work there if she'd had a problem with one of the other workers?

CHAPTER 22

"ho could Della have a grudge with? Well, there's Charley Campbell, for one," Susan said thoughtfully. "She killed Bobby Dyson, Della's half-brother. And then they found out she was actually a Jackson. I don't know why the Dysons didn't take Charley out as soon as they knew what had happened."

"Charley wasn't the one who killed him," Erin objected. "She was just the initial suspect, but she was cleared. And she didn't know that she had any Jackson blood. She is adopted."

"Do you really think that would matter to someone like Della? She's not exactly known for being forgiving."

"But why would she be so obvious?" Erin challenged. "Why would she use Melville stationery?"

Susan cocked her head to the side, considering, then nodded. "You've got a point. I think she's smart enough not to do that. But that doesn't rule out her husband or other sons."

Erin smothered a smile at the suggestion that Mr. Melville and the two older brothers were not that smart. She was sure that wasn't what Susan had meant.

"What are they like?" She asked. "What reason would they have to start a campaign like this?"

"I don't know if we will be able to figure out the 'why,'" Vic put in. "You can't always know why someone does what they do or their real motive. Sometimes they don't even know why."

"True," Susan agreed. "I've known some real winners in my time, if you want the truth. Sometimes, unraveling why they do something can be impossible. They're impulsive, or confused, or psychotic. Or just human."

"People are driven by feelings more than logic," Erin offered.

"Yes." Susan pointed at her. "You nailed it. You look at the things your friends do, going back to relationships that don't work, sabotaging themselves, wrecking something that took years to develop. And look at the behavior of strangers online. If you think that people always make sense, you don't have to go far to figure out it isn't true. Especially when people think they are anonymous or won't get called out."

A waitress arrived with a platter of freshly toasted, fragrant garlic bread Susan had signaled her to bring, and they each savored the delicious appetizer. The conversation was put on pause for a few seconds.

Then Susan resumed. "But all of that said... I can say that the Melvilles have plenty of reason to resent other families or individuals here in Bald Eagle Falls. They aren't exactly easy to get along with."

"That includes all of them?" Erin asked, "Not just Della?"

"Yes." Susan looked at Vic. "The clans are famous for being able to hold on to old grievances. They can hold on to a slight for generations, building up their anger around something as simple as one student beating another's grade or calling him a name. Or one woman winning the pie baking category at the Founder's Day Fair away from another who had swept the category for five years."

Erin shook her head in dismay. "How could we ever discover all the resentments over little things like that? You could talk to people for years without being able to ferret everything out."

"No one is expecting you to," Vic assured her. "It's the job of the police to investigate and find out who has been sending these letters."

"No one is expecting me to?"

"Well," Vic smiled slightly. "I can't say no one is expecting you to. But it isn't your job."

"My job is baking and keeping the bakery open."

"I know. But people have gotten the idea that you are talented at this kind of thing and expect you to try, at least. But I know. You can't do everything. And it's not fair to expect you to solve all the cases the police department is investigating. Or not investigating."

Erin pondered. "If Della is not the person sending the letters, then it isn't about the Melville family. The letters are written in a feminine hand. It couldn't be the husband or sons."

Susan smiled and helped herself to another slice of garlic bread. She tore off a piece and popped it into her mouth. "Are you saying that men can't write nicely? There are plenty of male calligraphers."

Erin's cheeks warmed. "Well, it wasn't exactly calligraphy. I just mean… you can tell the difference. Can't you?"

"Not necessarily. Some people can write in all different styles, especially if they have practiced a lot."

"Are any of the Melville men calligraphers?"

"I don't know what they do for their hobbies. I wouldn't expect it, but… you never know. There are men who do knitting or embroidery, cooking, making jams or preserves…"

Erin exchanged glances with Vic, smiling over a secret they shared.

Vic also had really nice handwriting, Erin realized. She always admired Vic's neatly printed price labels for the display case, and Erin knew that she had a beautiful loopy cursive hand as well. Had she learned to print and write like that as James Jackson? Was it something she had practiced and perfected before coming out as a transgender woman? Of course, a man could develop beautiful handwriting that Erin would have initially considered feminine.

"Okay," she admitted, shaking her head and rubbing her temples. "I can't tell just from looking at the handwriting that it was a woman. You've convinced me."

"Harold's father, Donald, expected to be a bigwig in the Dyson clan," Susan said, leaning forward and lowering her voice so that those at nearby tables wouldn't overhear her. "He figured being

Dwight's son-in-law would give him cachet, and he would be able to take whatever job he wanted to."

Vic rolled her eyes and shook her head. "Being married to a clan member, even a high-ranking one, doesn't give you any authority. And from what I've seen and heard, Della isn't actually that involved with the clan."

"Would you really know?" Erin asked tentatively.

Vic opened her mouth, then considered. "Well... I think I would see some signs. But I'm not close to her. She could be more involved than I think. But I don't think I ever even heard of her before they moved back here to Bald Eagle Falls, and I grew up in the Jackson clan. If she was that involved with the Dysons... I would have at least heard of her."

Erin had to trust that Vic knew what she was talking about. She looked back at Susan. "So Donald thought he would be able to be a big deal with the Dysons, but it turned out he wasn't. So he's disgruntled because of that. Wouldn't that make him turn against the Dyson bosses? Why target me or the bakery?"

"Maybe he thinks Charley or Willie or someone else loosely associated with you or Auntie Clem's had something to do with not being able to get anywhere in the clan." Susan shrugged. "You never know."

"And what about the other boys? Are they like Harold?"

About the only thing Erin knew about Harold's older brothers was that they had not watched him closely enough on the fishing trip to keep him from getting a fishhook embedded in his foot. Not very responsible. But then, she didn't know what they had been doing when Harold had been injured. They could have been on an errand for Uncle Nelson. Erin was just assuming they had been partying or goofing off instead of taking their responsibilities seriously.

Vic looked at Susan, brows raised, with nothing to contribute to the discussion.

"Harold's brothers, Anton and Salman..." Susan considered. Glancing at her watch, she knew she didn't have much more time to spend sitting at Erin's and Vic's table. She had work to do, and their dinners would be arriving shortly.

"I think they started life with the same misguided expectation that they would be something big in the clan. Maybe encouraged by Della, thinking that her sons would be in the running for the leadership of the clan, with Nelson not having any progeny and Bobby being… young and wild."

"So they might have thought that they would be in Willie's position before he was shot," Erin suggested. "Will they be now? With Willie out of the way and Nelson leading the clan? They are his nephews, so they would be in line, wouldn't they?"

"They could be, if the Dysons are going to follow family lines," Vic said. "But we don't know if they will. We didn't even know they were being led by the matriarchal line before Willie was installed and that men like Dwight were only figureheads. That was kept a very close secret. I'm amazed that no one in the Jackson clan ever had an inkling of it."

Susan made a small noise in her throat. "The thing about Anton and Salman is… they're not that bright."

Erin blinked at this. She had just assumed they would be like Harold, who was always quick to pick things up. If they were not, it would be pretty difficult for them to run the entire organization. Even a figurehead had to have some idea what he was doing.

"So even now, they're not likely to get a lot of recognition in the clan."

Susan shook her head. "No, not as far as I can see. Of course, I'm not in either of the clans, so I can only say what I see from the outside. I could be completely wrong. But I think Della has been pushing those boys to become something since they were born, and now she has to deal with the likelihood that they will never amount to anything."

Erin could see how that would cause a lot of anger and bitterness. From all of them. Della, Donald, and the boys. Resentments that might be directed at Vic, an ex-Jackson, for being connected with Willie Andrews, the man who had been picked over the boys to lead the Dyson clan. Or against Charley, who had been accused of taking out Bobby Dyson.

Susan looked at her watch again. "It's been nice, ladies, but I need to get back to the grindstone. Enjoy your dinners, and come back any time for a chat and whatever else you need. I know what it is like trying to get back to a normal life after losing someone close to you. I'm here for you."

"Thanks." Vic squeezed Susan's hand before she left. "You've been so kind."

"And I love a good bull session any time." Susan smiled. "Nothing like a bit of gossip to make the time pass faster."

CHAPTER 23

"Y"ou know who we should take some eclairs to?" Vic asked the next afternoon as Erin piped filling into one of the shells.

Erin shook her head. "Who?" she asked without looking up.

"Frank Grayson."

"The mailman?" Erin turned to look at Vic with a frown. "Why?"

"I just think… we take his services for granted. He is out there every day, come storm or sleet or… uh…"

Erin laughed. "Neither snow nor rain nor heat nor gloom of night," she quoted.

"Yeah! I knew it was something like that."

"So we should take Frank eclairs?"

"Definitely. And while we're there, we could ask him what he knows about who sent the letters. If there was anything about the sender or the envelopes that was different. Maybe he recognizes the handwriting or stationery from someone else…"

"Oh," Erin drew the syllable out. "Now I get it. You know Terry wouldn't want me interfering with a police investigation."

"They've had plenty of time to follow up with Frank. It's not our problem if they haven't. And all we're doing is taking him some eclairs out of appreciation. Like giving an apple to a teacher."

"Have you ever actually done that? Or known anyone who has?"

"Uh… no." Vic scratched her temple. "Where did we get that, anyway? Is it because apples represent knowledge? 'Cause of Adam and Eve eating the fruit to gain knowledge?"

"I assumed it was just because they were hungry. Early American teachers weren't paid much, and the students' families supported them."

"Oh." Vic shrugged. Her cheeks got a little pink. "Maybe that too."

"Maybe you want to give Frank eclairs because you are sweet on him."

Vic's cheeks turned an even deeper shade of red. "Erin Price! You take that back! You know I'm not sweet on anyone except Willie! I wouldn't even look at someone else."

"Oh, no?" Erin asked. "Hmm." She tried to think of who else Vic might take the occasional look at, despite the fact she was in a dedicated relationship with Willie. "You're always making comments about my Officer Handsome. So you must have looked at him from time to time."

"No. I never did. You're the one who talks about his cute dimple and… how ruggedly handsome he is."

"I've never said that!"

"Well, you should." Vic stuck out her tongue as she poured fondant over the eclairs Erin had already filled. "Because he is!"

They both giggled.

The icing on the eclairs had set enough to transport them by the time Erin and Vic were finished their shifts. Erin looked at her watch. "Did you really want to stop by and see if Frank is home? I don't know his schedule after he makes his deliveries, but we could see if he is home."

"Yes," Vic agreed quickly. "For sure, I want to know whether he knows anything about—I mean, I want to thank him for how diligent he is about the mail. In sleet and snow and all that. We are beholden to him for all of his work."

"It shouldn't take too long to tell him that," Erin agreed. "We can just drop the eclairs off at the door…"

"Well, that would be rude," Vic said. "We should at least go in and ask him how he is. You can't just 'ding dong ditch.'"

"He might be busy. I wouldn't want to interrupt him."

Vic shook her head. "You really are full of sass today, aren't you?"

Erin was feeling energized instead of tired at the end of her shift, silly and teasing and enjoying Vic's company even more than usual. What reason was there for *not* being happy on such a beautiful spring day? The eclairs had turned out beautifully, and everyone was putting in extra orders for them, which was great for business and gave Erin's ego an extra boost. She was good at what she did and enjoyed seeing her customers enjoying themselves.

Frank was home, and his eyes lit up when he saw the plate of eclairs that Vic and Erin had brought him.

"Oh, those look delicious! Come in, ladies. How nice of you to bring me something. People really don't do that, you know? Sometimes they give a tip at Christmas or New Year's, but I don't get a lot of presents. You wonder if people even see you, sometimes. You put the mail in their hands, and they are a hundred miles away. You could be invisible."

He opened the door wide for them and ushered them into his living room.

Erin stopped and stared. Rather than a conversational grouping of furniture and some side tables and bookshelves or an entertainment center, like she saw in most people's living rooms, almost the entire space was taken up by tables.

Not dining tables or coffee tables. Train tables.

Erin gaped at the scenery spreading out across the tables. Tiny buildings and streets. And train tracks. Double, triple, and quadruple tracks snaked around the table, with an electronic control panel to operate the switches and control where the trains ran.

"Oh, this is a-maz-ing!" Vic declared. "Oh, my word. I've never seen a setup like this. Why didn't I know you were a model train guy?"

Frank smiled, enjoying their reactions. "Are you interested in trains?" he asked Vic.

"I love trains. These are so cool! I had an uncle with a little model train setup, but it was nothing like this."

"It's the biggest layout in Bald Eagle Falls."

"I believe it. Look at it, Erin! This is fantastic."

Erin was looking. Vic was closer, blocking Erin's view of a lot of the details. She leaned in, looking closely at something.

"Come here! Did you see this? Look." Vic grabbed Erin's hand and pulled her over, as excited as a child in a toy store. "He has Auntie Clem's!"

Vic pulled her over to where she could see a miniaturized Main Street, with Auntie Clem's Bakery, the Book Nook, the General Store, and other businesses Erin was familiar with laid out in a line.

"Oh," she squeaked. "It's so cute!"

Frank was beaming. "I haven't replicated all of Bald Eagle Falls," he said, "but I have included many of the town's most popular locations." He pointed out a few features. "Your woods and Canyon Park. The most popular restaurants. The library. Town Hall and police department."

Erin got closer to look at the tiny police department. She laughed. Frank had taken a few liberties, and there was a jail cell within the suite of offices, even though the real police department had only a couple of interview rooms and did not have the facilities to hold arrestees. Any prisoners had to be transferred to the penitentiary.

"I love the little jail cell. We need one of those!"

"Right?" Frank agreed. "How can you have a police department without a jail cell?"

Erin gazed at the sad little felon being held in the jail cell, his tiny face despondent.

"Here's your summer house," Vic pointed to a little structure in the middle of the woods Frank had indicated, where Adele, the gamekeeper, lived. "And is this your house? It is!"

Frank had not replicated all of Bald Eagle Falls, and because of how his tables were set up, everything did not have the same layout as they did in real life. She focused on the house Vic pointed out. It did not have all of the same features as her house, but there was a yellow bug parked on the street in front of it and a two-story garage behind it, with a stairway running up to the loft apartment on the second floor.

Her stomach knotted, and she felt suddenly uneasy about the miniature Bald Eagle Falls. She felt as though Frank had been spying on her, studying and replicating the details of her life in his living room. She should be flattered that he had picked these details out of her life to copy into his setup. But instead, she felt like the subject of a peeping tom, a voyeur who had been spying on her for months without her knowledge.

CHAPTER 24

*V*ic was still exclaiming over all the details, including a policeman on patrol with a German shepherd. She was so excited about it. Erin smiled and tried to appear as engaged and interested as her friend. Vic had Frank run the trains through their paces, exclaiming over the different eras and styles of trains that were represented. Some of them had whistles or clacking wheel sounds.

Erin sat on one of the stools Frank had available for when he was working on various parts of the layout or had visitors who wanted to watch him run the trains. Frank put his plate of eclairs in the kitchen and offered Erin and Vic beverages, which they declined. Erin tried to figure out how to signal Vic that she was ready to leave.

"Oh, this is just amazing, Frank," Vic told him, finally starting to wind down, even though she kept peeking in the various windows or leaning down to get a better look at something in the scenes Frank had set up. "I know we need to get going soon; we don't want to monopolize all of your time. I wondered if you would mind... we were curious about the letters you delivered. You know the ones I'm talking about. Those clairvoyant letters."

"Of course I know which ones you mean," Frank sighed. His

fingers moved nimbly over his electronic controls as he sent three trains around the town in complicated patterns, avoiding collisions by a hair's breadth.

"I just wondered if you knew anything about where it came from. I guess everything is probably all sorted before you get it, so you don't see how it all comes in. But you must recognize some of the handwriting and stationery from people who send out a lot of mail."

"Sure," he agreed. "There are some mail pieces that I know came from a certain person even without seeing a return address."

"So I was hoping you knew whose stationery or handwriting that was. Do you know who sent those letters?"

"If I did, I would have told the police when they asked."

"Oh." Vic was clearly disappointed by his response. "You don't have any idea? I mean… maybe there are a few places it could have come from, or a few people use that kind of stationery."

He shook his head. "I haven't seen any stationery like that used in years. It's good quality, but it's old stock. You don't see stuff like that anymore. A few people still send handwritten notes or letters regularly, but if they are sending letters by post all the time, they turn over their stationery stock pretty quickly. Someone who sends out letters all the time won't have stock leftover from thirty years ago."

"How can you tell it's old?"

"You can tell by the weight and quality. The texture… the way the envelopes are put together. Like comparing antique, handmade furniture to modern, cheap stuff glued together by machines."

"Where would someone get that kind of paper now?"

Frank shook his head. "No one sells it anymore. Maybe at an estate sale or something like that. Something you found when you cleaned out your grandma's house after she died. It's something that has been sitting around for years. It wasn't purchased recently."

"I guess you heard that Cindy Prost said the watermark on the letters was the Melville coat of arms."

"Sure, I heard that. It's interesting to know the history of different kinds of stationery. But does that mean that paper came from the Melvilles?" He shrugged heavily. "I have no idea where it came from. Or if she's right about the coat of arms. Maybe that's what it looks like, but I couldn't tell you if that was what it was, or who might have a stash."

"Do the Melvilles send out a lot of mail?"

"I consider information about who mails what to be confidential," he said stiffly. "Like lawyer-client privilege or doctor-patient. It's not something I would share with someone else."

"There isn't any mail carrier confidentiality," Erin told him.

"I know that. But would you want me to tell your neighbors about what you send out or receive? What would happen if I started spreading information about what everyone buys and where they buy it from? What magazine subscriptions people have? Where their family members are writing from."

A lot of those details might be things people found embarrassing. Erin could understand why Frank felt like he should keep such details confidential.

"We aren't asking because we want to know people's secrets," she reminded him. "We're worried about the threats that have been made. I'm worried about the safety of my employees. You wouldn't want any of them to get hurt. Especially the kids."

Frank nodded slowly. He shrugged and grimaced. "I can't really tell you anything about it. Who might have written those letters. Who writes in that style. They are distinctive; I don't know where the stationery came from."

"Well… if you see or think of something, could you let us know?"

Frank looked from Erin to Vic and then at his model train layout. "That's why you came here today? Because you wanted to know if I could tell you who sent the letters?"

"Oh, no…" Vic protested.

"I didn't know whether you would know anything about the letters," Erin said. "Either way… you've been delivering our mail faithfully for two years, and you deserve some kind of thanks."

"But you came because you wanted to know whether I could identify the letter writer."

Erin shrugged, unsure whether to deny it. It sounded bad, like they didn't care about Frank as a person and were just using him. But Erin hadn't meant it that way at all.

"Well." Frank stopped the running trains and stood up from his seat. "Thank you for the eclairs. They look delicious. I'm not going to turn down a sweet treat like that. But... I think it is time for you to get on your way."

ow I feel bad," Erin told Vic as they returned to the house. "I didn't mean to make him feel used."

"The whole thing is my fault. It was my idea, and I was trying to get more information about the letters, not because I cared so much about him. He does deserve recognition for what he does and for being so dependable, but... I guess we should have taken a different approach."

"I don't know. I don't know what we could have done differently. Other than being upfront about being there to find out what we could about the letters' origin. Maybe if we'd said that's what it was all about, he wouldn't have felt like we were just being nice because we wanted something from him. Like we were trying to pull one over on him."

Vic was silent as Erin led the way across the backyard to the door. Erin unlocked the door and disarmed the burglar alarm.

"He does have a really cool train setup!" Vic said.

"Yeah. That was a pretty sweet setup. I never knew he did anything like that. Why haven't we ever heard about it?"

"I don't know. It can't be a secret. Anyone who goes to his house would know about it."

"Maybe he doesn't get very many visitors."

"That makes me feel even worse."

Erin nodded. "I know," she agreed. "Me too."

"Shall we have some tea?" Vic asked, heading for the teakettle. "I can play on my phone and keep you company while you do some planning."

She was clearly not ready to return to the loft apartment, where she would be alone.

"Sure. You should bring Nilla over, too. He'll be bored."

Orange Blossom, who had come into the kitchen yowling for food and attention, glared at Erin as if he knew exactly what she had just suggested. He and Nilla did not fight, but Blossom always made himself scarce when the dog was around.

"You can sit with me on the couch," Erin told him. "Nilla isn't allowed up there unless Vic is holding him. If he's being yappy, just ignore him. He'll settle down."

Blossom yowled crossly and rubbed against the pantry door, encouraging Erin to pay attention and get him treats and dinner.

"Back in a minute," Erin told Vic and Orange Blossom. She went to the door to check for any deliveries on the doorstep. Fiona from the flower shop was just pulling in at the curb in front of the house. Erin waited while she got out a flower arrangement from the back of the house and walked up the sidewalk.

"Looks like I arrived at just the right time," Fiona observed, smiling. "Where have you ladies been?"

"Just paid Frank Grayson a visit. Would you like to come in for tea? Vic is just putting the kettle on."

Fiona hesitated for just an instant, then nodded. "That sounds nice, actually. I don't get the chance to visit with you very often since we are both usually working at the same time, more or less."

"Come on in," Erin opened the door wider for her.

Fiona entered. She wiped her feet and bent over to scratch Marshmallow's ears when he hopped over to investigate the visitor.

Marshmallow sniffed at Fiona's fingers with interest. He didn't usually pay that much attention to visitors.

"You must smell like all the different flowers you cut and arrange all day," she suggested.

Fiona laughed. "I guess so; I never thought about it. Sometimes when I put my hand up to my face, when I'm eating or putting on lip gloss, I can smell something that I was cutting or arranging earlier."

"Come, have a seat. Vic will bring it out here."

Fiona sat down on the couch.

"I'll be just a sec," Erin told her. "I need to feed the beasts."

Orange Blossom was making a racket, complaining that neither Erin nor Vic was taking care of his needs. Erin went through her usual routine of making Orange Blossom chase a few treats, which she told herself was good exercise for him, and then giving him his dinner. Marshmallow followed her and she gave him some vegetables from the fridge.

"Fiona is going to have tea with us," she advised Vic, in case she hadn't heard.

"Yes, ma'am. It will be ready in a minute."

Erin returned to Fiona and sat down with her for some small talk while they waited for Vic to finish.

"You must enjoy the animals," Fiona commented. "Though I can't see when you have time for them! You work long hours with the bakery."

"It depends on the day. Terry is often here when I am not. And Vic and Willie—" She caught herself, "Sometimes Vic and I do not work the same shift, so she and Nilla are around too. She's going to bring Nilla over now so he gets some attention and socialization. He likes to play with K9, too; K9 wears him out, which is good for everyone."

Fiona nodded, her expression serious. "It's so nice that you and Vic are so close, in proximity and as friends. It is good she has someone she can be comfortable spending time with right now. People are often so isolated after a death."

"It's amazing how well we have gotten to know each other. Hard to believe that I didn't know her at all when I first came to Bald Eagle Falls."

"What I can't believe is that you took her in like you did."

137

Fiona shook her head. "A perfect stranger, and you just opened up your home to her."

"Well…" Erin looked for a way to explain it. "It just seemed like the right thing to do. She didn't have anywhere else to go. I couldn't let her sleep in the basement of Auntie Clem's. I couldn't kick her out. She needed someone."

"Most people will not take a stranger into their homes like that. You're lucky she didn't murder you in your bed."

Erin remembered how vulnerable Vic had seemed. A runaway teen, all on her own. Nowhere else to go. She hadn't been afraid to take Vic in. She hadn't worried that Vic would hurt her. Maybe if she had known more—that Vic had been raised in a violent crime family, physically abused, and was capable with a gun and in a fight —maybe then she would not have been so quick to offer Vic a room while she got back on her feet.

"It never even occurred to me," she told Fiona honestly.

"You're either a really good judge of character or really naive."

Erin laughed. "Probably more naive. But it worked out okay, so I can *say* I'm a good judge of character."

Vic got back from a quick hop over to her apartment with Nilla, who was yapping excitedly, claws clicking all over the floor.

"Shh, shh," Vic told him as she brought the tea tray in. "Calm down. This is teatime, not playtime. Settle down." She smiled at Fiona. "Hi! It's nice you could come over."

"Thanks. I just stopped by to drop off the latest arrangement," Fiona showed Vic the bouquet she had brought in, with lots of pink mums and baby's breath. "And Erin invited me in for tea. I hope I'm not invading your private time. You must get tired of being around people all the time."

"Well, sometimes," Vic admitted. "But this isn't bad; it's just a few people together. And we won't talk about how I'm doing," she said firmly. "Let's pick a different topic."

"Sure," Fiona agreed quickly. As someone in the service field, she was good at pivoting to do what her client needed. "You guys have had a bit of excitement at the bakery lately."

Erin wasn't sure that was where she wanted the conversation to go, but she acknowledged Fiona's observation. "Yes, it's been interesting, that's for sure. I guess I should be happy with anything that encourages people to gather at Auntie Clem's, but I wish the letter writer would just go away quietly."

"Is it causing you a lot of problems? Everybody must be worried about how the predictions are going to be fulfilled. Harold was lucky that he only got a minor cut. That could have been bad."

"He could have hurt himself worse," Erin agreed carefully. "You have to be careful in the kitchen. Working with knives takes attention and skill. If you lose focus, things can happen. But Harold was fine."

"I heard the police are working on it now. Is that because Harold was hurt?"

"No, it has nothing to do with Harold's accident. They are not connected. It was just because of... the third letter."

"What did it say?" Fiona asked breathlessly, her cheeks pink.

Erin looked at Vic.

"Even I don't know," Vic told Fiona. "It's a big secret. So that the police will know if someone... knows too much."

"So, does it warn about more blood? Another accident?"

"I can't tell you what it says," Erin pointed out. "We don't want to get cross-threaded with the police investigation."

"It was on the same stationery," Vic offered, looking down at her tea as she stirred in a little honey and milk. "Have you heard about that?"

"That it was Melville stationery?" Fiona asked. "Yes, I heard that. Can you believe it? Do you think Della Melville accidentally cursed her own son?"

"Nobody cursed Harold," Erin said firmly. "This is just a prank. Some silly letters to get people panicked and seeing things that aren't there. No one is cursed. There is no curse. Just a few vague letters."

Fiona looked at Vic to see if Vic was of the same opinion. Vic was not as adamant as Erin. "We can't always tell what is happening in the unseen world. But I don't know if there is any mystery associated with the letters other than where they came from."

"But they must have come from the Melvilles."

"If it even is Melville stationery," Erin said, "we don't know that it is. And even if it is, that doesn't mean it couldn't have been written by someone else who got their hands on it. It is old paper, so who knows, it could have been sold at a garage sale or something like that. Stolen or swiped without anyone knowing about it."

Fiona looked doubtful. "Why would anyone do that?"

"Misdirection. Maybe it is someone who has a grudge against the Melvilles."

"Oh." Fiona looked thoughtful at that.

"Do you know... someone with a grudge against the family?" Erin suggested.

"Well, there are a lot of old feuds and disagreements," Fiona said with a shrug. "People around here can hold on to the littlest slight for generations. It's our superpower."

"So you don't know about any specifically against the Melvilles? Or against Della in particular."

"She is a Dyson. Did you know that?"

"I heard that," Erin agreed with a nod. "I guess that means... there might be all kinds of clan politics around her."

"Mmm." Fiona sipped her tea, nodding. "She was never popular at school. Gave herself airs. Thought she was better than anyone else, and that she would be some big boss in the Dyson clan someday." Fiona laughed. "As if they would ever allow a woman to lead the clan."

Vic tried to cover up a snort with a cough, looking away from Fiona.

"She thought she could hold a leadership position in the clan?" Erin repeated.

Fiona nodded. "She was tough, believe me. A big bully. Pushed a lot of people around. Got in trouble for threatening people or bringing a weapon to school." Fiona shook her head. "And this is rural Tennessee. It's practically expected that kids carry pocketknives."

"What happened?"

"She was in trouble a lot during school. After she graduated...

Well, she worked for a while. In the city, I think. Got married and had kids like anyone else. Any of those ambitions she had about becoming an important clan member... faded away. People forgot about it."

"And you don't think she ever had a position in the clan? Did someone block her?"

Fiona looked at Erin like she was crazy. "It's just not something that is done. That's not the way things work around here. I'm sure she was blocked... by the clan leaders."

There were a few seconds of silence while Vic and Erin pondered this, and Fiona looked at them, expecting them to understand what was so clear to her.

"Was that the only thing?" Vic asked. "The only grudge that she had? Or was there other stuff?"

"Oh... I don't know. There were probably other things. I'm sure there were plenty of other petty grudges. Everyone has them, you know, but you don't always hear about them. I've been having a boundary dispute with a neighbor for years. It isn't like we would do violence over it, but when you know you're in the right, and someone else is trying to step all over you..." She shrugged. "You do hold on to things. I admit it."

"Who's your neighbor?" Erin asked, wondering whether it was the Melvilles and Fiona was trying to be circumspect about it.

"Tara Waldon."

"Oh." Erin nodded. She couldn't picture the two women having a fight. Especially not one where they harbored bitter feelings against each other for years. They were both such nice, pleasant women. And Tara was a trained mediator. She must be able to manage her own disputes. "Well... I hope you got it straightened out."

"It hasn't been resolved. We're still fighting over it. I'm right. I've got the surveys. But she thinks it was historically Waldon land, that she can prove that it has been in the family for generations from old family journals, and the surveyor was wrong when he marked the boundaries."

"Oh. Well, that makes sense," Erin nodded. But it would be

difficult for either one of them to prove what had happened generations ago. "That must be stressful."

"Believe me, it is. Especially when it's been going on for so long and stretches indefinitely into the future…"

"How do you ever solve something like that?" Vic asked. "If your survey and your title show one thing, she doesn't have a leg to stand on, does she?"

"She takes it to court. Proves to the judge that it was improperly surveyed and registered." Fiona shook her head. "The lawyer says she's got no chance of winning, but that doesn't mean I get out of going to court. I still have to jump through all of the hoops just to prove that what I know is mine is really mine."

Erin pondered the different problems. Land rights and boundaries. Della Melville's belief that she and her sons were destined to lead the Dysons. She had heard of other disputes over the years over things like a borrowed cup of sugar or a failed business. Humans seemed to have an amazing ability to hold on to a grudge. She didn't know how she would have reacted if she had ever been in any of those situations. She was more likely to brush an argument aside and forget about it, even if she thought she was in the right. She was an avoider. Stay away from confrontation at all costs.

"Did you read the first two letters we got? The ones that are posted at the bakery?" she asked Fiona.

"Yes…?"

"Did they make any sense to you? Do you know what they are talking about?"

Fiona shook her head slowly. "I don't know. What do you mean?"

"Well, you've lived in Bald Eagle Falls all your life, and you hear about things that are going on in town. I just wondered whether you had any insights."

Erin pulled out her phone and repeated the words of the first two letters.

A recipe long forgotten stirs trouble anew— vengeance and blood will soon ensue. Tread carefully, I see danger brew!

When the bakery opens its doors, beware those who seek more than pastries and s'mores.

Erin looked at Fiona. "Do those sound like... any real dispute that has been going on? Some 'long-forgotten' argument between friends? Something that might have resurfaced for some reason? And the reference to the bakery... that must mean that they are customers, or that someone is looking for something other than just baked goods, or... maybe the sweet stuff is talking about someone's reaction. That they want more than just platitudes."

Fiona and Vic were both looking at each other, shaking their heads and frowning. Vic put her teacup down.

"It could be anything, Erin. I mean, isn't that what you've been saying all along? That it could be talking about anything? That the writer is just trying to get people all uptight?"

"Yes, but what if that's not the case? Maybe the vagueness is just the writer not wanting to give anything away too soon. Could it be something real? Like your property line dispute?" Erin looked at Fiona.

"It isn't me," Fiona laughed, putting her hands up. "I didn't write those horrible rhymes."

"No, I know that. But is there something that people who have lived in Bald Eagle Falls forever would know of? I'm not the right person to ask, because I've only lived here for a couple of years. We need someone who knows about what's gone on over the years. Things that might have seemed like they went to sleep... but now are coming up again?"

"You should go to the library," Fiona suggested. "They have the old newspapers on microfilm, and you can look through them to see what community disputes were reported. If it was something important enough to make it to the paper. You can talk with Betty, she's a librarian over there and she remembers everything she's ever seen. If it was something that wouldn't make it to the papers, she might still know something from old letters or journals or published books and histories."

Erin nodded. "Yes!" she agreed, her spirits lifting. If the letters referred to some real dispute, one that the third letter said resulted from a betrayal between friends and was important enough to lead to murder, maybe she could track it down in the town's recorded history. Clementine had kept a lot of information in her genealogy files too, but the stuff at the library would be properly cataloged and organized, and Erin would have a better chance to find what she was looking for.

"I'm going to do it," she said. "I'm going to go to the library and find out what it was all about."

CHAPTER 26

*E*rin was drowsy when Terry arrived home and came into the bedroom to talk to her. She tried to explain to him about the library and how it would help her to figure out the mystery of the anonymous predictions.

"How are you going to know what this dispute is?" Terry asked. "Even if you find it, how will you know that is what the letters are talking about?"

"I know," Erin told him firmly. Her eyes were shut against the hallway light, so she couldn't look him directly in the face. "I'll know when I see it."

Terry rested his hand on her. "I don't want you investigating this, Erin. I think going to the library and asking questions about it are mistakes. If someone is making threats, you don't want to push them into something. You just leave this to the police."

"Mm-hmm," Erin agreed.

"Erin. Are you listening to me?"

Erin let herself drift back to sleep.

In the morning, Erin made her coffee and went to work with Vic as usual, but once it was a reasonable hour, she called some of her part-time employees to see if anyone could cover her for the afternoon. Charley agreed to come in, so Erin was free to go to the library in the afternoon and to try to find the root of the threats.

"*What* are you looking for?" Betty repeated, frowning at her and readjusting her glasses.

"I am looking for anything in the newspapers or any histories of the town that talks about longstanding disputes between townspeople. Stuff that their children or grandchildren might still be holding on to today. Or if the original people involved in the dispute are still alive."

"But that is very broad. I don't think you have any idea how many 'disputes' go on in a place like this. You could read all day and not find them all. You could do research here every day for weeks and still be finding new things that people were arguing about. In a small town, it is practically a sport."

"Well, I have to try," Erin said. "Especially anything to do with the Melvilles or the Dysons."

"Oh." Betty's mouth was pinched into a small O. "I don't think that is a good idea. You might think all these things have been put to rest now, but it isn't true. Just look at the feud between the Jacksons and the Dysons alone. How many generations it has been going on and all of the heartbreak it has cost. You can't resurrect these things. It will only cause more trouble."

"The trouble is already here. I want to stop the letters and stop the writer from doing anything... drastic. I don't want any more trouble at Auntie Clem's."

"Digging up old fights isn't going to stop anything from happening. It is going to cause more trouble. It is going to get you in trouble."

"So you're not going to help me?"

Betty looked torn. Erin didn't know if there was a purpose statement for librarians, but if there was, it probably included never refusing to help a patron looking for information. Betty refusing to help Erin find the right resources to look for evidence of old disputes in Bald Eagle Falls went against everything she stood for as a librarian.

"You know where the microfilm readers and newspapers are," she told Erin. "I will... pull some additional resources that might be helpful. But that doesn't mean I think it is a good idea. I think you should give it up and go back to baking."

"My employees are doing the baking this afternoon. If I can find what I am looking for, I can go back to baking tomorrow. But sitting around waiting for the next letter isn't doing anyone any good."

Betty shook her head, but she promised to bring Erin what she could, and Erin headed over to the microfilm room to look through papers.

At least stored on microfilm, they were not dusty or moldy and did not make her sneeze.

But Erin quickly discovered the truth of Betty's warning. At least one community dispute was mentioned in each of the weekly Bald Eagle Falls newspapers. Every single week. How was she supposed to know which ones had been resolved and which were still ongoing or had been recently resurrected?

When she had been there an hour, she looked at the fresh page in her planner where she had resolved to write down all the disputes she could find. She had written two columns of brief notes, each line representing one dispute. Her page was completely filled.

Should she only write down the ones that seemed like they might be significant? Maybe things like a stolen pig or a borrowed cup of sugar that had not been replaced should be left off the list. It was true that they might have been carried throughout the years and generations, but she was getting bogged down by way too many possibilities. She needed to focus on the big stuff and hope to identify which one had recently been resurrected.

She thought about telling Terry in her half-asleep state the night before that she would recognize the dispute when she found it.

Now she doubted it. She felt no closer to finding it now than she had been the day before. In fact, she felt bogged down now by all of the details and possibilities.

Erin looked through the list that she had written down. She started a new page, writing down only the most important items on the list. Things that had been big, that had affected the Dyson family. Things that still might be festering, bothering someone even though they had happened years ago.

How long ago? She had grabbed the roll for one of the earliest newspapers, but looking at the disputes she had noted, she wondered if it was too long ago…

The first verse had referred to a long-forgotten recipe, so that had to be a longstanding dispute. It couldn't be something that was only a year or two old.

She kept the spool she had started on, and moved on to the next edition.

CHAPTER 27

*E*rin was deeply immersed in her research when her phone buzzed. She didn't look at it right away. She knew that Vic was looking after everything at Auntie Clem's, and anything else could wait until she was free. She thought she had turned her phone to Do Not Disturb, but maybe it had not taken or the phone had shut it off again for some reason. Technology was flaky. Erin accepted that it just didn't always work the way it should.

But her phone vibrated again. Erin pushed a button to send the call to voicemail. It started vibrating again as soon as she took her hand off of it. Erin looked at the phone to see who the caller was.

Terry.

She could see a couple of missed calls and texts below the most recent notification, stacked up in groups. She had assumed that everything could go on without her, but apparently, she had been wrong.

Something was going on.

She tapped Terry's name and put the phone to her ear. "Terry?"

"Erin. Where are you? You haven't been answering."

"I'm at the library. I told you where I would be."

"I need you to come over to the police department. Right away."

She swallowed and her stomach felt tight and heavy.

"Terry, what's wrong?"

"Just get over here. Talk to me before anyone else. Understood? Don't call Vic or anyone else. Just come here."

"Um… okay. I'll be there in a few minutes."

"Drop everything else. I'm serious. Leave whatever books you have out on the table and come here immediately."

"Okay."

Erin picked up her planner and shoved it into her shoulder bag. She clutched it to her and hurried to the door.

"I have to go," she told Betty, as she nearly ran into the librarian returning with a stack of books. "It's an emergency. I'll call you back when I know what's going on."

Betty was not quick enough to answer before Erin was gone, dashing for the outside door.

She had driven, so she didn't actually have to run to the police department, but by the time she reached the main doors of the police department, she was drenched in sweat.

"Clara, Terry called—"

Clara waved her through. "He's in his office."

It was a little disconcerting dashing into Terry's office. The last time she had been in there, he had been sharing it with Rodney Stayner, and it had been crowded. Now that Stayner was gone, it seemed half empty. Terry's items had not yet expanded to fill the space. Erin didn't know if they planned to get another police officer to fill Stayner's position. As far as she was concerned, they did need another person to cover the work. But whether they could get someone or not was another story.

"Terry."

He looked up from his paperwork, phone glued to his ear. He held up one finger to get her to wait, talking urgently to someone. Erin tried to sort out what he was saying, but couldn't tell what was going on. It sounded like a medical emergency, but why would he be dealing with that instead of a medical professional? And why had he called Erin?

"Call me back," Terry instructed. He dropped the handset back into its cradle on the desk and looked at Erin. He shook his head. "We have a problem."

"What is it?" Erin's heart pounded. She had no idea what it was, but it had to be serious for Terry to order her attendance and instruct her not to talk to Vic or anyone else. She dropped into the chair across the desk from him.

"You filled an order for the Historical Club meeting today."

"Yes. They ordered eclairs." She swallowed and tried to answer fully without waiting for him to ask further questions. "We did like we did for the ladies' tea and cut them crosswise so that people could have a few bites instead of having a whole one each. They were also going to get a fruit tray from the grocery store to have something lighter. People could have a bite of eclair and some fruit… or a few pieces of eclair…"

"Who made those?"

"I did. Like all of them. It's a picky recipe, and the timing for baking and cooling is crucial, so I've been making the shells myself. The others have whipped up some of the fillings and glazes. Then we fill them an hour or two before the event so they're nice and fresh."

"Who made the fillings?"

"I don't know… Harold and Vic. I think Bella made the fondant for this batch. We've been making so many lately, I couldn't tell you who made what, other than that I always made the shells."

"This is important, Erin."

She shook her head. "What happened? Did someone react to something? We always follow a checklist to make sure the ingredients match what we put on the labels."

"I know you're careful. But something went wrong."

Erin's eyes burned. She blinked a few times. "What happened?"

"Everyone is sick."

Erin didn't think she could feel any worse. Her heart raced so hard it felt like it would burst from her chest. She was again soaked with sweat. She felt like she was going to throw up.

"Everyone?"

Terry nodded. "Everyone who ate the eclairs. Symptoms range from mild to severe. We have several people on their way to the hospital in the city. A few others are under observation here while we scramble for more transportation with people who can provide first aid en route. A few who are only mildly sick. Could just be psychosomatic because they are expecting to get sick. But we won't know until everyone has been treated and tested."

"There wasn't anything in those eclairs that could have made anyone sick. You know that. Everyone has been eating them. They're very popular."

"Except for this batch. Something has happened to this batch."

"It's been tampered with."

Terry nodded. Erin brought her hands to her face, covering her eyes. She tried to slow everything down. Slow her heartbeat, her breathing, her thoughts. It was an emergency, and she was good in emergencies. She needed to help. She needed to give Terry and the medical professionals the information they needed. She rubbed her eyes, wiping away the tears that threatened to overflow. It wouldn't do anyone any good if she broke down.

"I made dozens of the shells and froze them so they would be ready when orders were filled. They were not specially made for the meeting. I don't know if all of the eclairs served at the Historical Club meeting came from the same batch. The vanilla cream was split between a few orders today. The book club at the Book Nook got some too. Have you checked with them?"

"Vic checked, and they were fine. She didn't suggest to them that they had been poisoned," Terry said with a dry smile, "she just asked them for feedback as a new product offering. How the flavor and texture were, and observed them for any adverse signs. They were just fine."

"Then it has to be the fondant topping. Or else someone contaminated them between the time I finished preparing them and when they were served."

"Which was?"

Erin focused on the timeline. "I finished them at eleven o'clock.

They chilled in the fridge. They were to be picked up and taken to the Historical Club at two."

"Picked up by who?"

"Annie Parks at the school." Erin took her hands away from her face, and she looked at the time. Twenty past three. "They would have served them at three. That's really quick. That's not food poisoning."

"No. We don't think so. Some people did report a strange after-taste. That didn't prevent some of them from having three or four pieces."

"All of the ingredients were fresh. There wasn't anything questionable. Nothing that had been stored for too long. Nothing that hasn't been used in other products or orders today."

Terry didn't say anything. He looked at her.

"The letters," Erin said. "The third letter that predicted death."

CHAPTER 28

"Samples are being taken of all the food," Terry said. "Sheriff Wilmot is getting a search warrant for Auntie Clem's and he will gather samples of ingredients there as well. And look for anything else suspicious."

"You don't think it was anyone at Auntie Clem's," Erin protested. "You know us. You know that no one at the bakery would have done anything like this."

Terry nodded. "Of course not," he agreed in a voice that was too flat. "But we have to conduct a proper investigation. If we were ever reviewed by another authority, we want everything to be regular and all laid out the way it is supposed to be. We can't show a bias toward or against anyone. The investigation has to be neutral."

"I know... I know... but you have to know that none of us would do anything to harm anyone."

"I know you didn't do anything, Erin. But you still need to be investigated like anyone else."

"But the others—Vic, Charley, Harold, Bella, everyone—you know that they didn't have anything to do with it either."

"I know that we can't judge from the outside what is going on inside a person's head. And I don't know the others as well as I know you. But the police department can't just assume that we know people well enough to make that judgment. If you could tell who was a criminal by looking at them, there wouldn't be any need for the police. And we would already have caught the person who has been sending those letters."

"You do think it is related to the letters, don't you? This isn't just a coincidence?"

"A coincidence that a letter-writing campaign against the bakery, which predicted death at a friend's hand, just happened to take place in the days before a poisoning by baked goods? No, we don't think it is a coincidence."

"Did you find out anything about the letter? Were there any fingerprints? Anything that you could follow up on?"

"We cannot tell a suspect anything about the course of the investigation."

"A suspect? But you just said—"

"What I know and what we can put down on paper are two different things. I told you, we have to pursue this investigation without any bias. You *are* a suspect."

"Then why are you talking to me?"

He gazed at her. "I'm just having a conversation while we wait for the sheriff to become available. I can't take part in questioning you."

"But what—"

Erin decided she'd better shut up. Terry had already overstepped propriety by telling her what had happened and asking her the few questions he had. That conversation might be off the record, but this was not. She didn't want to get Terry in trouble.

"This wasn't anyone at the bakery," she assured him. "We both know that. This was directed *against* the bakery. It didn't come from within. This is someone attacking Auntie Clem's, just like it has been from the start."

"And those letters have been directed to you. Can you think of any reason why they would be coming to your attention rather than anyone else at the bakery?"

"I don't know. Just because I am the owner, I assume. I don't think… I don't think the threats were against me personally."

"Are you sure of that?"

"Well, no, how could I be? I don't know who sent them or why."

"Is there anyone who might have a grudge against you for something?"

Erin had to look at Terry's face to see if he was teasing. She shook her head. When she had gone to the penitentiary with Adele, she had been forced to confront exactly how many people she'd had a hand in sending there during the time she had lived in Bald Eagle Falls. People who had committed murder, been involved with the clan, with drug dealing, with other crimes. And while those people were behind bars and had not been the ones to send her the letters, they could have partners outside the prison.

And there was everyone in the Jackson and Dyson clans. She had been too involved in their business. In revealing old, hidden secrets. In supporting and employing Vic and Charley.

"I… uh… can't think of anyone specific," she told him, her cheeks warm. "No one who has been in contact with me, sent me letters or other messages."

"You would tell me if you had received something."

"Yes. Of course. I would come to you or the sheriff right away."

"Not like when Crazy Theresa was sending you messages."

She swallowed. "I haven't had any messages other than the letters. And you have seen all of the letters."

"Good."

There was a knock, and Erin looked up to see Sheriff Wilmot standing in the doorway, having knocked politely on the open door to get their attention.

"We've got the warrant," he told Terry briefly. "You and Tom go over there together and stay with each other the whole time. Working together, eyes on each other, not in different rooms."

Terry nodded. "Yes, sir." He rose to his feet. K9 swiftly got to his as well. K9 sniffed at Erin as they walked out of the office and looked at Terry, confused about why Erin wasn't going with them.

"Come on, boy," Terry encouraged. He looked at Erin and nodded. "I'll see you later. Do what you can to help the sheriff, but… be careful what you say. Remember that you are a suspect, and you can refuse to answer at any time."

He cleared his throat and walked away, not looking back. Erin sat where she was, uncertain what to do.

Wilmot nodded to her. His expression was serious. But he had to know that she hadn't had anything to do with any tampering with the eclairs. She would not poison her own baking. What reason would there be to do that?

"Miss Price, if you would join me in the meeting room," he invited.

Erin did as he asked. She got up from the chair feeling numb, removed from herself. Terry hadn't said who from the Historical Club was in serious condition and who was only mildly affected, and she started thinking about it as she walked with the sheriff to the interrogation room. A few people in the club were quite old and frail. It tended to attract an older demographic. Young people were not generally that interested in history.

"Is everyone okay?" she asked Wilmot. "Tell me everyone is going to be okay."

"I wish I could." He motioned Erin into a chair and closed the door. On the security camera that hung in the corner of the room, a red light blinked on. Recording. "I would like to say that this was just another prank and that whoever tampered with those eclairs was just trying to get attention, like with the letters. But this has taken it to the next level. I don't know what was put in those eclairs, but it could have serious consequences."

Erin thought of all of the things that could have been added to the eclairs. Digitalis, belladonna, rat poison, eye drops, some household product… there were so many possibilities, some of which she had experience with. Who would have done that? Poisoned a whole room of people just to tell them that she wasn't kidding with the letters? Just to fulfill the prediction in the latest letter that someone would die? Erin pressed her hand over her stomach, feeling nauseated, but tried not to let Wilmot see how much she was affected by the news.

But why was she trying to cover up her reaction? If someone later reviewed the recording, did she really want them to think she was unemotional? Unaffected by the news that people were in serious condition? Did she want them to believe that this was just routine for her?

But she felt safer not showing everyone how she felt. She wanted to keep her thoughts and feelings private.

"Who is the worst?" she asked. "I know that you can't tell me everything, but… I can't bear thinking this happened because of my eclairs. I've been having so much fun with them. And then someone comes along and tampers with them. Adds something to make people sick… it makes me sick just thinking about it."

"I know," Wilmot acknowledged. "I want you to run through the process. When the eclairs were made, who had a hand in it, how they were delivered to the Historical Club…"

"I made the shells myself," Erin had already covered this ground with Terry. He'd made it easier for her to tell it a second time, calmly and clearly, without getting flustered. "I've been making and freezing them, and then we just take out the frozen shells when we are ready to make a batch for an event. A lot of people have ordered them, so we've had a lot on hand. The shells used for the club meeting might have come from a couple of different batches. Then we just fill them and deliver them to whichever customer had ordered them."

"And the fillings? Are those made in batches as well?"

"Smaller batches; they are always served fresh, not frozen. We could pre-fill them and just thaw them for the event, but I prefer to use fresh ingredients as much as possible. The shells are just so finicky, I need to make them myself and give them my full attention."

"Who would have had access to the fillings?"

"Any of the bakery employees. Or everyone who was on today."

"Who was that, please? Was Harold Melville there?"

"Vic, Charley. Harold would still have been in school. He gets release time some afternoons, but the eclairs would have been delivered to the Historical Club by then."

"Was there anything to stop any other employees from showing up to chat for a minute or drop something in your office? How often did people come and go when they were not on shift?"

"Pretty rare."

"Did anyone drop by while you were there?"

"No."

"Did anyone come to the back door for any reason? To make a delivery, ask a question, pick up day-old bread?"

"We had a delivery, I think. Some flours I was waiting for. No one else."

"And the deliveryman would have been allowed into the kitchen."

"Yes. On his way to the storage room."

"But those ingredients would not have been used in today's eclairs?"

"No. None of that stuff was opened yet."

"We will be taking samples of all open goods."

Erin swallowed and nodded. "Of course. You need to rule the bakery out as the source of the contamination."

"That's right."

"They must have been tampered with after they were delivered."

"Who would have had access to them at that point?"

"I don't know. You would have to ask them. I don't think anyone was policing them. We've never had anything like this happen before. Anything like the Historical Club or Book Club... we would just deliver the trays, or they would pick them up, and then they would put them in the kitchen or wherever until it was time to serve them. No one would be standing over them. They wouldn't be locked up."

Wilmot nodded and made a couple of notes. Erin was sure this came as no surprise to him. Unless there was a rash of poisonings, who would be concerned that a platter of eclairs sitting on the counter or in the fridge until the meeting started might be tampered with? It was difficult to fathom that it had really happened. She waited for them to tell her it was just a joke. Just April Fool's Day or *What Would You Do?*

"I just can't believe any of this." Erin shook her head. "How did it come to this?"

"How did *what* come to this?" Wilmot questioned, his eyes sharp.

"What I thought was just a weird prank... someone looking for attention. How did it end up being... lives on the line? Who would do that?"

"That is what we intend to find out."

CHAPTER 29

*C*lara knocked on the door and came into the interview room without waiting for Wilmot to invite her in. He looked irritated, scowling at the intrusion. Clara bent down and put a message slip on the table before him, whispering in his ear, "Martha Erasmus has passed."

Erin felt her eyes widen, and a lump swelled in her throat. She barely knew Martha Erasmus, a gray-haired, elderly woman who occasionally came to the bakery but never had anything to say, just pointing at what she wanted from the display case and whispering. She was not one of the women who liked to gossip and was usually there alone. Erin thought she was a widow, but knew little about her. She was a little surprised that Martha was in any club, but was glad she shared a hobby with others in the community. Maybe her life hadn't been as lonely as Erin had thought.

Wilmot was looking at Erin, obviously able to read on her face that she had heard Clara's whispered message.

"Clara, get Miss Price a glass of cold water. I have to go. Erin? Erin?"

Erin tried to focus on him. She rubbed her forehead. "Sorry, what?"

"You can stay here for as long as you need to. Call someone if

163

you're feeling unsteady, okay? Don't drive. Terry can drive your car home later."

"Where are you going?"

"I need to pursue the investigation. I may reach out to you with more questions, but for now, you're free to go home. Sorry to cut this off so abruptly. You know we are short on manpower, and I can't be in two places at once."

Erin nodded.

Wilmot got up, picking up the phone message slip, and walked out of the room. Clara returned with a glass of water and handed it to her.

"Can I get you anything else? Do you need something to eat? A cup of tea?"

Erin shook her head. "No, that's okay. Nothing else. I'll go home. I'll feel better once I'm home."

"Be careful. Do you want me to drive you?"

"No, I'm okay. Really."

Not like Martha Erasmus.

What was going on in Bald Eagle Falls? Who had done such a dreadful thing? Would Martha be the only fatality? Everyone at the club had been poisoned. What if there were other deaths? She couldn't understand someone being so reckless. This wasn't a targeted, finely tuned attack, it was scattershot, taking out innocent people without any regard for their safety.

Erin drank the water that Clara had provided her and felt a little steadier. She wanted to get home. It would take some time for the whole situation to become real. Maybe once she heard more about what had happened, she would understand and could give the police department some kind of assistance.

She left the meeting room and gave Clara a little wave on the way out but did not stop to talk.

There was no point in going to Auntie Clem's to see how things were going there; the police had a search warrant and would be searching the bakery and taking their samples, trying to figure out what had happened and to eliminate Auntie Clem's as the source of the poison.

There were several people gathered outside the town hall talking. Erin guessed that the rumors were flying and everyone was speculating on what had happened and trying to predict what the police would find. Were they speculating that it was someone at Auntie Clem's? Were they still targeting Harold?

Maybe the poisoning proved that Harold was not involved. He was, after all, at school. He could not have slipped over to the community center to poison the eclairs.

As Erin left the building, the gathered townspeople quieted to turn and look at her. Erin saw Tara with them, her face pale and eyes red. She waved Erin over and clutched her arm.

"Oh, Erin, you heard what happened?" She had a weepy, almost hysterical tone. "I can't believe this."

Erin nodded. "I know. I don't know what to say. It's crazy. I don't know how someone could have done this."

"Do they know who did it? Do they have any idea?"

"I don't know for sure. They are just starting the investigation. But it must have happened at the community center. It couldn't have happened at Auntie Clem's."

Tara closed her eyes and pressed her fingers to their corners as if plugging any leaks. "Are you sure?" she asked. "You can't watch everybody in there all the time. Even if you are working with someone else, you have someone in the kitchen and someone out at the front. You don't see what they are doing when you're not looking."

"There's no way it was anyone at Auntie Clem's. I trust my employees."

Tara shook her head. She looked at Erin, opening her eyes again and squinting at her. "You can't know what is in anyone's heart. You might think you can, but believe me after years of mediating disputes, I can tell you that you can't."

"If it was someone at the bakery, then the Book Club would have gotten sick too, but they didn't."

Tara looked surprised at this. "What?"

"The Book Nook ordered eclairs too. We did up a big batch that was split between the two orders. But no one got sick at the

Book Club. So it happened at the community center, not at the bakery."

"Or someone tampered with the eclairs once they were split into orders, and only poisoned the ones going to the Historical Club."

"Why would they do that?" Erin demanded.

Tara sniffled, and the other women looked on, everyone shell-shocked by the news.

"But at least everyone is okay," Tara said, taking a deep breath and letting it out. "It could have been worse. If it had been cyanide or strychnine or something…"

"Martha Erasmus died," Erin told her. "They just got word. Before I came out."

"What?" Tara's eyes were wide and round.

She sought solace with the other women, grabbing Mary Lou and hugging her as if she were the one in need of comfort. "She couldn't be dead. I thought everyone was only sick. How could this happen?"

Mary Lou patted her gingerly on the back and nudged her away as soon as she could do so without being offensive.

"It is sad," she agreed. "And dreadful to think that someone we know could do something like this. Just when I think that all of the secrets in Bald Eagle Falls have been unearthed and we can let our guards down…"

Erin felt the same way. She would think that everything would finally settle down and return to normal, and for a few months, everything seemed quiet. And then something awful would happen.

She supposed that's the way it was everywhere. Life was never quiet and idyllic forever. Everyone had their own challenges. But she did seem to get more than her share of unexpected deaths.

She rubbed Tara's back. The woman wore a vibrant pink jacket that set off her dark hair and eyes. And it was smooth and silky under Erin's touch. It was too hot for Erin to wear a jacket, but those who had grown up in the area tended to find the cooler weather chilly and wore jackets when Erin would have smothered in them.

"Did you know her well?" she asked Tara, giving her a chance to express her grief.

"No, not well," Tara admitted. "I saw her sometimes at the community center or other events. She was very involved." She sniffled. "I just can't believe it. I can't believe that anyone would target her." Tara looked toward Auntie Clem's Bakery.

"The police are there now," Erin told her, "but they aren't going to find anything. They are just going to eliminate the bakery as the source of the contamination. It wasn't anyone at the bakery."

"I'm sure you wouldn't hire anyone you thought might be a danger to the public," Tara said, though she didn't sound that certain. "But that doesn't mean that you didn't do it anyway."

"I know my employees. People may think that Harold had something to do with it because of the stationery, but he didn't. He had nothing to do with the notes and nothing to do with the poisoning. He wouldn't do anything like this. Where would he even get poison?"

"The school," Cindy suggested, "they have a good chemistry lab, and who knows what chemical cleaners and other toxic substances they have. He had a whole array of products to choose from."

"He's not that kind of person."

"That's what people always say about serial killers," Cindy argued.

"No, it's not," Erin retorted. "You think people said that about Dahmer? Or Charles Manson?"

Cindy opened her mouth and closed it again.

"I want to help," Tara told Erin, holding her arm again. "I want to help you to figure out who did this."

"I'm not... I'm not investigating it. The police are. I'm not going to try to figure it out."

"You're not?" Tara shook her head, not believing it. "Erin Price? You're always trying to figure it out."

"That's not true. It's just that... sometimes I stumble across a clue. Something that cracks the case."

Or, if the truth were told, because the culprit confronted her before she even figured it out. But that wasn't going to happen this time, because she wasn't going to investigate it, and no criminal types were going to get anxious and come after her.

She'd had enough of being in the spotlight. It wasn't all it was cracked up to be.

"If you don't think it is Harold, then who do you think it is? It obviously has something to do with the bakery. Why have all of the letters been sent to you?" Cindy asked.

"I don't know who it is."

"Come on," Tara said, tugging at Erin's arm. "I'll walk you home. I really do want to hear what you think."

Erin resisted at first, then let Tara encourage her along. She didn't want to stand there talking with everyone about the tragedy and trying to defend her employees. She wanted to go home or back to the bakery, and since she couldn't go to Auntie Clem's, it would have to be home.

As far as telling Tara what she thought, Erin had no answers, so there wasn't any risk of telling her anything dangerous. She didn't want *Tara* to be targeted by the letter writer herself.

"Have you ever met Harold's mother?" Tara asked as they walked toward the house, Erin leading at a leisurely pace so she wouldn't get sweaty and out of breath.

Erin answered with caution, not wanting Tara to think that anything she had learned about Harold or his mother pointed at him as the letter writer.

"I've met her a couple of times. She is..." Erin shrugged. "A protective mom, I guess. She wants to look after her kids. Make sure that they have the best she can give them. That they have whatever opportunities she can give them."

Tara cocked her head slightly. "You think she's pushy?"

"How did you get that from what I said?" Erin demanded, embarrassed. "I didn't say that."

"But you do, don't you? You think she's overprotective. Pushes her kids too hard. Maybe her husband too?"

Erin shook her head. "No, no!" she protested.

Tara laughed. "I've known them a lot longer than you have,

Erin. If you think she's any of those things, you're right. It just means you're perceptive. She's always been 'that mom.' The one who thinks that if she pushes hard enough, her children will turn out to be the perfect little mini-mes she wants them to be."

"I would never say anything like that."

"Of course not. You're too nice. But you can be honest with me. I've been around here long enough to know something about most of the secrets around Bald Eagle Falls. And Della Dyson being a bit of a… harpy is not a secret. Everyone knows that."

"I'm sure she only has their best interests in mind."

"I'm sure she does," Tara agreed with a laugh. "And her own. Well…" She looked at Erin's house as they arrived. "I know you probably have things that you want to get to. Or some time to yourself. So I will say goodbye here…"

"Thanks… I would invite you in for tea, but it has been a crazy day. I am going to crash as soon as I get inside."

"Of course, dear, don't you worry about it. You need to take care of yourself first. You're so caught up in always nourishing everybody else that you forget about yourself."

Erin really didn't. She wasn't nearly as self-sacrificing as some people seemed to think she was. She had just as many self-serving habits and viewpoints as anyone else. Nobody spent every hour of the day serving others.

"I was sorry to hear about Martha Erasmus," she told Tara. "I'm sorry that you lost a friend to this killer." She shook her head. "I can't believe she went from writing letters to poisoning old ladies. Why would she do that?"

"Maybe she didn't intend for anyone to die. I hope… that's the only one. It would be terrible to lose more members of our community over this craziness."

CHAPTER 30

*E*rin had her wish and was able to crash at home for a
couple of hours, just lying on her bed as if she were sick
with a fever, letting the events of the day and the previous week
wash over her. It was hard to accept that the juvenile prank had
turned into a murder. Maybe more than one, if anyone else from
the Historical Club didn't make it. She hoped they all would, but a
lot of those people were old and frail. Not a good target for a
poisoning prank. Tara was right; maybe the writer had never
intended to turn into a killer, but had just been trying to get more
attention. Perhaps she just wanted a few people to get sick. Enough
for everyone to know that there had been a poisoning. That she was
really serious about her predictions.

Erin's phone vibrated, and she picked it up to take a look at it.
A text from Vic.

Are you up for company?

Erin closed her eyes. She didn't want company, but Vic couldn't
fairly be called company; she was more of a sister to Erin than any
of the foster sisters she'd ever had. Even she and Reg had not been
together for that long and had not been that close while they were
together. They hadn't had that much in common, other than
sticking with each other because they were both rejects and

outsiders, foster kids who came into and out of people's lives with barely an acknowledgment.

Vic was an outsider of another sort. Rejecting her old life and forging ahead with something new. Erin always thought she should take a cue from Vic and be bold and courageous in pursuing what she wanted instead of being so tentative. She'd started a bakery, hadn't she? And not just any bakery, but a gluten-free bakery in a small town where everyone had told her it was impossible and she was bound to fail. She had loyal customers. She had won over those who had thought that anything gluten-free had to be the texture of cardboard or crumble to bits at a touch. Erin had faced them all down and pursued her dream. Not everyone could say that.

Come on over, she texted back to Vic.

She intended to be in the kitchen by the time Vic made it over, but she was still struggling to get herself off the bed, where she had collapsed.

"You look tired as a one-legged man in a butt-kicking contest," Vic observed.

Erin couldn't help laughing. "Well, that's about right," she agreed. "Thanks for noticing."

"I was going to ask for a ride, but I'll see if Jeremy is around. You don't look like you should be going anywhere."

"No, I've been napping for a couple of hours. I need to get up and do something for a while, or I won't be able to get to sleep tonight and make it to the bakery in the morning."

"Will it be open?"

Erin opened her mouth to ask why, then remembered it was being tossed by the police. "They'll be done by then," she said with confidence. "It doesn't take that long for a simple search."

"It didn't look that simple."

"There's only so many bags of flour they can sample."

Vic sat down next to Erin on the bed. "Are you okay? I felt bad I couldn't talk to you about what was happening."

"It's okay. I understand they wanted to get our stories separately and ensure everything lined up."

"Yeah, but... I don't know. I still feel like I should have gone over to the library and talked to you as soon as I knew there was something wrong."

"No, you needed to help the police. I was fine. I *am* fine. You don't need to worry about that. You do what the police tell you to and keep out of trouble. I don't need my assistant put in the clink."

Vic grinned. "You think Terry would throw me in jail?"

"No, I don't… unless you were really being a problem."

They both smiled. "So, where did you want to go?" Erin inquired. "The car ride."

"Well, I was hoping to see Willie for a couple of hours. It's not the best timing, I know, but I wanted to get him caught up. He needs to know what's happening in the area, even if it isn't directly related to the clans. We don't know what might have a connection that only he would be aware of." She sighed. "I'm missing him. And craving some hot chicken."

Though Erin had lived in Tennessee for the first few years of her life and for the last couple of years, she had not gotten used to their spicy fried chicken. She was a wimp, preferring her chicken crunchy and savory, but not fiery hot.

"I think we could manage that," Erin agreed. "If I don't have to make supper, I can manage a little drive out to the back of beyond."

"Really? You look tired, so don't tell me it's okay if it's not. If you can't drive…"

"I can drive. But I want biscuits and gravy."

"Of course," Vic agreed. She knew how wimpy Erin was about hot spices. Maybe the same quirk of genetics that gave her an incredibly acute sense of smell had also made her more susceptible to hot spices. She didn't see how Vic could eat the hot chicken without even breaking a sweat when Erin couldn't have a bite without succumbing to tears.

"I'll call an order in to the restaurant and we can pick it up on our way out of town."

"Be careful what you order," Erin warned. "Get Terry's usual order instead of Willie's."

"Oh—you're right. I hadn't even thought about that." Vic nodded. "Good point."

Erin went to the bathroom and splashed cold water on her face to make sure that she was, in fact, alert enough to drive. In a few minutes, they were both ready and on their way to meet Willie.

Erin drove out to where she had dropped Willie last, but he was nowhere to be seen. She knew he was supposed to be in hiding, but she had thought that she would still be able to see his encampment.

"Do you think he is still here?" she asked Vic, looking around.

"Yeah, he's here." Vic looked around with the sharp, experienced eyes of a hunter. "And I'm sure he's either got eyes on us already or will soon." She opened the bucket of chicken. "This will draw him out!"

Lacking a tailgate or even a proper trunk on the VW, they found a log to sit on and started to spread the food out. Vic was right, and in a few minutes, Willie was there, grinning at the spread.

"How did you know?" he asked. "I'm gettin' tired of fish and squirrel."

"Squirrel?" Erin squeaked, though she knew it was a backwoods favorite. She didn't know why she was more squeamish about eating squirrel than eating chicken.

"Or rabbit," Willie offered. "You don't know what camping is until you've had a good roast rabbit."

In light of Erin's ownership of Marshmallow, the thought of eating rabbit was even more reprehensible than squirrel. It was akin to eating cat or dog. People didn't eat pets!

Willie and Vic snickered at Erin, but didn't tease her any further. Willie helped himself to a piece of chicken and bit into the crispy fried skin. The smell of the hot spices burst into the air, and Erin took a step back.

"Would be good if you could drive me to another mine today," Willie suggested. "If you have a few minutes. I don't want to stay in one location for too long."

"Yeah, as long as it doesn't get too late," Erin agreed.

He gazed at her for a minute, studying her expression. "Did something happen? You're pale."

"Just tired."

"She's not just tired," Vic disagreed. "There was a poisoning. The Historical Club meeting, if you can believe it. And Martha Erasmus was killed." Vic looked at Erin and then back at Willie. "We don't know yet how everyone else fared. They sent us on our way once it turned into a murder case."

Willie leaned forward. "The Historical Club was poisoned? The entire club?"

Erin nodded. "Everyone who was there today, anyway. And with my eclairs!"

"If I had to choose the way to go…"

Erin smiled her appreciation, but his admiration of her eclairs was bittersweet. How was she going to continue serving them? She still had several dozen shells in the freezer.

CHAPTER 31

"hy the Historical Club?" Willie asked, frowning.

Erin looked at him and then at Vic. She shook her head. "I have no idea. I thought it was… just random."

"It must have been targeted. Why not one of the other groups that ordered eclairs? They've been pretty popular lately, haven't they?"

"Yes. Maybe those are the only ones the letter writer would have access to."

"Does that mean that they are a member of the Historical Club?" Vic suggested.

"Maybe…" Erin thought about it. Who would have access to the eclairs at the community center? From her experience, the community center's security was not the best. And during an event, the doors were left unlocked and anyone could walk in and out of the building. There was no guard or gatekeeper, no security to keep them from getting in. The kitchen door had a lock, but it was usually left unlocked and sometimes propped open. People were not concerned that someone would walk in and steal the club's snack.

Or poison it.

Such a thing had never happened before, so why would they worry about such a thing?

"It could be a member," she admitted, "but then wouldn't it look suspicious if they didn't eat the eclairs?"

"Not necessarily." Vic shrugged. "People are on diets. Diabetic. Allergic. Avoiding sugar or desserts or fat. Or they put it on their plate and made it look like they had eaten it."

"Terry said that everyone at the Historical Club was sick."

Or had he? He'd said that everyone who had eaten the eclairs was sick. So maybe not everyone had sampled them.

"They did all get taken to the hospital though, did they?" Vic asked.

"No. Not everyone was that sick. Terry said that they were keeping an eye on everyone, but only the most critical ones were taken to the hospital. We don't have enough vehicles to rush people into the city, and I think the rest were at the clinic, or maybe still at the community center under observation."

"You wouldn't want to just send everyone home in case someone had a delayed reaction or something more subtle," Willie agreed. "What poison was it? What were the symptoms like?"

"I don't know, he didn't tell me."

"Gastrointestinal," Vic offered. "At least to start with. That's what Terry said to check when I went to talk to the book club. Nausea, vomiting, diarrhea. Make sure there was no one in the bathroom sick. And watch for anyone with a headache or confusion."

Willie considered this. Erin could tell he was thinking some-thing through, so she waited, not saying anything.

"So, that would have been easy enough for anyone at the Historical Club to fake," Willie pointed out. "The more acute cases were sent to the hospital in the city, but the milder cases—some nausea and cramping—it would be easy enough for the poisoner to pretend that they were having the same symptoms as everyone else, and no one would know that they hadn't actually eaten any of the eclairs."

"Or he could have poisoned all of the eclairs except for a few in one corner, and the poisoner ate one or two of those," Vic suggested. "He eats them, even gets a little cream in the corner of his mouth, and pretends to have symptoms, and no one would know any different. Unless they can detect it in the blood and take samples from everyone."

"They weren't doing that. We would have heard about it if they were. They'd have to send everyone to the city or the clinic to take blood. And people could refuse. They might be able to get a warrant to search Auntie Clem's, but to take everyone's blood? There's no way." Erin shook her head.

"Not likely," Willie agreed. "They could recommend that everyone be tested so that they could be treated properly, but they couldn't insist. I don't think your poisoner would have any trouble avoiding tests. Just say they were afraid of needles and were only having mild symptoms. No one could force them."

"Do they even know what the poison was?" Vic asked.

"I don't think they've had time to identify it yet," Erin said. "Not that they told me. They were going to take a bunch of samples from the ingredients at the bakery. And I guess they must be taking and testing blood from the people who were taken to the hospital."

"They'll figure out what it was eventually," Willie said.

They were quiet for a few minutes, eating and thinking about the poisoning. Erin felt a little queasy, even though she knew everything she was eating was perfectly safe.

"You don't think it was anyone at the bakery or anything to do with the bakery, right?" Vic asked Erin. "I mean… the letters were directed there, but it didn't have anything to do with us, did it?"

"No. I keep telling everyone, it has nothing to do with the bakery or Harold."

Willie cocked his head slightly and looked at Erin. "Harold?"

"Harold Melville. You probably don't know him. He's only been in town for a short time. His parents used to live here, but they went to Nashville for a while when Harold was younger."

"I know who Harold is."

"Oh, okay." Erin hesitated, unsure why this sounded alarm bells for her. She tried to follow through on the implications. "How do you know who he is? Because you knew him when he was a little kid?"

Willie's brows drew down. "His mother is one of the Dyson family. One of Dwight's kids."

"Oh. So you know her from way back, before Harold was even born."

"Yes, from back then and from more recently. She has three boys and is quite intent on getting them into the clan's leadership."

Erin swallowed. "I guess I heard that. But her older boys aren't... the best leadership material?"

Willie snorted. "They might be adequate for some positions in the clan, but the leadership... no. It takes a lot of intelligence, as well as..." He searched for a word. "Craftiness? Savvy? Understanding how the political structure works in the clan. Who has influence no matter what position they are in, who you have to court and what their motivations are. You have to know people and how to handle them. And not get involved in all of the petty disagreements between members."

He shook his head.

"Not my area of expertise or something I want to spend my time doing. I prefer more solitary pursuits..." He made a motion to indicate their surroundings; in the backwoods, the nearby mine where he worked alone, his only company Vic and Erin, and they would not be staying.

"Harold is pretty good with people," Erin observed. "He's bright and picks up things pretty quickly. But he's sort of... naive..." She thought about it. "I mean, that's understandable in someone so young. But even for his age. He seems a little... trusting. Guileless."

"He will need to overcome that if he is going to step up to take a place in the leadership."

Vic and Erin exchanged looks.

"But I thought Della's boys didn't have a chance of getting into the clan leadership," Vic said slowly.

"The older boys, no. They are the stereotypical thugs. Big,

brash, quick to take action, not so quick to think things through, the kind who think they know everything when they don't have a clue."

"But Harold is the opposite," Erin said. "He is a thinker. Doesn't just jump into things. And…" she swallowed, "I know he's been doing things with Nelson. They go on these fishing trips…"

Willie nodded. "One of the ways he gets to know the boys. Who they are, their skills, and how they will react."

Erin thought about the stories she had heard from Harold. The fishhook story. How, as a six-year-old, he had gone to Uncle Nelson for help, hadn't tried to pull it out himself, and hadn't cried when Nelson had pushed it through his flesh to cut off the barbed end. Nelson had learned a lot about Harold's nature through that experience. And he kept inviting Harold on the fishing trips.

Willie was watching Erin.

"Does Harold have a chance of getting into the clan's leadership?" she asked, a lump of dread in her stomach.

Willie took his time in answering. He looked for another piece of chicken, considering them all carefully before finally choosing a wing and nibbling at the edge. Erin was becoming more used to the spicy particles floating in the air.

"Nelson has been grooming Harold as his heir for some years," Willie disclosed at last.

"But Nelson didn't even know he was going to lead the clan," Vic protested. "Until you made him your heir and 'died,' he didn't think he would be leading it. He was setting up his own faction within the clan."

Willie nodded his agreement. "The clan was being led by Mona, with Dwight as the figurehead. Nelson was likely to take over as Dwight's heir, though there were a number of children who aspired to the position, and a certain amount of infighting and politics to be selected. Bobby being killed changed the balance and Nelson was definitely in the running. But he didn't like the way things were being run and he did set up his own faction within the clan, planning to break off from the main clan, eventually."

"But then, when you made him your heir, he became the only one with the authority."

Willie nodded. "The bloodline through me, the figurehead through Dwight, and the powerful faction he had been building within the clan, all merged together."

"And he wants Harold to be his heir," Erin said slowly, "because he doesn't have any kids of his own. And he doesn't want it to go to any of his siblings or lieutenants."

"He's been planning and building for a long time," Willie acknowledged. "He has a vision for the future, and is one of the few people with the foresight and patience to play the long game. Especially in the world of organized crime, where politics and leadership could shift in a day."

Vic shook her head, her eyes wide. "He wants Harold to be the next leader of the clan after him? But he's such a sweetie! He would never agree to something like that."

"He is not necessarily being given a choice. His mother has been pushing for her children to be considered since before he was born. Nelson has been taking him on these trips, grooming him, bringing him in close, since he was a child. He won't have the option to say that he wants to be an accountant or whatever he wants to do with his life."

Vic looked like she would argue this, insisting that Harold did have a choice.

"Look what happened to me," Willie pointed out. "My parents took me away from the clan since I was a baby and I decided to have nothing to do with them after serving my five years as a soldier. They still got me, after decades of saying no, and I had to die to get out of it. You think a fifteen-year-old kid can resist all of that pressure?"

CHAPTER 32

*E*rin and Vic were quiet on the way home after giving Willie a ride to the next mine he wanted to stay at. Erin was glad that their idea for Willie to stay in the wilds and operate his mines was working out for him. He certainly seemed happier out there in the wild than he had been cooped up in Vic's apartment.

Erin had never enjoyed camping and a life of deprivation. She preferred her flush toilets, HVAC, and a comfy bed to sleep in. But she was glad Willie was enjoying it.

On the way home, all she could think about was Harold and the life that his family intended for him. She had enjoyed Harold since she had met him. His chipper attitude and enthusiasm, his joy in his work and the results of their labor, his quick mind in learning new things, and his care for others all worked together to make him a pleasant employee and someone she enjoyed seeing and talking with when he was on shift.

His whole personality would be crushed if he were forced into the leadership of the Dyson clan. There would be no more chipper, cheerful Harold, excited to try a new recipe or method. She didn't know what profession he planned to go into, but whatever his hopes and dreams, they would be crushed if he were installed as the head of the clan.

Vic was quiet, apparently lost in similar thoughts. Or maybe she was just sad to be leaving Willie in the wilderness instead of bringing him home with her. Erin pulled the car into the garage, and they both sighed.

"Well, have a good sleep," Vic said. "I'll see you in the morning."

"Tomorrow will be a better day," Erin promised.

"Yeah, I hope so."

Erin walked into the house through the back door and could smell Terry's aftershave and sweat as soon as she walked in. She was glad he was home.

"Hello," she called out, making sure that she didn't startle him. If he were watching a video or had his earbuds in for some other purpose, he might not have heard her entrance through the back door. It was best not to surprise a law enforcement officer.

"Oh," Terry stepped into the kitchen. "I just got home and was wondering where you were. Over at Vic's?"

"She and I went on a supply run for Willie. Took him a few things."

"He still out in the sticks?"

"He seems to enjoy it." Erin rolled her eyes. "I don't see the attraction, myself."

He chuckled. "Why is it women don't generally enjoy sleeping under the stars?"

"A lot of things are more difficult for women, biologically speaking, than they are for men. And that's not even considering their responsibilities if they have to make the meals and care for the young 'uns. The men drink beer and lie around in a boat or a duck blind to provide for themselves, while the women get to do all the real work."

"Men split firewood too."

"And build the fires," Erin agreed. "Since lighting a fire is obviously men's work. Except when it's women's work."

"Men do a little more than lie around and drink beer."

"Maybe. Not that I've seen."

Terry smiled. He checked the fridge and grabbed himself a can of beer, obviously inspired by their conversation. "Have you eaten?"

"Yes, thanks."

He popped his can open and sipped the drink. "I assume Willie is working his mine out there, not just sitting around drinking."

"Yes. He's got that to do. And he says he's eating squirrel and rabbit, so he must be hunting. And fishing. Though I didn't see any equipment."

"He's resourceful. Reckon he has supply caches at all of his mines in case he ever needs them."

"I guess so." They both drifted toward the living room and settled into the couch. Erin snuggled up to Terry, needing the warmth of his body and the comfort of having him close. She sighed. She really needed it. She let out a long sigh. "Tell me no one else died."

Terry put his arm around her and squeezed her close for a few seconds before releasing her and resting his arm on her shoulders.

"No one else died. Martha Erasmus was the only one."

"How many others were hospitalized? Is anyone else still really sick?"

"Two others are still in the hospital. Most of the others were just treated at the clinic. Symptoms treated until they were out of the woods. Some people are still feeling pretty rough tonight, but they will recover."

"Poor Martha. I feel so bad for her family. Do they think she got more of the poison, or was it just because she was frail?"

"The medical examiner will have to do more extensive testing. They haven't figured out what the poison was yet, though they are thinking it was something organic. A plant rather than a chemical."

"Like foxglove or belladonna?"

"Something milder than that. And there didn't seem to be many heart or neurological effects, most gastrointestinal."

"Maybe the poisoner didn't think it would kill anyone."

Terry nodded. "That's possible. They might have thought that it would just make people nauseated or make them throw up. But even so… they are still going to prison. Even if they didn't think it would kill anyone. That is a risk you take if you tamper with food. It isn't accidental. It is reckless."

"Manslaughter or murder?"

"It depends on how they are charged, what the DA thinks they can prove, and the jury."

Erin closed her eyes. She had to believe that the police would find the person responsible, and they would go to prison. Whoever had poisoned everyone at the Historical Club meeting would be caught and punished for what they had done.

CHAPTER 33

*H*arold was scheduled to work the next afternoon, and Erin picked him up at the school as she had done before, alert for anyone who might have evil intentions against the boy.

Harold looked so vulnerable, walking from the school to the car. Skinny, not yet filling out his adolescent frame, unarmed, carrying a heavy backpack full of schoolbooks. His bag looked like it weighed more than he did. He thanked her for the ride as he put his backpack into the back seat and then sat down beside her. He sighed. He was looking paler than he had before. She worried he wasn't getting the sleep or the sun he needed to stay healthy. Was he lying awake at night worrying about the letter writer and what they would say next? What the townspeople would accuse him of? If they all believed that he was the poisoner, Erin didn't imagine they were making life too easy for him.

"How are you holding up?" she asked him.

Harold looked out the window rather than at her. "It'll all blow over soon enough," he told her. "That's what Mom says. People get all riled up over things and throw around accusations and such, but they'll get over it."

"Are you getting a lot of grief from people? I'm worried about you."

"Mom made everyone shut off their phones last night. And we got the dogs to keep anyone off the property. I was worried about getting a brick through the window. Or worse. But the dogs won't let no one get that close."

"That's good. I guess there are benefits to living 'out in the sticks.'"

Harold nodded, a slight quirk to the corner of his mouth. "I didn't really like moving all the way out there after Nashville. In Nashville, there were places to go... I could walk to the store... go to the movies, stuff like that. Here, I can go places after school or if I'm in town for another reason. But there isn't anywhere to go in walking distance of the house."

"That can't be easy."

"It's not bad, it just means I have to plan if I want to go somewhere. But now..." He sighed again. "I can't really go anywhere alone. I like being independent. But all of this stuff means I have to have someone with me. I don't want to get jumped by a bunch of vigilantes who think I'm writing crazy letters or poisoning people."

Erin wanted to pat Harold on the knee and tell him it would be okay, but she didn't want the gesture to be taken the wrong way. So she just shook her head. "I'm sorry all this is happening to you. You don't deserve that."

He looked at her briefly. "I'm glad you don't think it's me."

"I know you, Harold. And anyone who knows you has to know that you wouldn't do something like that. You wouldn't do anything to hurt anyone."

"Yeah." Harold looked wistful. "I wouldn't want to do that."

Erin pulled into her parking space behind Auntie Clem's. She looked at Harold.

"Your Uncle Nelson..."

"Yeah?"

"Does he want you to be in the clan? Helping to run things, I mean?"

It was probably not proper to ask him. It was probably one of those things that Erin should not do if she valued her life. But she wanted to hear it from Harold's own mouth. To know what was going on in his head and what he thought about this destiny.

Harold rubbed his head. "I guess so, yeah. It's not something I ever wanted or asked for. My mom says it is a privilege and that I should be grateful and take advantage of it. I'll have all the money and power to do what I want. But I was never interested in that part of the business."

Erin stopped with her hand on the door handle. "What do you mean, *that part* of the business?"

"Well… it's not all illegal, you know. It isn't all about violence and trafficking drugs and that kind of thing. There are legitimate business segments, too. I wouldn't mind that. Being a businessman. Like Miss Victoria's boyfriend, before he got back into the clan. Or like you with the bakery. I think it's cool, having a venture like that to run."

"What does Nelson think about that?"

"I haven't talked to him about it very much. He knows that I like business and that I'm doing this school course and the work release at Auntie Clem's. He says it's good experience, and he's proud of me for doing it." Harold allowed himself a smile at that. "But we haven't really talked about… how I could work for the clan but not get involved in any… messy stuff."

His Adam's apple bobbed as he swallowed.

"Messy stuff," Erin repeated. In her mind, she saw Mr. Inglethorpe on the kitchen floor. She had seen some terrible things, and she didn't want Harold to have to witness them too. He deserved to have a childhood and to grow up to do what he wanted to do with his life. She hated the thought of this kind, thoughtful young man being forced into a life of crime.

"Do you think he would let you?" she asked. "I know he has other businesses; he even had one with Willie for a while. I don't know what happened to it. Maybe he would be happy to have you working in one of his businesses."

"I don't know. I haven't asked if it is okay. I know… my mom would think that was selling out. She thinks I need to do... what Nelson's doing now."

"Running the entire organization."

"Yeah." Harold rubbed his forehead. "I can't believe that people think I would threaten people or poison them. I'm trying to figure out how to have my own life, the life I want, and they think I'm some mass murderer. I've seen people die, and I don't want any part of it."

"You have?"

Harold looked around, and his hand moved to the door handle as if he would get out of the car to escape answering her question. But then he stopped and just sat there. "It's not something I can talk about, even with you. Your husband is a cop. If you told him what I told you, I'd be in big trouble."

Erin didn't offer to keep Harold's secret and not tell Terry about it. If Harold had been a witness to a mob hit or some other violent death, she wouldn't promise not to tell Terry or another cop about it. He obviously wasn't just talking about watching his elderly grandmother take her last breath when she reached the natural end of her journey. He wouldn't be worried about what she would tell the cops if that were the case.

"Does your mom know you saw this?"

He stared straight ahead and didn't answer.

"If your mom knows and didn't care or thought that was good, then you know her opinion about you and the clan. If she doesn't know... maybe you should tell her about it and see what she thinks. She might surprise you. Maybe she doesn't want you involved in anything like that. Maybe she just wants you in the family business and hasn't thought about what impact that might have on you."

"I know I'm just a wimp. I shouldn't be bothered by something like that. It's the way the world works. It's the circle of life, right? Even Disney talks about how you're born, and you live your life, and then you die, and that's just normal and natural and not something to cry about." He took a deep, shuddering breath and didn't shed a tear. "Uncle Nelson likes it when I show him I'm tough. When I don't cry over nothing like a little kid."

Erin ran her fingers around the outside of the steering wheel, thinking about it.

"I was really upset when I heard about Martha Erasmus dying yesterday. And... I cried about it."

"Was she your friend?" Harold bit his lip, looking stricken.

"No. I barely knew her. But I still cried about it. It's normal to be upset when someone dies. Even if you don't know them. People cry when TV show characters die. People that don't even exist."

"It's fine for *women* to cry. But it isn't fine for a man. Especially not one who... wants to become something in the Dyson clan."

"But that's not really what you want, is it?"

"It is. I just don't want... the other stuff. I like the thought of being in charge and people listening to me. I want my mom and Uncle Nelson to be proud. I want to do something real, to be important."

"But not who you would have to be if you were in the clan. Or what you would have to do to get there."

Harold let out a long breath. "It's just something I have to figure out," he said. "You can't help." He opened the car door before Erin could argue and headed for the back door of Auntie Clem's.

Vic looked into the kitchen from the front when they entered. "Oh, there you are. Thought you got lost!"

"Sorry, we were just talking," Erin said. "Lost track of time."

Vic raised a brow questioningly, but Erin shook her head. She wasn't going to share what she and Harold had discussed.

"We'll get to work here," she assured Vic. "Unless you need someone to spell you out front. Do you want me to take till for a while?"

"No, it's all peachy," Vic assured her. "Carry on!"

CHAPTER 34

*T*he bells on the door jangled loudly when Melissa flew into Auntie Clem's with a handful of brightly colored flyers. She flapped them in Erin's direction, ignoring the customers lined up in front of her.

"Town hall meeting," she announced. "To discuss the issue of the letters and the incident at the Historical Club."

"The incident?" Erin repeated.

Melissa's face flushed.

"You mean the poisoning?" Erin demanded. "Do you think that not calling it what it was makes it less scary?"

"Well… I guess I do, yes," Melissa admitted, surprising her. "I don't like to scare people; if someone hasn't heard about what happened, I don't want to shock them. I want them to find out gradually. From somebody else, preferably," she said with a self-deprecating laugh.

"I thought you liked to spread *important* news." Erin decided at the last minute not to say bad or tragic news. It was less judgmental. But the truth was, Melissa had a long history of eagerly spreading bad news, especially if it had something to do with someone in her audience. Erin didn't know why she would be avoiding calling a murder a murder now.

She took one of the flyers from Melissa. She didn't need more than that. She wasn't going to be passing them out. If Melissa wanted to distribute them, she would need someone other than Erin to pass them along. She looked over the details.

"What's this got to do with you?" she asked. "Are the police putting on the town hall meeting?" She wasn't sure how events like this were planned and managed. She'd never been to one before. Even the fire on Main Street that had burned down the original Auntie Clem's Bakery had not warranted one. Or if it had, she hadn't been invited. But it looked like everyone was invited to this meeting. Not at the community center, Erin noted. That was probably too close to the tragedy to be used for the purpose. Instead, it was in the school auditorium.

"No, the police are not in charge of it, though they will be making a statement. The town council is in charge of it. But I do some administrative work for them now and then, so I said I would help to get the flyers distributed and posted wherever there is a community bulletin board." Melissa handed flyers to each customer and then looked at Erin expectantly.

"I'll put it on the bulletin board," Erin agreed.

"Great. Well, I'd better head out and make sure everybody knows what is happening."

"So is this just a session to inform people about the poisoning? Or is it a discussion about how we can help the police or keep people safe, like with a neighborhood watch, or what?"

"It will be a discussion," Melissa said slowly. Her eyes flicked toward the kitchen. "About... directions the police should be investigating, how to deal with disreputable characters on our streets and threats to our community."

Erin's skin crawled. That significant glance toward the kitchen told her everything she needed to know about who would be targeted as a disreputable character or threat to the community.

And what to do about him.

"A witch hunt."

"What?" Melissa demanded. "Witch hunt? Of course not. But people need to know of anyone who might pose a threat to the community. We can't just ignore the dangers out there. We need to protect... the vulnerable populations in Bald Eagle Falls."

"Like school kids. Children who have been the targets of bullying."

Melissa smiled with her teeth, but no friendly concern in her eyes. "All vulnerable populations. Including *seniors*."

Erin nodded. "Okay. Glad to know what is planned."

Most of the customers Melissa had handed flyers to had left them on the small tables at the front of the bakery, and Erin left them there. They were picked up the rest of the afternoon and evening by other customers. And there were other customers who had picked up flyers at other establishments who discarded them onto the tables with the others.

The end result was that when Erin turned the sign over to Closed, locked the bolt on the front door, and closed the blinds, there was still a messy pile of flyers left on the tables. She gathered them up, glanced at the bulletin board to ensure one was displayed there, and carried them over to the recycling bin. She could feel that something in the middle of the pile was a different weight and shape from the flyers. She flipped through them and pulled out an envelope.

White, old stock, personal size. With her name written in now-familiar handwriting.

Erin nearly tossed it into the recycling bin with the rest. Why open it? Why give it any attention or scrutiny?

What would happen if she tossed it and pretended that she had never discovered it? The sender would assume that it had remained buried in the fliers. They couldn't blame her for not disclosing it if she didn't find it. Not her fault they had left it mixed in with the flyers. Trying to make another covert delivery to her, like the one left on the sidewalk on a day when the postal mail would not be delivered.

But it was Friday, a day when the mail had been delivered. For some reason, the sender had chosen not to use the mail this time. Did that mean they didn't trust Frank to deliver it? Or to keep quiet about it? Had he approached the person he believed was the sender and warned them he wouldn't deliver another one and keep their secret?

Or was there another reason the letter had not been mailed?

"Erin?" Vic was looking at her. "We're about done... was there something else...?"

Erin dropped the flyers into the recycling bin and was left holding the envelope so Vic could see it.

"Oh, no!"

Erin nodded.

"We do not need another letter today! You haven't opened it yet? You oughta call Terry. Don't bother opening it. Let him deal with it."

She was right. Erin put the envelope down on the counter and pulled out her phone. She dialed Terry's number, hoping he would not be busy with something else and would be able to answer right away. It went to voicemail. Erin hung up.

"Voicemail. Should I just keep trying to get him? Take it home with me? Leave it here? Stay here with it?"

"Text him and leave it here," Vic suggested. "When he's free, he can get the keys from you and come get it."

"I shouldn't just take it home with me?"

"If you want to. Do you want to be looking at it all evening until he gets home?"

"No."

"Just leave it here," Vic repeated.

"What if it's important?"

"Then he'll pick it up as soon as he's free."

Erin still hesitated.

"You could call the main dispatch line," Vic suggested. "They can send one of the others over or page Terry."

Erin nodded. "Okay... I'll try that."

She should have thought of it herself, but her brain was not working after the shock of discovering another letter.

When were they going to stop? A woman was dead. Would the letter be an apology? Mocking?

A threat that more would follow?

CHAPTER 35

The dispatcher paged Terry, and although the time seemed to stretch out unbearably long, he was at Auntie Clem's within half an hour. Each minute passed with the painfully slow ticking of the clock on the wall. Erin had always enjoyed its friendly noise, but now she was seriously considering climbing up on the counter, taking it off the wall, and removing the battery. She stared at it while Vic tried to engage her in discussion, but Erin couldn't get her mind to focus on anything but the envelope in her hand and what it meant to them.

She couldn't believe that the letter writer was still sending new messages. Didn't she know what had happened in town? How close the scrutiny was getting? Everybody in Bald Eagle Falls knew about the letters now. And if they did not already, they would soon understand that they were not psychic predictions, but the sick taunts of a cold-blooded killer. It wasn't a discussion of whether the Bible said that psychics didn't exist or that people should avoid them; there was a predator in their midst. Someone prowled around them like a wolf, waiting for the moment of weakness when it would pounce and take down the vulnerable.

And the author of the letters still had the gall to send another.

Finally, Terry knocked on the back door. Erin went to the door and looked out the peephole. After confirming it was Terry, she opened the door and handed him the letter.

Terry took it gingerly by the edges, looking surprised. "You shouldn't be handling it," he told Erin. "Where did it come from?"

"I couldn't help it. It was just with a bunch of other papers, flyers for the town hall, and I pulled it out. I didn't open it," she pointed out.

"No," Terry agreed. "We'll get the crime techs to do that. Ensure we don't contaminate the letter inside with any transfer evidence."

Erin stared at the envelope. "But what if it is something that we need to know? What if we can prevent... whatever it is threatening."

"We'll have to wait and find out."

"How long will it take?" Erin looked again at the clock on the wall. "Will they open it tonight? Run any fingerprints or DNA so that we'll know by morning? And tell us what it is threatening so we can try to head it off?"

"It won't likely be that quick. The courier for the crime lab in the city will pick up around ten tomorrow morning, and it will go into the queue. Even if it is marked as urgent, there's no guarantee it will be processed tomorrow. It will probably wait until Monday."

"And then it will be dealt with in a day or two, and maybe they'll have results for us by Christmas?" Erin said sarcastically.

"Well..." Terry's cheeks took on color, "we can only get the results as fast as it can be processed. I can't *make* them handle it any faster."

"Do you have to wait for the courier to pick it up tomorrow? Can't you take it to the crime lab right now?"

"I'm not sure that will get it into the queue any faster."

"You don't think you can convince them to process it any faster if you talk to them face-to-face? And tell them that it might be a threat of violence that you can avoid if you can identify the sender?"

"Anything is possible, but that's not usually how it works,"

Terry warned. "The lab just processes stuff as it comes in. Usually, the crime has already occurred, and we are trying to identify who did it weeks or months later. Or to build up enough evidence to prosecute the case."

"This person killed yesterday. They have already escalated from threatening notes to murder. What if we can prevent another one?"

"Are you saying I should open it?"

Erin stared at the offending envelope. Of course she wanted Terry to open it. She had to know what it said. But she hadn't wanted to take that responsibility on herself. She nodded wordlessly.

Terry looked at the envelope critically, then shook his head. "It needs to be opened in a controlled environment, where there is no possibility of us contaminating it."

Erin sighed noisily.

"We could drive it to the lab, though," Terry suggested. "See whether they will open it immediately so that we at least know what it says. I don't know how long it will take them to process it for fingerprints or transfer DNA, but we can at least do that much without compromising the evidence."

Erin took a breath in and nodded in agreement. "Yes. We can do that? What are we waiting for?"

Terry laughed. "You're not impatient at all, are you?" But he sobered. "I agree… if anything in this letter points to something we can avoid… we need to know what it says right away. I'm sure they can open it today so that we can at least see what it says."

Erin looked at Vic. "I'll take you home so you can take care of the animals and I can park the car. We'll drive to the city in Terry's."

"Lights and siren?" Vic asked enviously. "You get all the fun."

"Did you want to go into the city? It could be fun with all of us."

"Nah. You guys go. I'll hitch a ride in with someone on the weekend."

"We're not going to have fun," Terry pointed out. "We're going to get the evidence processed so that we can prevent harm."

"And that isn't fun?" Vic challenged. "And you are bound to stop for food. That's like a date."

Terry shook his head. "If everything is done here, why don't we lock up? We'll get on our way as quickly as possible and Erin can tell me on the way how you found the letter."

CHAPTER 36

*E*rin was glad to be doing something proactive. She was also glad that she had not succumbed to temptation and opened the letter, hopeful that there would be some evidence inside that the tech would be able to use to identify the letter writer and put a stop to the disruption and murder. She did not want to have to deal with another murder, especially one they could have prevented.

After Erin had given him all of the details she could about the discovery of the letter, she asked about the poisoning and if they had been able to find out anything about what poison had been used and who'd had access to the eclairs at the community center. Unfortunately, the police hadn't been able to make much progress on it, and it would be a while before the lab was able to identify the poison that had been used.

"But if it was organic," Erin said slowly, "foxglove or something like that... then you won't be able to trace who had access. Because anyone could have just picked it in the woods somewhere and prepared the poison."

"It would have to be someone who knew what they were looking for, someone who could recognize plants and had the ability to prepare it," Terry said, "but that could be pretty much anyone."

"But not Harold. He wouldn't be able to prepare it at his home without someone noticing. I think his mother would have noticed if he was boiling up some foxglove on the stove."

"Would she have stopped him? You're assuming that it was something she would have disapproved of."

Thinking back to her discussion with Harold, Erin had to admit that Della might have actually encouraged this murderous behavior.

"Well, I know it wasn't Harold anyway. He wouldn't do something like that."

Terry looked at her and didn't repeat that Erin couldn't know what was in someone else's heart. She'd heard it enough times over the past week or two and didn't want to hear it again.

"So that's a dead end unless you find out it was some rare or sophisticated poison."

Terry nodded. "Unfortunately, yes. And there were no fingerprints on anything at the community center. Or rather, everybody's prints on everything. There isn't anything that wasn't touched by anyone but the poisoner."

"And no security cameras. No one who shouldn't have been inside the community center. No one who disarmed the burglar alarm," Erin ran through the various scenarios in her head, trying to find some way that the killer might have left some trace of his or her identity.

"We're at a dead end unless more evidence comes to light," Terry sighed. "Maybe somebody will remember something that they saw."

But it wasn't likely. A witness would have come forward immediately, when it was still fresh in his mind and he found out that it had been a deliberate poisoning.

Despite the lights and siren, it still seemed like it took a long time to get to the city. Terry had called ahead to the crime lab to make sure that he would be able to get in once they got there to turn the evidence in. While it was irregular, it was apparently not against the rules.

They were met at the door by a heavyset man with black-rimmed glasses and a white lab coat. He had a lanyard around his neck, but the identity card was stuffed into his jacket pocket so it wouldn't swing around and get in his way.

"Dr. Lenton," he introduced himself, not offering his hand as he ate a sandwich. He motioned them into the building, through an airlock, into a lab. There were a few people working, who looked up to see who it was and then went back to their jobs.

Dr. Lenton had abandoned his sandwich on the other side of the airlock. No contaminants allowed in the crime lab. He took the evidence envelope that Terry proffered, with the envelope that Erin had discovered inside it.

"Erin's prints will be on the envelope," Terry said. "I only handled it by the edges, but I can also give you my prints for elimination."

"Yours are already in the system. Records are kept of law enforcement officers' prints. You'd be surprised how often they touch something they shouldn't."

Terry reddened. "Probably not as surprised as you think."

Dr. Lenton chuckled. "Tell me about the urgency of this piece of evidence."

"We have been receiving these letters with predictions or threats of violence and death. The writer apparently followed through with a mass poisoning yesterday in which one person was killed. We are afraid this may be another threat and hope that it will be something we can head off."

Lenton looked at Erin. "And you brought this witness because…"

"Oh. Uh. We're together. And Erin is the one who the letters have been addressed to, and maybe that means she'll be able to make a connection that I wouldn't be able to myself. Of course I'll distribute the letter to all of the law enforcement officers in Bald Eagle Falls, and hopefully we will be able to interpret the threat and put a stop to the letter writer."

The technician nodded. He went to a clean workstation and withdrew the smaller envelope from the larger one. He examined it under a magnifying glass mounted on an articulating arm, taking his time to look for any minute details. Then he took a sharp knife and slit the end of the envelope.

Erin and Terry watched with avid interest, quiet and waiting patiently as Lenton pulled out the folded letter with tweezers. He examined it under the magnifying glass, then eventually tweezed it open.

"Okay, you wanted to see the contents of the letter? Don't touch, but you can come over here." He moved to the side slightly to allow them a clear line of sight.

A twist of fate, a shocking turn,
    In silence waits a lesson learned.
    When wires cross and light ignites,
    The thrill you seek brings fraught delights.

Erin read it and shook her head, frowning. "Okay... what do you think? Is it a threat? There's no talk of blood or violence in this one. No murder."

"A shocking twist of fate..." Terry murmured. "Crossed wires usually refers to a miscommunication. The rest of it... seems like nonsense just put together to make it rhyme. Thrill seeking? You are not a thrill seeker. Maybe the sender is, but if there is anyone who is definitely *not* a thrill seeker, it is you."

Erin felt like he was putting her in a box. Maybe one that said, "doesn't know how to have fun." But she had to admit that he was right. She wasn't looking for thrills. Erin wasn't looking for something exciting or dangerous. She liked to bake bread during the day and return to her cozy home and her pets and Terry at the end of the day. She liked having her own place, running her own business, and not having to report to anyone.

She wasn't going to be sky diving or bungee jumping any time soon.

"What does 'fraught delights' mean?"

Terry shook his head. "I have no idea."

"Does that mean something I will be happy with or worried about? Or is it something to do with her, the writer? Is *she* looking for thrills and delights... no matter the cost? She enjoys seeing us squirm, right? That's the whole point of delivering these letters."

Terry held his phone over the letter to take a picture of it.

"Yeah... At first, we thought that the letters were just a prank, just trying to get people's attention. But then, with Harold's accident... things changed. Maybe she got a taste for actual violence then. Decided she would try her hand at it herself..."

"But she didn't have anything to do with Harold's accident. I was right there. He was the only one around."

"I know. But people immediately started talking about the blood, started talking about how it was the fulfillment of the prediction. And maybe that turned her on. She wanted more. Not just hoping that the letters would coincidentally be connected with something that happened, but..."

"But doing it herself."

Terry nodded.

Erin considered. "So... does this letter tell us how she will do it? Or just warn us that she's going to try again?"

"The electrical references could mean something. Or it could just be a theme. I'm not sure where to start." He tapped on the screen of his phone. "But I'm going to send this out to the others and hope that one of them has a good idea. Sometimes, there are obscure references that you don't even know are there."

"Like it could be from a book or a play."

"Maybe."

Dr. Lenton inched over, and Erin and Terry stepped back from the counter. "So, I will examine the letter for fingerprints and traces of DNA in case the writer touched the page without gloves at any time. Anything else that we should be looking for?"

"Can you tell... anything about the paper?" Erin asked. "I've been told that the watermark is the Melville family crest, but I don't know if that is true. And the mailman, he said that it was old stock. Not something modern."

Lenton scrutinized it. "I agree it is not modern. Thirty, even fifty years old. Linen, I would guess. And the watermark... watermarks usually indicate the manufacturer, not the sender. I don't recognize this one, though. I'll have to do some research and see if I can find any mention of it."

"Okay. I don't know if that will help us get any closer to the sender. But it's worth a try."

"Of course."

"Is there anything else we *should* be looking for?" Terry asked.

Lenton returned to the envelope and moved it back under the magnifying glass with his tweezers. "The paper stock and handwriting match the envelope. How was it delivered? No stamps, so it didn't come through the mail."

"No, it was left for someone to find it."

Lenton grunted and nodded. "Not very helpful. I will also do a DNA swab of the seal on the flap." He indicated the flap that he had not attempted to lift, having simply slit the end of the envelope. "If the sender licked it rather than using a sponge, there is the possibility of a DNA sample."

"That would be helpful," Terry agreed. "You never know. You would think that all criminals nowadays would do everything possible to avoid being discovered by DNA or fingerprints. Still, a surprising number of criminals are caught by very basic investigation and stupid mistakes."

"They aren't all geniuses masterminds like on TV," Erin repeated what he had told her before.

"Luckily, no. The culprit is usually exactly who you think it is."

CHAPTER 37

*W*hy is it called a town hall meeting if it isn't held at the town hall?" Erin asked as she and Terry both prepared to attend the meeting. Terry was putting the last touches on his uniform, and Erin was looking at herself in the mirror, wishing she had something a little more polished to wear. There seemed to be a gap in her closet between casual wear, her bakery clothes, and a little black dress suitable for a gala or party.

"Well, it's a *type* of meeting, not one that has to be held in a particular space. A town hall meeting is a chance for constituents to talk to their municipal elected officials about a particular issue. In this case... the letters and the poisoning. It's a chance for people to clear the air and for the mayor and town council to gently nudge them away from any vigilantism, which is a concern right now."

"You mean people taking matters into their own hands?"

Terry nodded. "We don't want citizens 'helping' us and taking down someone they think is guilty. Whether the person is guilty or not really doesn't make a difference. Vigilantism doesn't help anything. Vigilantes are just as likely to break the law, destroy evidence, or make it impossible to prosecute someone as they are to help. Innocent people can be targeted, injured, or even killed. We need to do everything we can to assure people that the police are handling it and they don't need to take it on themselves."

Erin nodded. Terry tactfully didn't point out that he often felt Erin was crossing that line and getting too involved as a citizen in something that should be left to the police. But Erin wasn't a vigilante. She had no interest in violence or capturing criminals herself. She just wanted the right people brought to justice.

"Are you worried about Harold?"

Terry brushed invisible lint from his shoulders and nodded. "Of course. We don't want a teenager being targeted with violence. I don't want anyone to get hurt, and he is certainly a person of interest in the letter writing."

"He didn't write those letters."

"That's not what I mean. The question isn't whether he wrote them or not. The problem is that he has been identified by citizens as a viable suspect, and they can't understand why the police haven't arrested him. They are demanding answers, and we don't have the evidence to charge anyone with anything."

Erin nodded. "I've been really worried about him. And not just because of the letter-writing."

Terry motioned toward the door. "Let's get on our way. What exactly are you worried about with Harold? Because his mother is a Dyson?"

"No, just a Dyson. Nelson's sister. One of Dwight's children."

"Among many. As far as I can tell, she isn't directly involved in any of the clan business. You could check with Beaver; she might know more about it. But I don't think you need to worry about Harold being pulled into a life of crime. Things are pretty quiet in Bald Eagle Falls."

Erin chewed on her lip as she and Terry walked out to his truck. Willie obviously knew more about the situation than Terry did. But should Erin tell him about it and potentially make Della and Harold Melville the subject of a police investigation or what they considered harassment? She especially didn't want to put Terry in the path of the clan.

Crazy Teresa could have killed him. Frank Ward, the cop who

had been with Terry at the time, had been stabbed and narrowly escaped death. Remembering seeing the hilt of the knife protruding from his back made her nauseated. She never wanted him to be that close to the Dyson clan again.

And when Erin and Terry had faced Mona due to Erin's research into what had happened to Hannah Dyson, she had thought it was the end of the line.

Terry looked at her after they got into the truck, with K9 sitting in the second-row seat of the extended cab. "What is it?"

"I guess I'm just anxious about the meeting. And about Harold."

"Harold will be okay. We'll make sure of that."

She nodded and sipped coffee from her travel mug. Terry didn't say anything as he drove to the school. There was an area reserved for police and the other officials who were there for the meeting.

They had arrived early, before everyone had assembled. Terry and K9 were to walk around the gym and surrounding areas to look for anything suspicious or out of place. Other people were busy setting up chairs, AV equipment, and signage. The audience would be kept away until everything was properly checked out and ready to go. No one wanted either the letter writer or a vigilante to decide this was the place to make their next move.

Erin hadn't been given any assignments, but she could help with things like setting up chairs. She joined the other volunteers setting up the folding chairs. But that job was finished pretty quickly.

Jazz was up at the front, checking the settings on the sound system. Erin looked around for anything else she could help out with. Everything seemed to be under control. She walked up to the front to chat with Jazz while he worked.

He smiled at her approach. "Miss Erin. How are you today?"

"I'm good, thanks. How about you?"

"Right as rain, missy. You sticking around for the show today? Reckon there might be some fireworks."

"I hope not! The idea is to settle people down, not rile them up."

"Sure… but you never know how people are going to respond. Some folks are like rattlers. You try to pet 'em, they're just gonna strike."

Erin laughed at the colorful metaphor. "Well, I hope not!"

Jazz threw a series of switches and frowned. "Something is not hooked up properly here. Good thing we're here in enough time to test it out. You would think that the school has enough assemblies to know how to set up their sound system properly."

Erin nodded. She remembered the endless assemblies and events that had taken place while she had been in school. There was at least one thing every week, sometimes more than that. The staff should know the system and proper settings inside and out.

Jazz looked behind him at the electrical cord leading up to the control board. "Would you make sure that is plugged in securely?"

"Sure." Erin followed the snaking cord. There were mats placed over it where it crossed aisles so people would not trip over it.

She reached the wall outlet and saw that the plug had pulled loose. It was dangling precariously from the socket, not pushed in far enough to get any juice. The cord was stretched too tightly, angled up from the last mat, in a position where it was likely to trip someone or get pulled out again after she pushed it in. Erin grasped the cord and pulled on it to ensure that she had enough slack, then pushed the plug into the socket so that it would connect. She looked at Jazz and gave him a wave.

Jazz flipped switches, nodding in approval. Erin heard a slight hum from the audio system. A bit of feedback?

"Can I get a mic test?" Jazz called out.

Melissa Lee, talking to one of the town council members, heard Jazz and turned toward the microphone.

Erin caught a whiff of something hot, like an electrical heater that was malfunctioning.

As Melissa reached for the microphone, the words of the verse came into Erin's head.

A twist of fate, a shocking turn, In silence waits a lesson learned.

When wires cross and light ignites, The thrill you seek brings fraught delights.

The unplugged cord.
The electrical hum.
That smell.
A shocking turn.
When wires cross.

Erin started to run. "Melissa!" There were too many people talking and too many other noises going on; Melissa didn't hear her. "Melissa, no!" Erin screamed, sprinted, and tried to get there in time to stop her.

One of Melissa's hands closed around the microphone, the other around the microphone stand. There was a crack, a flash, and Melissa stood there rigidly, eyes wide, hand glued to the microphone in her hand.

"No!" Erin hit Melissa in a flying tackle, knocking her off her feet, both of them crashing to the hard gymnasium floor, skidding and rolling away.

CHAPTER 38

There was a babble of voices around them. Jazz was yelling at everyone to stay back from the equipment and to unplug the cord. Erin righted herself, getting to her hands and knees, and she grabbed Melissa, a bigger woman than she was, and rolled her onto her back.

"Melissa! Melissa, are you okay?" Erin gasped.

"Ow!" Melissa complained, reaching her hand up to rub her head. "What did you do that for?"

"To save your life! The writer—the letter writer—messed with the wiring of the sound system." Erin gasped for breath, her heart going a mile a minute. "It shocked you. It could have electrocuted you!"

"Whew," Melissa blew out her breath. "My head is buzzing like a tree full of bees. Oh, goodness."

She started to get up. Terry and others were there, stopping her.

"Stay where you are, Miss Lee," Terry told her, putting a hand on her shoulder and pressing her back. "Take a minute to recover and let someone take a look at you. Are you okay?" He took both of her hands and looked at them. Then he put his fingers over her pulse. "How are you feeling?"

"Wishing I'd had a second cup of coffee this morning." Melissa pulled her hands away from Terry and rubbed her eyes. "That was a jolt like no other."

"I'm calling an ambulance," Terry advised. He reached for his radio and informed the dispatcher of their need.

"I'm just fine," Melissa protested. She pulled her dress up slightly to look at her bruised knees, bloody with a friction burn from the gym floor. Her elbows were in similar condition. "Ow. Just need some bandages. I definitely don't need an ambulance."

"They'll want to check your heart. Do an EKG and make sure everything is in order."

"I barely touched the microphone. Erin should try out for rugby. Wow. I haven't been tackled like that since I was in school."

Terry turned to Erin. "And you. Are you okay? Did you get a shock?"

"No. I didn't feel it. Just hitting the floor. I'm going to have some bruises." She looked at her palms and knees. "And some scrapes, like Melissa."

"We'll get both of you some bandages. Those must sting."

"Yeah, like a burn," Erin agreed, shaking her hands to cool them, which didn't really help.

"How did you know Melissa was going to get a shock?"

"I just… I could smell it was hot, and I remembered the words of the letter."

Terry's eyes met hers.

"Can we get some room?" He requested. "Everyone move back. Give these ladies some breathing space."

It was a few minutes before the other law enforcement officers and civic leaders managed to get the volunteers and rubberneckers to move back, giving them space.

Jazz was at Erin's side, worried, unwilling to be pushed back without talking to her first.

"I don't understand what happened!" he insisted. "There is a GFCI outlet; this should not have happened. This equipment is old and flaky, but nothing like that…" He looked at Terry pleadingly. "How could the mic have been hot? That can't happen."

"It was tampered with," Terry told him. "Intentionally. It wasn't something you did wrong. This was intended to hurt someone."

He thumbed the screen on his phone and looked at the picture he had taken of the letter the day before.

"When wires cross and light ignites."

Erin nodded. "A shocking turn."

He shook his head. "How did she get access to this equipment?"

"Where was it before it was set up here?"

"In storage. They set it up yesterday in anticipation of the town meeting."

"And who has had access to the gym since then?"

Terry shook his head. "Too many people. I'll have to find out if there's any log kept or any security cameras."

"In here?" Jazz questioned. "No. Nothing in here. In the hallways, maybe. Or the outside doors. But there's nothing in here."

He looked around. Erin also glanced around, looking for cameras on the walls or up by the ceiling in the corners.

"They just get knocked out in a room like this," he explained. "Basketballs, volleyballs, dodgeballs, kids goofing off. Even keeping the cages around the spotlights intact is nearly impossible."

"Is there any way the town hall meeting can still be held?"

Erin turned to look at the mayor, who looked a little embarrassed by his own question, but didn't back down.

"This is just more evidence that the situation is getting out of hand. We need to do something."

Terry's mouth was a thin, unyielding line. "I think it's obvious that it will not happen today. We have victims who need to go to the hospital. We need to investigate what happened here and who had the chance to tamper with this equipment. It is a crime scene. This was attempted murder."

"Not murder," the mayor cajoled. "No one was seriously hurt. It couldn't have resulted in death."

"It could have," Terry maintained. "Erin was very quick to intervene and break contact between Melissa and the electrified equipment. If she had not, and no one realized what was happening…"

"But is it really tampering? It could just be an accident."

"We will investigate that question. At the moment, I'm going with tampering. It shouldn't take long to figure out whether we are dealing with a frayed wire or someone intentionally creating a short and disabling the GFCI socket."

The way he said it made it clear that he had no doubt that Melissa's shock had not been an accident.

"We still need the town hall meeting," the mayor maintained. "This will get out of control if we don't stay on top of it."

Terry shook his head. "Not today. We need a chance to look over the equipment. We can't use it."

"What about another sound system? We must have a portable sound system in town that could be borrowed."

Terry tilted his head, not disagreeing.

"If we bring in another system that hasn't been left here for someone to tamper with, what about that?"

"Okay. If you can find a totally separate, stand-alone system that can be used and doesn't rely on any of the electrical in this building… then okay. We'll move this to a secure location, test the new system to make sure it is safe, and continue with the town hall meeting. Minus a couple of participants," Terry said, looking at Melissa and Erin.

"I'm not going anywhere," Erin said flatly.

"Erin, you need to be checked out."

"I'm not the one who was shocked. All I did was hit Melissa. And the floor."

"I'm not leaving either," Melissa insisted, following Erin's example. "I wanted to be a part of this discussion, and I'm not leaving. If someone wants to get rid of me, they're going to have to try harder than that."

"That's what I'm afraid of," Terry said seriously.

"You think this was aimed at me?" Melissa shook her head. "I'm just helping out with setup. I'm not the one they want to silence."

"I still don't think dangling the fact that you survived electrocution in front of them—whoever it is—is a good idea."

Melissa folded her arms and looked at Erin. Erin shrugged and looked at Terry.

"You both need to be checked out."

"Later," Erin said. "We have other things to do today."

"Yeah, we do," Melissa agreed.

Terry shook his head and rubbed the space between his brows. "The two of you are a pain in the..."

"Officer Piper!" Melissa chided.

"The bar has a karaoke machine," the mayor said. "So does the community center. They can be used as stand-alone amplifiers. They have an internal battery so you can take them to parties. On the beach or wherever. As long as it has been charged, they won't need to plug it in here at all."

"Use the one from the bar," Terry advised. "If someone foresaw us going ahead with the town hall meeting despite this incident, they might anticipate us switching to the community center sound system. But not the one at the bar. I want it tested at the bar before it is brought here."

"We're going ahead!" the mayor called to the others who were already assembled and waiting for word.

An anemic cheer went up. Not everyone was as intent as he was to continue with the meeting after the demonstration of the letter writer's intentions.

Erin took a deep breath and nodded at Terry. "I guess we'd better get ready, then."

"The first order of business is to get the two of you taken care of. At least let the paramedics check you out and get your floor burns bandaged."

CHAPTER 39

*I*t was a while before everything was set up. Erin and Melissa were examined by the paramedics who had arrived and pronounced to be in good health as far as their field testing showed, though they did recommend getting a follow-up EKG done and checked by a cardiologist, just to be safe. Heart rhythm problems were nothing to sneeze at.

The sound equipment was brought over from the bar. It turned out that the system used two wireless microphones, so they could have one up at the front for the speaker to use and one to be passed around to members of the audience who had questions or comments so they didn't have to waste time going back and forth to the microphone at the front.

They tested both microphones to ensure they worked and set the volume to a comfortable level. Erin winced at a moment of feedback, her heart immediately speeding up again in case she might have to perform another rescue. But nothing exploded or shorted, and she was left sitting there, gasping for breath.

It was half an hour late when they finally let the audience into the gym, and people were not happy about having had to wait in line. It wasn't a great note to start out on, but what were they supposed to do? The new system had to be set up and tested if they wanted to go ahead with the town hall meeting. At least they hadn't had to send people home with the news that the meeting had been canceled.

Erin hadn't felt great about the town hall meeting in the first place. She was afraid it was going to stir up more trouble than it was going to solve. But the town council seemed to think it was the solution to their problems. Erin was crossing her fingers that it wouldn't make things worse.

She watched the audience come in with travel coffee cups from home or the family restaurant. She felt bad that there were no baked goods for refreshments. But the organizers had decided that after the poisoning of the Historical Club, it was not a good idea for them to provide any food that could be tampered with. And Auntie Clem's was closed for the day, so people couldn't even stop by the bakery to get treats of their own.

Erin knew it was for the best, to ensure everyone's safety, but that didn't mean she had to like it. She was so used to catering at such events that she felt guilty about just sitting in the audience watching people drinking their own cups of coffee and nothing to eat.

The seats filled quickly, and people were anxious for the meeting to begin. The town council obliged, with the mayor himself standing up to welcome everybody there and to apologize for the late start due to an unforeseen equipment malfunction. He outlined the procedure they would be following for questions and comments once the floor was open for comments.

He extended condolences to the family and friends of Martha Erasmus.

"We are a family here in Bald Eagle Falls," Mayor McCormick said mournfully. "It is a great loss to all of us. Her sudden passing raises questions about what is going on in our community. What predator might lurk among us with the intent to harm other innocent members of our family."

A murmur ran through the crowd.

"We have a report from the sheriff on the investigation into Martha's death."

Sheriff Wilmot went to the mic and gave a brief recap of the circumstances of Martha's death and assured the townspeople that they were looking into it, pursuing all leads, and waiting for lab reports to get back to the medical examiner in the city so that they would know exactly what they were dealing with. Nothing to indicate that they were any closer to finding the killer than they had been the moment she got sick.

Erin watched and listened to the audience. They did not seem to be any happier about the report than Erin was. It didn't escape them that he didn't know who the killer was and was apparently not even close to finding out.

Wilmot sat back down. There were a few more uninformative comments from members of the town council, and then the floor was opened up to questions from the community members.

Tara Waldon, attractively attired in a bright blue blazer, was one of the first to speak, beginning by thanking the police department and town council for everything they had done so far.

Then, with a puzzled smile, she asked, "Can you tell us when you're going to arrest the perpetrator?"

"We are still investigating Miss Erasmus's death," Wilmot reiterated. "When we have enough evidence pointing to the identity of the poisoner, we will proceed."

"You don't know who it is?" Tara asked, bemused.

"I'm sorry, we are still investigating the circumstances of her death. If and when we have enough evidence to charge someone, we will not delay."

Tara looked around at the other people sitting around her, then sat down.

Cindy Prost received the mic next. "There's no doubt who's behind these threats and attacks," she said aggressively. "So explain why you are not arresting Harold Melville."

"I am unable to discuss the course of our investigation so far or the evidence we have gathered," he said gravely. "We do not have the evidence to arrest anyone at this point. It is still an active investigation, and we are pursuing all leads."

"The notes are written on Melville family stationery. What more evidence do you need?"

"I cannot comment on the evidence. But I assure you, we will make an arrest when we have the evidence to do so. You are jumping to conclusions about the origin of the paper and the writer that cannot be verified."

"We all know it is Harold," Lottie insisted, standing and taking the microphone. "Why are you hesitating? Why are you covering it up?"

"We don't know that it was Harold Melville. There is no evidence that he had the paper or letters at any time or was at the community center when the food was poisoned."

"It was his family stationery. He tried to make people believe that the predictions were true by cutting himself. And I heard a rumor that there was another letter delivered yesterday?"

Who had told her that?

"I cannot confirm or deny the existence of another letter." Wilmot did not comment on the other accusations.

"Are you saying that Harold getting hurt was just a coincidence? That he just happened to have an accident that fulfilled one of the predictions?"

When Wilmot opened his mouth to answer, Lottie cut him off. "Or are you saying that the writer of the letters really was clairvoyant? That there was witchcraft involved?"

"I'm not saying anything of the sort," Wilmot said firmly. "We would ask that the citizens of Bald Eagle Falls keep their heads. Don't let this become a witch hunt."

Erin suspected he was going from a previously developed script, and it was unfortunate that he had decided to use the phrase "witch hunt" in his answer when Lottie had just referenced witchcraft. A murmur went through the crowd.

"We would ask citizens to report any leads or suspicious behavior to the police and let us investigate. Please do not take matters into your own hands. Actions by citizens can be dangerous and can compromise evidence so that it cannot be used at trial. We want to be able to bring Martha Erasmus's killer to justice. Don't hamper our investigation."

"If you want to bring the killer to justice, why have you not arrested Harold Melville?"

The sheriff took a deep breath and let it out again noisily, blowing into the microphone. "I have already answered that question, Miss Sturm. Please pass the microphone on to the next person with a comment or question."

Lottie sneered at him, but handed the microphone to the usher who was walking it around to the audience and sat down.

Several other people stood up, echoing Lottie's and Cindy's words, demanding to know why justice wasn't being done and specifically why they couldn't arrest Harold Melville when everyone knew he was the one who had been writing the letters and was, therefore, also Martha Erasmus's killer.

Erin shook her head. So much for it not turning into a witch hunt.

Mary Lou stood up. She smoothed her hair and her pantsuit, neither of which needed it, and waited for the microphone to make its way over to her.

"I have known Harold Melville for many years," she said. "I remember him from before his family moved to Nashville. And he goes to school with Joshua."

Erin knew Harold was a couple of years younger than Josh, and the two boys were not close. Mary Lou was trying to make it sound like she knew Harold better than she did, especially since his family had moved to Nashville when he was just five or six.

"I have never known Harold to do anything violent or to be involved with anything questionable. And Josh has never had anything but good to say about him. Josh and Bella Prost also know each other, and Bella works with Harold at the bakery." Mary Lou looked at Cindy, Bella's mother. "Has Bella ever had anything negative to say about him?"

Cindy avoided Mary Lou's gaze, but when Mary Lou didn't continue, she was forced to answer. She shook her head, cheeks pink.

"I realize there may be questions about Harold's family connections, but I have not known Harold himself to break the law." Mary Lou looked around at the townspeople sitting around her. "Maybe we should let the police continue their investigation and believe they will act on the evidence."

Erin could feel the words, "And not make this a witch hunt," hanging in the air, but Mary Lou did not finish with that. She just looked around at the people sitting in the audience, gave Lottie and Cindy a particularly stern look, and sat down. She passed her mic back to the usher.

CHAPTER 40

Even though Auntie Clem's was closed for the day, there were a few things Erin wanted to take care of. So when the town hall meeting finally ended—with no one particularly satisfied with the results—she headed over to the bakery.

There was an unfamiliar car in the parking lot behind the building. A dusty, black pickup truck with a big dent in the passenger side door. Erin's stomach clenched at the sight of it. She hesitated after pulling into her usual parking space, looking at it and wondering whether she should get out, go home, or call Terry. She did not want to chance being attacked all alone in the bakery parking lot.

The dented door opened, and a gangly, familiar figure stepped out of the truck. Harold. Erin got out of her car to talk to him.

"Harold? What are you doing here? We're closed today. Because of…" She made a gesture to encompass everything, at a loss of words to cover all the reasons they had chosen to keep the bakery closed for the day.

Harold nodded. "I know." He scratched anxiously at his acne-pocked face.

The other door of the truck opened and the driver approached. Clearly a relative of Harold's. His facial features were very similar, but he was probably ten years older than Harold, his face fuller and his body broader and well-developed.

"Miss Erin, this is my brother Anton," Harold introduced him.

Erin did not offer to shake hands. She was nervous about the stranger, even if he was Harold's brother. He had an air of menace that was utterly absent from Harold. There was a hardness to him. A recklessness that made the hair on Erin's neck stand up.

"Hi. Nice to meet you," she told him in a flat, neutral voice, not inviting any contact.

Anton nodded, his eyes going over Erin. "I want to thank you for looking after the boy," he said. "Picking him up at the school and not letting anyone bully him here."

Erin nodded. "Of course. Harold is a good worker. People are a little crazy right now, and I wouldn't want anything to happen to him."

"A lotta people are making accusations. Saying he is the letter writer and poisoned those people. But he didn't have nothin' to do with that."

"I know."

"I wanted to know…" Harold swallowed hard. "What happened at that meeting? I didn't think I'd better go to it, but I need to know what they said."

Erin sighed. She didn't like to be the one to tell him that he was still the scapegoat, still the one everyone was pointing to. Calling for him to either be arrested or run out of town. She didn't know people could still be "run out of town" in this day and age, but apparently, in rural Tennessee, it was still a thing.

"About what you expected," she told Harold gently. "There are still a lot of people who think that you wrote the letters and that, by extension, you were the one who poisoned people at the Historical Club."

"It's that woman," Anton growled. "Old bat is always trying to make trouble for us."

Erin assumed he meant either Cindy or Lottie. She had to admit they were frequent troublemakers, enjoying making a scene or upsetting people. It was all done under the guise of being good

Christian women, calling out evil in others and warning the public about the pitfalls and hazards around them. Erin had a pretty good idea that they didn't care about everyone else's safety and salvation as much as ensuring everyone knew of their own superiority.

"I'm sorry," she apologized. "I wish I could change people's minds... I've done my best to explain to people that it couldn't have been you. But..." she rolled her eyes, "I guess people just want to keep believing what they believe and not be inconvenienced by the truth."

Anton gave a bitter laugh. "You're right about that."

Harold stared down at his feet, scuffing his toe in the gravel. "I know," he agreed. "They've been trash-talking my family for years. Since before I was born. You can't talk people out of it."

"Well, I'm sorry that they're so prejudiced against you. It isn't fair."

"They can't run us off'n our own land," Anton said. "That woman thinks she can turn everyone against us, and we'll just give up and leave. But we won't."

Erin nodded. "Well... hang in there. I'm sure it will blow over. The police will figure out who is behind all of this, and people will forget they ever suspected Harold of anything."

"We can hope, but I'm not crossing my fingers," Anton said flatly. "Come on, kid. Get back in, and we'll head for home."

Harold nodded at Erin, murmuring his thanks again in a low voice, and he followed Anton back to the truck.

CHAPTER 41

*A*s the truck drove off down the back alley, Erin heard
another vehicle approaching from the other direction. The
old sedan slowed as it drew up beside Erin. The car stopped, and
the driver rolled the window down to talk to her. It was Tara, her
bright blue jacket cheerful on what had become a dreary day.

"I thought Auntie Clem's was closed today?"

"Yes, it is. I just stopped by to do some paperwork and ensure
everything will be in order for when we open on Monday."

"No ladies' tea tomorrow?"

"No. Hopefully, on Monday, everything will be back to
normal."

Tara made a motion in the direction Harold and Anton had
departed in. "Was that the Melville boy?"

Erin sighed and nodded. "Yes. Poor Harold is having a pretty
tough time. It isn't nice feeling like the whole town is against you."

"My family having experienced some of that, I can sympathize,"
Tara said with a grave nod.

"Oh, did they? I'm sorry to hear that, too."

"Well, we don't get to choose the circumstances we are born
into, do we?" Tara's mouth pressed into a thin line.

Erin wanted to just take care of things at Auntie Clem's, but she didn't want to invite Tara inside with her, so she needed to find a way to politely disengage from the conversation. But she couldn't very well leave it on that note.

"What happened with your family?" she inquired. "I understand if it is sensitive and you don't want to discuss it."

"My sister was terribly bullied in school. She was interested in a boy, and she wasn't popular, so of course he mocked and humiliated her. Said horrible things about her to make himself more popular with his crowd."

Tara shook her head and rubbed her forehead, reflecting on what had happened decades before.

"I suppose I should count myself lucky that she was not bullied into suicide. Instead, she ran away. They drove her out of town, those people. She hadn't done anything wrong, and they acted like she was some pariah, a less-than-human they could grind into the ground."

"Oh, that's terrible. I'm so sorry. I'm glad she got out while she could. Did she... how is she now? Did she go on and... find her way?"

Tara bit her lip. "I never saw her again. I've tried to reach out a few times in the past, but even when I could find her, she wouldn't respond to me. She broke with everyone and everything to do with Bald Eagle Falls."

"That must have been really hard on you. Were the two of you close?"

"We were sisters; of course we were close. But now... it's like that part of my life was a dream. Like it never even happened. No one remembers anymore. And anyone I went to school with... either they don't remember, or they don't want to talk about it. They just want to put it in the past. That's what it is like, you know. They don't want to remember how they treated Ash, how dreadful they were, and that they were in the wrong. So they pretend it didn't happen."

"Other people were involved too, not just the boy she was interested in.?"

"Of course. They were a clique, all looking for each other's approval. And being mean to Ashley was the way to get it. Get everyone laughing and making fun of her."

"That's really terrible." Erin had been the brunt of enough bullying, shaming, and canceling as a child in foster care when there was no one to protect her. No siblings who wanted to step up, no real friends, no parents who cared about her.

She was glad that Ashley had gotten out of Bald Eagle Falls and hoped she had started a new life somewhere that she didn't have to endure the shaming she had endured as a teenager.

Erin stepped toward the bakery's back door, hoping to find a crack in the conversation that would allow her to escape.

"But Ash leaving wasn't the end of it," Tara said, her lips pale and her face a frozen mask. She opened her door and got out of the car. To follow Erin into Auntie Clem's or head her off if she tried to duck out of the conversation. "My parents had been saving all of their money to pay for the land we were living on. Renting from the property owner. But instead, the property owner sold to *his* family, and we were kicked out!"

"Oh... oh, that must have been so... discouraging. I'm so sorry that happened. Your family must have felt persecuted, dealing with all of that."

Tara nodded, rigid jaw muscles emphasizing her clenched teeth. "Yes, exactly. That's exactly right." She nodded. "We lost the only home I had ever known. That was *our* land. The owner had always promised to sell it to my parents once they could raise enough money. And instead... *his* family strolls in and scoops it out from under us. Kicks us out of our home."

"That sounds tough." Erin inched again toward the door. She knew she should be more empathetic. Tara obviously still felt traumatized by this move, which, from her age, must have happened thirty-five or forty years ago.

With the number of times Erin had been forced to leave her home and her current family, she found it hard to understand how having to move once with her family could have been so hard. But she understood the pain of her sister being bullied and running away from home, never to return.

"It surely was," Tara agreed. "We fought it. We fought hard, took the landowner to court and everything, trying to hold him to the promise that he'd made. Or my parents did, I mean. I was still a kid, so I had no say in anything. But seeing how the court system worked—or didn't work—led me to getting into mediation later in life. Helping others in conflict to come to a resolution instead of one party losing and the other winning."

"So I guess something positive came from it."

Tara glared at her in response, and Erin tried to explain that she wasn't trying to negate Tara's experience or to say that it had been good that it happened.

"I just mean… you brought other people peace and helped them find ways to work things out. *That* was good. Not that your family was taken advantage of."

"I supposed you might see it that way."

"Well… I hate to be rude, but I have a few things I need to attend to here." Erin took a couple of quick steps toward the doorway. "I'll see you Monday. Will you be by?"

"I suppose so, since I can't get anything from the bakery today or tomorrow."

"Yes, sorry for the inconvenience. I hope things are sorted out soon so we don't have to worry about the letter writer or being poisoned. It's all kind of scary."

"I'm sure the police will find some clues sooner or later."

"I'm sure they will. These things take time, but they'll sort it out eventually." Erin reached the door and unlocked it. She gave Tara a smile and wave and let herself into the bakery, pulling the door shut behind her.

CHAPTER 42

*E*rin decided that with Saturday and Sunday both off, it was time to spend some time on Clementine's genealogical files. It could be overwhelming when she only had an hour or two of time, because she had to spread files and books all over the place, with sorting piles that she had to step around.

Orange Blossom had also decided that he liked it when Erin got out the genealogy, because he liked to lie on top of whatever she was trying to read and refuse to move. If she ignored him, then he was likely to start jumping from pile to pile, making them slide around. It made Erin long for the time when, as a kitten, he had been afraid to climb the stairs to the attic room when she worked on it.

She just had everything pulled out and arranged the way she wanted it when the doorbell rang. Terry was on shift, so it wasn't for him. It wasn't Vic because she didn't bother to ring the bell; she just let herself in.

She didn't know who it might be. Maybe a delivery.

Erin picked up Orange Blossom and descended the stairs with him. She looked through the peephole and opened the door for Susan Brown.

"Hi. How's it going?"

Susan nodded. "As good as can be expected," she acknowledged, looking serious.

"How can I help you?" Susan didn't normally come to the house, so Erin wasn't sure what to expect. Maybe Susan wanted to see Vic or was passing out flyers or coupons for the family restaurant.

"I'm just helping to pass the word around that we are having a little memorial for Martha Erasmus tonight. I know it's short notice. You aren't expected to bring anything or to get dressed up. It's just a chance to get together and share some remembrances."

"Oh, okay. When and where?"

Susan gave her the details. Erin put Orange Blossom down and grabbed her planner to write it down. "Okay. I'll get there if I can," she promised.

"Great, I appreciate it. Let Vic know, too, and Officer Piper? Anyone you see, really. And if you see Frank, we're trying to get ahold of him especially."

"Frank Grayson? The mailman?"

Susan nodded. "Mail carrier. Or whatever we're supposed to call them these days. Yes, he didn't tell anyone where he was going, but no one has been able to reach him, and I know he would want to come. I'd hate for him not to find out about it until after it's over."

Erin nodded. "He's not answering his phone? That seems strange."

"Maybe he broke it, or he's out hiking and it is out of service. I don't know. I just know that no one has been able to reach him."

"I didn't know he was a member of the club."

"Really?" Susan raised her brows. "He is our Treasurer."

"Oh! Has someone gone by his house?"

"We've split up the lists, so I'm sure someone will be ringing his bell this afternoon."

"Okay." Erin nodded slowly. "Well... hopefully, I'll see you there tonight. And Frank."

Susan nodded. She gave a little wave and walked down the sidewalk, heading for Mrs. Peach's door. Erin closed the door and thought about it.

A few minutes later, she was calling Vic.

"Do you have anything you have to be doing right now?" she asked. "Something you can't leave alone?"

"No," Vic said, sounding surprised. "What's up?"

"I'm going over to Frank's house. I think something might be wrong."

"I'll be right over," Vic promised, wasting no time on questions. "Meet you at the car."

Of course, they could walk over to Frank's, but Erin wanted to get there as quickly as possible. She had a bad feeling in her gut. He should have been at the Town Hall meeting, but she hadn't seen him there. She had decided he was staying away because he didn't want to be asked too many questions about the letters and who had sent them to Erin.

But now she doubted it. Would he really have stayed away because of that? And if so, what was his reason for not answering his phone when other members of the Historical Club called him?

CHAPTER 43

$\mathscr{E}$rin grabbed her shoulder bag and hurried out to the car. By the time she had locked up, Vic was descending the stairs from the loft. They didn't stop to discuss the need to reach Frank; they just quickly got into the VW. Erin backed the car out.

"Susan came over to invite us to a memorial for Martha Erasmus," Erin explained. "Tonight. Just a casual get-together. But she said they hadn't been able to get Frank. He hasn't been answering his phone. And he's the treasurer for the club, so he should be answering anything from the members."

"He didn't tell anyone he would be out of town?" Vic asked, though it was obvious from her tone that it was more of a rhetorical question. She knew that Susan wouldn't have said it was strange not to be able to reach him if he had told anyone that he would be out of town.

"I guess not."

"And he isn't one of the members still in the hospital?"

"Terry said that all of the poison victims were back home now. So he's not at the hospital."

"Well, that is odd," Vic mused.

Erin nodded her agreement. In a few minutes, they were parked in front of Frank's house. Erin didn't dawdle or worry about what she was going to say; she just hurried up the sidewalk. A few flyers were protruding from Frank's mailbox.

She knocked on the door and rang the doorbell. "Frank? Are you home?" she called through the door.

There was no response. She waited for footsteps or some other sound within, for a twitch of the curtains or a shadow falling across the peephole or the little window beside the door. But there was no movement.

"You don't think…" Vic's hand was over her mouth. "You don't think something's happened to him, do you? Maybe he wasn't out of the woods with the poisoning, even though he said he was feeling better. Maybe they let him go too soon."

"I don't know," Erin admitted. But her body was definitely telling her something was wrong. She knocked again, then put her hand on the doorknob. She hoped it would turn in her hand, but it didn't.

"Should we call the police?" Vic suggested. "Get a welfare check."

Erin nodded. "Go ahead."

Vic pulled out her phone. Erin dug around in her bag to find her wallet. Vic was frowning as she watched Erin while waiting for the emergency dispatcher to answer the phone. It was taking longer than it should. She must be occupied with another emergency.

Erin selected a credit card and slid it into the crack between the door and the jamb. She felt the bolt of the simple doorknob lock, and she fiddled with it for a few moments before there was a click, and she pulled the door open.

"Erin, did you just—" Vic started to accuse, but the dispatcher apparently came on the line at that moment, and she was occupied with deciding what to tell the dispatcher.

Erin pushed the door open and stepped in. "Frank? Yoo-hoo? Are you here, Frank?"

She walked into the living room where his train layout was and found him on the floor. "Frank! Are you okay?"

The stupidest things came out of her mouth at times like this.

Are you okay? When the guy was on the floor, not moving? She knew he wasn't there because he'd needed a nap.

She hurried over. Looking in, Vic decided she didn't need to fudge her answer to the dispatcher to say why they wanted a welfare check or to explain why or how they had gotten into the house. Her voice climbed higher as she said she needed an ambulance.

Erin got down to her knees and reached for Frank's pulse. She didn't want to touch him. Didn't want to feel the cold, waxy skin and have to tell the police that there was no hurry for the ambulance. Frank's face was pale, and there was a pool of blood beside his head. Not bright, liquid blood, but dark and dry.

But when she touched him, his flesh was not cold and stiff. He was still warm. Erin touched her fingertips over his wrist and felt the quick scurry of his pulse.

"He's alive," she told Vic, her voice choked. "Have them get first responders here as soon as possible."

Vic relayed the message. "Is he breathing?" she asked.

Erin nodded. "Yes. He's breathing. No need for CPR."

She was glad. Things had not gone so well the last time she had tried CPR.

"Can you wake him up? Shake him and call his name."

Erin looked at Vic to see whether these instructions had come from the dispatcher. Vic had the phone pressed to her ear and gave a nod, waiting for Erin to try.

Erin didn't think this was a good idea. She had seen what could happen when trying to rouse an unconscious drunk, and she didn't want to be within arm's reach if Frank came up swinging.

"Try it," Vic encouraged.

Erin moved back from him. "Frank!" she shouted. "Frank, wake up!"

He didn't stir.

"And shake him," Vic reminded her, making a shaking motion. Why wasn't *she* the one getting close enough to shake Frank awake?

She had met Vic's abusive Pa and suspected that she wasn't the only one with experience in waking a violent drunk. There was a reason Vic wasn't any closer than she was, and it wasn't just to watch for the first responders and open the door for them.

Staying as far back as she could, Erin shook Frank's shoulder and again called his name and told him to wake up. There was no tightening of the muscles, no response.

"No," she told Vic. "That's not doing any good."

Vic relayed this back to the dispatcher. "Maybe a blanket," she started to tell Erin, but then they could both hear the approaching siren, and there was no point in trying anything else.

A police car pulled up. Erin could see through the living room window that it was Tom Banks. He exited his car, retrieved a case from the trunk, and walked up to the house.

"Ladies." He looked down at Frank, taking everything in. "Have you checked the rest of the house?"

Erin swallowed and looked around. "No. This is as far as we came." It hadn't occurred to her that someone else might be in the house. Either injured like Frank, or someone who might intend them harm. It was obvious that Frank's injuries had been sustained some time ago. His wounds were no longer bleeding. The blood was completely dry.

Tom put down his medical case. "Give me a minute. I'll be right back to assist."

Tom made a quick circuit through the house, opening and closing doors and checking out each corner, closet, and alcove before he returned. He nodded. "All clear. Let's see what we have here."

He checked Frank over carefully and reported back on his radio that the victim was stable and that he would wait for the ambulance to arrive.

"Not much we can do at this point," he told them apologetically. He pulled a silver emergency blanket from the medical kit, unfolded it, and tucked it around Frank.

"Do you think... he had an accident?" Vic asked.

"I suppose so," Tom said. "We'll get what information we can about his injury from the doctor once he's been examined. I'll review the site to gather any evidence. Did you touch anything?"

Erin shook her head. "Just the doorknob to get in."

Vic shook her head, still standing back from the injured man.

Erin had been hoping that when Tom started to tend to Frank, he would come around. He would move or groan or give some indication that he was going to be okay. But he didn't.

He lay there, still as death.

She looked around the room, gathering clues about what had happened. Had Frank just fallen and hit his head? It seemed unlikely that something would happen to him in the middle of his living room. He was used to sitting at his train controls or crafting new items to insert into his scene. A tree here, a house there, adding some new little detail about the homes and businesses she was so familiar with in Bald Eagle Falls.

Erin leaned over the little town on the table, taking it all in. Frank could not represent every building in the town, so he had to select the ones he was most familiar with, or that had the most significance. Was it flattering or creepy that he had decided to represent Erin's—or Clementine's—house? Maybe he had just selected the oldest houses. The ones with the longest history.

A little yellow VW bug was parked on the street in front of the house. Erin looked over the rest of the layout. There were some houses that were scattered at the edges of the city, back against the beginning of the trees, in front of the painted backdrop of the mountain. She recognized the little green and white Melville bungalow. In front were a young man and woman, cheerful, waving.

Another siren sounded, and in a few minutes, an ambulance pulled in front of the house. Erin was relieved. At least Frank would now get the medical care he needed. She didn't need to worry that she had just sat back and done nothing.

She and Vic retreated from the house so they were out of the way while the paramedics evaluated Frank and loaded him onto a gurney.

"What do you think happened?" Vic asked.

Erin sighed. "I don't know. He was hit on the head. Or hit his head on something. But I don't see much he could have hit his head on in there. Did you?"

"Well, maybe he dropped something and hit his head on the table when he bent down to retrieve it."

"Maybe."

They weren't exactly marble counters. They were lightweight plastic folding tables that could be transported by one person. Erin didn't know if hurting his head on a table like that was even possible. Not without help.

While she and Vic were standing outside waiting for Frank to be taken care of, Terry drove up to the scene. He and K9 got out of the truck and approached Erin.

"You guys called it in? What happened?"

"We don't know exactly what happened," Erin told him. "We came by to check on him because Susan said that he wasn't answering his phone. She wanted to make sure he knew about the memorial for Martha tonight. I was worried about him being out of touch, especially when it was people from the club. His friends, not just telemarketers or... local businesses."

"Nosy bakers, you mean," Terry said with a knowing smile.

"I could understand it if he ignored me," Erin agreed. "He doesn't know me and might not want to talk to me about... anything that has happened. But when his friends from the club are calling, I would expect him to answer. Especially when they were all just poisoned. It is the kind of thing that pulls a group together..."

"Unless he thought that someone in the group poisoned everyone else."

"Is that what happened?" Vic asked with a gasp.

"We don't know yet. It is still under investigation. But it had to be someone who was not out of place in the community center. Someone who could come and go without attracting suspicion."

"Do you *think* it was someone else in the club?" Erin persisted.

"I don't know. It is a possibility."

"Who else is a member? I didn't even know that Frank was part of the club, and he was the treasurer."

"If you want to know who the members of the club are, you'll have to talk to them. I can't give you any information about the investigation."

"Well, I guess we're going to the memorial," Vic commented to Erin.

"I guess so," Erin agreed. She'd been planning on going anyway. But it was fun to watch Terry's face flush as he deliberated on whether to tell her to stay away from it and not ask any questions. Would there be any point?

CHAPTER 44

Frank was taken to the hospital in the city, and Vic and Erin went home to have supper and get ready for the memorial. Susan had told them it was casual, so Erin wore her usual work clothes, which were neat and professional. Vic chose to go with a coral dress that fit her willowy figure like a sheath, and put her fine blond hair up into a sleek bun, pinned in place with a band of pearls.

"Wow." Erin looked over her. "Now I feel way underdressed."

"I just wanted to dress up. I know everyone else will be casual, but sometimes, a girl just wants to dress up a little. I picked up this dress in a little vintage thrift shop in the city. You like it?"

"It's amazing."

Vic laughed in pleasure. She adjusted her assets and looked down at herself critically. "Will it set people talking? Bring up the whole transgender conversation again?" She seemed anxious at the thought.

"Definitely," Erin told her. "Considering you're going to outshine every cisgender woman in the room."

Vic flushed. "I have to check my makeup."

Erin shook her head. She gathered her things together,

throwing her phone and planner into her shoulder bag. "You look perfect, Vicky. Let's go."

Vic had a little pearl-encrusted clutch, probably also from the vintage thrift store. Erin didn't know how women survived an evening with such a small purse. Even if she tried to keep her belongings down to just the necessities, what she might need in an emergency, she needed something at least three times the size of Vic's little clutch.

They drove to the community center. Erin wondered before going in whether there would be refreshments, and if so, whether anyone would be brave enough to eat them.

They followed the voices inside to the multipurpose room adjoining the kitchen, the same room where Melissa's wedding reception had been held. There was a good turnout, and Erin was sure more people would be coming.

Rather than everyone sitting in rows of chairs and a formal program, there were loose groups of tables and chairs, and people circulated freely, talking to one another, sitting down, standing up, and visiting someone else.

Erin fit in with her casual professional outfit. There were a few women in dresses, mostly the older ones, and none had the glamour that Vic did. Murmurs and whispers followed as she glided across the room.

The members of the Historical Club had name tags which included their offices within the club where appropriate. Erin was surprised at how many there were in the club. Mostly women, but some men, too. Mainly in the older demographic.

They chatted and listened to stories about Martha Erasmus and her life. Conversations drifted to other things. The letters and the poisoning. Harold Melville and his possible involvement in the events. And then to past events, most of which were before Erin's time. She listened to the discussions of various families who had come and gone, making their home in Bald Eagle Falls and inter-marrying. Scandals and achievements.

Forget going to the library to find out about the conflicts and grievances in Bald Eagle Falls, or going through the tedious process of searching for anything possibly relevant in Clementine's genealogy files. The members of the Historical Club had it all on the tips of their tongues.

Sitting down at a table after helping herself to the appetizers that had been strictly guarded by a large man with folded arms who stared at everyone who approached, Erin started to relate to Vic the story that Tara had told her about how her sister had been bullied and run out of town and her parents evicted from the property that they had hoped to buy. They were joined by Fiona and Susan. Susan leaned in, looking amused.

"Is that what she told you?" she asked Erin. "So Tara is still up to her old tricks."

Erin raised her brows, confused. "What?"

"Do you know... Tara got drummed out of the Historical Club? She isn't allowed to be a member."

Erin and Vic exchanged astonished glances.

"Why?"

"Because she rewrites history for her own benefit. Makes things up. She's a pathological liar."

"You're kidding. So... this story about her sister? You don't think it's true?"

"I know it's not," Susan said. "She's a little older than I am, but I remember what happened. There was a lot of talk about it at the time. We all went to the same school, so it didn't matter that I was a few years younger, I still heard everything."

"What happened, then?"

"Ash wasn't the one who was bullied and made fun of. That was Tara. She was a screwed-up little misfit. Ash was popular. A gorgeous blond, like Vic here," Susan tilted her head toward Vic. "And a sweetheart, too. No 'mean girl' vibe."

"Was there a boy? Or was it just... everybody bullying her?"

"Tara had a major crush on Jason Tuney. And he had no use for her. He was the one who was such a bully. I couldn't understand what anybody saw in him. But maybe they were all in awe of him because of the family connection."

"What family connection?"

Susan waved the question away. "Jason bullied and humiliated Tara mercilessly. It was sickening. Like I said, she wasn't popular or easy to get along with, but I still felt bad for her. He was really nasty."

Erin shook her head. "Poor Tara. I didn't realize she was talking about herself."

"Well, maybe she can't stand to admit it actually happened to her. She rewrites the details to suit her."

"So what happened to her sister, then? Did she really run away and cut off all contact, or did she make up that part, too?"

"Run away?" Susan repeated. "Hardly. She married Jason, and they lived here for a while. I don't know if they're still together or not. Probably not, since Jason was such an entitled jerk and not a very nice person, but you never know. Some couples stay together despite predictions of the worst."

"So she's not the one living by herself. Tara is."

"Yeah. I would feel sorry for her if she wasn't always sticking her nose into other people's business the way she does. To hear her tell it, she had a great career mediating disputes. But she just can't give it up now that she's retired."

After the number of times Erin had been told to stop interfering in things that were none of her business and to stop stirring things up, Erin could empathize with Tara. It wasn't so easy to stand by and let things unfold the way they were going to when she could see a way to help or to see justice done. Stepping back often seemed impossible. Or, on the flip side, she tried to stay out of something, and people accused her of being involved in it anyway. There was no winning, especially once people judged her to be a busybody.

"What about the story of her parents being evicted from their house?" Erin asked.

Susan looked at her and shook her head, lips pressed together. "Sounds like more of Tara's inventions. Her parents retired to Florida, I think. No state income tax, you know."

"Uh... yeah. So, nothing she told me was true? She was so upset about it."

Fiona had stayed quiet until now and now spoke up tentatively.

"I think it all centers around her crush on Jason. She hoped to convince him to choose her over Ashley. But he was so cruel to her... I think something snapped."

Erin tried to reconcile it in her mind. She was picturing what Tara had described. The sister that withdrew, became suicidal, and eventually ran away, separating herself from her family forever. That was what made sense to her. Not a woman who mediated other people's disputes and told outrageous lies about the past.

"Something snapped... how?"

"She became obsessed with him, with getting him. She didn't withdraw, like you would think; she kept trying to convince him they were destined to be together."

"I don't know all of the details," Susan contributed. "If you want the inside scoop, the person to talk to is Della."

"Della Melville? Harold's mom?" Erin was floored.

Susan and Fiona nodded. "Yeah."

"How would she know the details?"

"Because Jason is her half-brother," Susan said.

"Another one of Dwight's children?"

Fiona nodded. "He's older. From his first wife?"

"But not the same wife as Della. Or Nelson."

"Right." Susan shrugged. "He's been married a lot. Then I think he stopped getting married and has just had... mistresses. Less trouble with division of property and support."

"So Tara is Harold's... aunt?"

"Well, sort of, but not really. She's the sister-in-law of Harold's uncle. He probably knows who she is, but I doubt they've ever had anything to do with each other. Since Tara hates Jason and his family."

"Except that she's obsessed with him," Fiona said. "So you could say she loves him."

"Love, hate... same thing for some people," Susan contributed.

Erin's brain was working away. Was this the connection? Someone who had been "done wrong" by Harold's family and the Historical Club?

Tara had seemed eager to help Erin and had provided support, suggestions, and frequent mentions of Harold and his family.

Could this whole thing have something to do with an old grudge between Tara and her sister, who didn't even live in Bald Eagle Falls anymore?

Erin put her hand on Vic's arm as Susan and Fiona talked to another of the ladies in their church group.

"We need to talk to Della."

"Do you think it's related?" Vic asked doubtfully. "I mean… everybody has problems with relatives. And you're going to find connections between everyone in Bald Eagle Falls. If you want to find a connection between me and… Sheriff Wilmot or Terry, you could. You just need to dig a little. We're all kin somehow, and there are all kinds of old arguments and grudges. Add in love triangles or unrequited love, and there's all kinds of drama going on under the surface in every family."

"It's all related," Erin told her firmly. "I'm sure it is. But I need Della to confirm it."

"Do you think she'll talk to you?" Vic dashed cold water over Erin's hopes. "She's not… well-known for being friendly. She's a bulldog about her boys and anyone who might threaten them."

"Which is why she *will* talk to me. If she wants this harassment to end, we need to identify the culprit."

"What if it *isn't* Tara?"

"Della is the one who knows the full story, so if we can talk to her, we can figure it out." Erin dropped her voice. "I don't want to accuse Tara of something she had nothing to do with. The last thing we want to do is to paint someone as the villain when she had nothing to do with it. We need to find out what happened between the two families and whether Tara could be the one writing those letters. This could be just the break we needed."

Vic bit her lip and nodded. "Okay… I'm game. If you think talking to her will give us what we need, let's go for it. I would love to be able to tell Harold that it's all over."

"The poor guy," Erin agreed. "He's been such a trooper facing this. He doesn't deserve to have all of this… ugliness."

"Great."

They stood up and started to make their way across the room, saying their goodbyes and making apologies for leaving so early. They had to work early, so they needed to get to bed... She felt a little guilty for lying to everyone about why they were leaving, but as she'd told Vic, she didn't want to publicly accuse anyone.

CHAPTER 45

*A*s they left the community center and walked across the parking lot to the car, Erin tried calling Terry. He didn't pick up, so she sent him a text informing him where they were.

"Okay." She settled into the driver's seat. "Let's go have a chat with Della."

Vic readjusted several times in her seat. Erin glanced at her and realized that the dress she had put on for the memorial might not be the most practical thing to wear to Della Melville's house out in the sticks.

"Do you want to go home and change?"

Vic readjusted her dress again and shook her head. "No, I'm fine. It's not like we're hiking or something. Just walking from the car to the house."

"Long as we don't have to change a tire or something."

Vic laughed. "If you blow a tire or end up in the ditch, I am not changing the tire or pushing you out. You're just going to have to call for help."

Erin giggled. As she drove toward the Melville property, she realized that she *had* previously been in an accident coming home from the Melvilles'. She had been run off the road and ended up in the ditch, just as Vic had said. She'd been on her own, concussed and confused as to what had happened and where she was. Terry had been able to find and rescue her.

That wasn't going to happen again. Dressed up or not, Vic could at least call for help if there were any problems.

"What?" Vic asked, looking at her. "What did I say?"

"It's just... that time I did end up in the ditch out here."

"Oh, mercy! I'm sorry, I forgot all about that!"

"It's okay. I'm fine."

"I didn't mean to joke about it. That was really scary. I don't want to give you flashbacks or nightmares."

"I'm okay," Erin promised. "I'd kind of forgotten about it, too. Weird, because you'd think it would stand out in my memory. It was kind of a big thing. But... maybe my concussion made me forget about it."

"I'm glad."

It took a little while to drive out to the Melville farm. Erin was afraid that she might not remember all the turns, but even in the dark, she managed to get there without making any wrong turns.

Frank had made a nice replica of the farmhouse for his train layout. She had recognized it immediately, and looking at the real thing now, she was struck by how true to real life the model was.

Dogs barked and menaced them, keeping them from opening the doors of the car to get out. Erin watched them and waited for someone to come out of the farmhouse to take care of them.

A dark figure approached, silhouetted by the lights of the house, a shotgun in hand.

"Who's there?"

Erin rolled her window down a couple of inches. "It's Erin Price. I was hoping to talk to Della for a few minutes."

"What for? Harold do something wrong?"

"No." Erin squinted at the figure. It looked like Anton, but she wasn't sure it was. Anton should have recognized her car, which he had seen a few hours ago.

"Who's there with you?"

"Victoria Webster. Harold knows her from the bakery."

The figure approached. The man got right up to the window

and peered inside. It was not Anton, but someone similar in appearance. Harold's other brother. He eventually nodded and ordered the dogs back to the porch, where they settled down and waited.

"Come on out," the man invited.

Erin and Vic opened their doors and approached the farmhouse. The wooden siding was a soft green with white trim around the windows and doors. A pretty white porch featured both a rocking chair and an upholstered patio swing with a striped canopy.

The man looked them over again, his eyes lingering on Vic for longer. He licked his lips and motioned to the side door of the house.

"Thank you. Sorry not to call ahead," Erin told him, wondering if she had imposed too much on their hospitality. "I guess I probably should have."

"We've had some trouble lately. People coming out here to make trouble for the kid."

"Oh, I'm sorry to hear that. Harold never said anything about it. Did you report it to the police?"

"Why would I do that?"

"Well... they could charge the people who are doing the harassing. Put a stop to it."

"We don't need the cops to do that. Chase and Bruno are enough for that. And my trusty 12-gauge." He gave the gun an affectionate pat.

Erin hoped the troublemakers didn't come back out with Molotov cocktails or something else that could cause a lot more damage than a box of eggs or a brick through the window. But she hoped to put an end to the harassment with the information she was there to gather from Della.

They entered the home and wiped their feet. Erin looked around. It was a comfortable, pleasant bungalow, no different from any other home in Bald Eagle Falls. She had been there before and didn't remember anything unusual from that visit. Except for the car being forced into the ditch afterward.

That wouldn't happen this time. The only ones who knew they

were coming out to the Melville place were Erin and Vic; and Terry if he had picked up his messages.

"Ma," the man called, "you've got company."

So he was the other brother. Erin tried to remember his unusual name.

Salman.

Salman motioned to the couch, and Vic and Erin sat, Vic immediately tugging down the hem of her dress. Salman eyed her bare legs, but dropped his eyes when footsteps approached from the direction of the kitchen.

Della Melville entered her living room and looked at Erin and Vic, scowling.

"What is this?" she demanded. "Why are you here?"

"I was hoping to talk to you about something that happened a long time ago," Erin said, "but it might have something to do with the current trouble. I thought if we could sort it out... we might be able to put a stop to the harassment of your family."

Mrs. Melville jerked her chin at Vic, her face twisted in an angry scowl. "Why did you bring her? You think I want someone like that in my house? I don't know why Salman let you in."

Erin immediately jumped to Vic's defense. "Vic is my right-hand man, and she is every bit as concerned about Harold as I am."

"Your right-hand *man*," Della sneered, "and a Jackson. You disrespect this household by bringing him in here."

"Vic is not a Jackson anymore. She's changed her name and broken with her family. And she was never part of the clan."

"I didn't mean to diss you by coming here," Vic said. "Erin asked me to come along, and I did. I didn't want her to come by herself, and I wanted to help Harold. I didn't think... I thought that since Harold knows I don't have anything to do with the clan, you would understand that."

"Harold is not experienced in the ways of the world. It's my job to guide him, not the other way around."

Vic blinked, unsure what to say to this. She looked at Erin.

"I don't think we have to be here for a long time," Erin said. "If we could just have a quick discussion, then both of us will be out of your way."

"I will not entertain a Jackson."

Vic moved to stand up. "I'll just wait in the car."

"Mom, no." Harold came into the room. He had obviously overheard most of the conversation. "Vic can stay here. She isn't a Jackson. And her boyfriend was Willie Andrews, the leader of the Dysons. If he doesn't have a problem with her, why should you?"

Della hesitated, screwing her face up. Erin suspected she wanted to snap back something derogatory about Willie, as most Dysons would have done before he had been appointed the leader of the clan. But since he had been the waited-for heir and had become the leader, they could not say anything negative about him without it being considered sedition. And since he had supposedly been assassinated to get him out of the leadership position, he was now something of a martyr.

And one didn't say nasty, seditious things about a martyr.

CHAPTER 46

*H*arold sat in an easy chair, making it clear that he planned to stay for the conversation. Despite Della's claim that she didn't take guidance from him, he seemed to have put her in her place quite neatly and was going to keep an eye on her.

Erin tried to give him a grateful look without being too obvious.

"I should probably have called before coming. I'm sorry about that. I just got caught up and wanted to ask you about this as soon as I could."

"What?" Della asked.

"I have just been learning some things about Tara Waldon's history, and I was told that if I wanted to know more about what happened, I should ask you."

Della shook her head. "That *woman*."

"I know... but I need more details. Susan Brown said she had a crush on your half-brother, Jason."

"A crush. Sure. If that's what you want to call it. She was obsessed."

"But he didn't like her. He liked her sister, Ashley."

"He married Ashley. So I would say he liked her, yes."

"And he wasn't very kind to Tara."

"So? That excuses her behavior?"

"I don't know anything that happened after that. Other than that she lies or makes up stories to rewrite what really happened. So I can't get the real story from her, can I?"

"No," Della agreed. "That one has always made-up stories. It was a while before we figured it out. She made a lot of trouble before we realized she was making everything up."

"I can imagine. So… I asked Susan what the real story was about her and her family getting kicked out of their home. Tara told me how the landowner had sold it to someone else instead of her parents when they had been working for years to raise the money to buy it."

Della snorted. "*This* property, you mean?"

"*This* property?" Erin repeated, pointing down at the ground beneath their feet.

Della, Harold, and Salman all nodded. Things became clearer.

"So Tara lived here, and then you bought it?"

"Not me personally," Della said. "I was too young. Dwight bought it for Jason when he and Ashley got married. A home for the newlyweds. With the approval of Ashley's parents."

"But *they* lived here. Ashley, Tara, and their parents."

"Yeah. But they wanted to move into town. Ashley wanted to stay here and set up house with Jason."

"No one evicted them. Or bought the land out from under them."

"No. They were all part of the decision. All but Tara, of course. She had no say in anything. She was still a child."

"And she didn't want to move. She didn't want to leave the farm."

"She thought she should be able to stay here with Jason."

"When he was married to Ashley?"

"She still thought that he would change his mind, get rid of Ashley, and accept Tara. They could live happily ever after."

Erin shook her head.

"I don't understand how she could have wanted to get together with him when he had treated her so badly," Vic said. "Wouldn't she want to be as far away from him as possible? Hate her sister for marrying him, maybe. But wanting to stay here and set up house with him?"

"She's not right in the head," Della said flatly. "That has been obvious for many years. I don't know how she has gotten along for so long, passing as normal. Her parents should have put her in an institution for people like that. Instead, everyone else had to decide how to deal with her... psychotic behavior."

Erin leaned forward. "What did she do? She was just a teenager when they moved into town, wasn't she? What *could* she do?"

"She tried to kill her sister. Figured she would have a chance of getting Jason and getting her home back if Ashley was out of the way."

"Land sakes," Vic murmured.

Della nodded. "They said they would put her away for good. But within a couple of weeks, she was back again, stalking Jason and Ashley. They said they couldn't hold her. She was perfectly logical and lucid when she talked to them. Explained how everything was just a big misunderstanding."

"She's so good at explaining things. Figuring out what people want to hear and telling them that," Erin contributed, thinking over her conversations with Tara. A bit bossy and self-righteous, but that wasn't exactly unusual. Erin had run into her fair share of bossy, self-righteous women in Bald Eagle Falls.

"Police couldn't do anything. She wouldn't be here when they showed up. She would have an alibi and a reasonable story when they caught up with her and questioned her. Her parents didn't want to say anything that cast her in a bad light. After all of the trouble at school with her being humiliated and bullied, people wouldn't look at them kindly if they accused their own child of something."

Erin shook her head. "That must have been so hard. I'm surprised that Jason didn't—" Erin stopped. While it was surprising to her that a mobster—or the son of a mobster if he wasn't in the organization—wouldn't just take the matter into his hands to order a permanent solution.

Della looked at her knowingly. "I asked Dwight once why he didn't do anything about it. He said Tara was Ashley's sister, and Ashley didn't want anyone to do anything."

"And eventually, it just blew over?" Erin suggested.

"Do you think someone like that ever gives up? You look in the news. See how many people have been stalked for years and years. They never give up."

"Then what happened?" Erin thought of how sad Tara had looked when she talked about poor little Ashley being bullied and eventually running away, never to be seen again.

"Ashley and Jason left." Della shrugged. "There was only one way to get away from her harassment. They left and never came back."

"Where did they go?"

Della shook her head. "I have no idea."

"They didn't keep in touch?"

"They have never contacted anyone since they left. The only way to escape her was to disappear completely. If they had told anyone where they were going, she would have found out."

"And you're sure... she didn't kill them? You've never heard a word from them since?"

Della scoffed. "How could she do that? A teenage girl? Killing two people and hiding their bodies so that no one ever found them? The police looked into it. They never found anything to indicate foul play."

Erin thought about Crazy Theresa and how her parents had disappeared. She had only been a teenager at the time, and Jack Ward was sure she had killed them and disposed of their bodies, possibly burying them somewhere on the property.

"So then... what happened after they were gone? You bought this property?"

"It is still in Dwight's name. When I got married, he invited us to live here." Della looked around. "We had all the boys in this house. It was a good place for them to grow up. But when I had...

a falling out, we decided to go to Nashville, try city living, spend some time on our own, away from the family."

"Get away from the clan?" Erin suggested.

"We had some things to sort out. But eventually, I knew we had to come back here. So we did."

"Anton said that someone kept trying to make trouble for the family. An old woman."

Della pushed her hair back from her face, looking rueful. "We're all getting older. Kids think anyone over thirty is old. He should have kept his mouth shut." She sighed. "Yes, he meant Tara. Telling everyone that Harold had something to do with those letters and… everything else. That was just the latest. She comes around here, asking questions or making accusations. Talking about what it was like when she was a girl and how we've changed things. It isn't her property, it's ours!"

Erin nodded slowly. No wonder they had guard dogs and approached strange cars and visitors with a shotgun.

"That must be exhausting. Did you tell the police what's going on?"

"Tell them what? That she visits? She's not making threats or breaking the law. If she was, we would take care of it ourselves. But a dotty old lady—yes, that's me calling her old now—coming around to reminisce over the house she used to live in? You don't wipe out an old woman because she is irritating. Big risk, little reward."

"But now she's been making trouble for Harold in town. Riling people up."

"She never says anything directly to him. But you know she's talking to people, telling them that it must be him."

"Do you think she's the one who wrote the letters?"

"What?" Della sat up straighter. "You think *she's* the one who wrote them? And then said it was Harold?" A wave of red rose from her collarbone. "That *witch*."

"I don't have any proof, but could she have gotten her hands on your old stationery?"

"She's been through the barns and outbuildings. Snooping

around. Says she just misses the old times. I don't know of any stationery, but Donald has boxes of stuff from his father's estate that we've never been through."

"You never suspected her of being the letter writer?"

"I thought she was just taking advantage of the situation."

"When Cindy said the watermark on the stationery was the Melville coat of arms? You didn't think Tara might have taken it from here?"

"I've never laid eyes on the stationery. Or any Melville coat of arms."

CHAPTER 47

I thought Cindy was making that up about the coat of arms, or it was a mistake," Harold contributed. "I mean, it's not like we're royalty or something. There may be a family crest, but I've never seen it on anything."

"And if there is, how did Cindy know about it?" Vic asked. "Do you know random family crests? I mean… maybe you know your own, but how would you know anyone else's? Unless you're an expert or it is your hobby, I've never heard Cindy say anything about any kind of family history before."

She had a good point. Erin looked at her, nodding. "Maybe Tara told Cindy something about it or happened to mention it in passing, so it was already in her mind when she looked at the paper."

Vic cocked her head slightly. "That isn't exactly easy to plant in conversation."

"No. I guess not."

Della waved her hand dismissively. "I think you've wasted enough of our time. You came here to learn about Tara Waldon's sad, sorry life, and now you have been told. It is time for you to go back home before someone misses you."

She stood, prompting everyone else to rise as well. Erin's head was still whirling with the revelations about Tara's past and how different it was from what Tara herself had related. They all followed Della toward the door.

She didn't have any independent confirmation about which story was true. Della's story could be just as fake as Tara's. The truth could be something completely different or fall somewhere in between. Erin had to be careful not to jump to conclusions based on just one person's say-so.

She would have to go back to the library to see whether anything had made it into the paper about Ashley's and Jason's marriage or the purchase of the farm. She could search up the land transfer as well and find out whether it was held by Dwight Dyson, though that wasn't proof that Della's story was completely factual. She could go to the Historical Club and see what information they might have about what had happened.

Erin stopped short. Vic, behind her, bumped into her and apologized. Della looked back, irritation clear on her face at the delay.

"The Historical Club," Erin said with realization. "I thought that they were just an arbitrary target. A show of power by the letter writer, or escalating from threats to random violence. But it wasn't random at all."

"What do you mean?" Della demanded.

"The Historical Club, or someone in it, knows the real story about what happened with Tara and her family. She didn't want anyone to spill the beans. So she poisoned them. Tried to get them out of the way so her motive wouldn't come to light."

"Ooh." The note of realization came from Vic. "Of course. But did she want to make them sick or kill them? She couldn't think that she could kill them all and not get caught..."

"I don't know." Erin shook her head slowly. "Would just making them sick keep us from learning Tara's history?"

"Well, it did at first. Everyone was busy looking at who could have poisoned them instead of the motive behind the letters. Until you decided to go to the memorial service."

Della shrugged. "What does it matter? If she was the one who poisoned everyone at that meeting, she can be charged with that and with Martha Erasmus's death. Whether she meant any of them to die or not."

"This is crazy," Erin murmured. "Would she really do all of this to... what? Get back at the Dyson family because Jason humiliated her and was not interested in marrying her. Does that make sense?"

"Since when does it have to make sense?" Vic asked. "People who do things like this are not following a logical progression. We've seen that. They are just reacting. They get pulled off on a tangent, something that doesn't matter to anyone else. Make a mountain out of a molehill."

Della motioned impatiently to the door. "If you don't mind. You said you would only be a few minutes, and I think that ship has sailed."

"We want to help Harold," Erin pointed out, looking at him. "I know that's what you want too. I don't think this was a waste of time."

"That remains to be seen," Della said, her expression grim.

She was right, of course. It was one thing to have a theory. It was another to prove it. And put together enough evidence for an arrest and to put her behind bars for an appropriate amount of time.

Even if they gathered enough evidence to prove that Tara had written the letters, turned people against Harold, and poisoned the Historical Club members, she could still avoid real consequences. If she managed to plead it down—arguing that she never intended anyone actual harm or that she was not mentally competent at the time—she might spend only a short time in a medical facility until she was declared stable and no longer a threat to the public. Or she might serve just a couple of years and be free to start her old tricks again.

Della opened the door to usher them out.

CHAPTER 48

*I*t was a quiet night. The darkness was complete, and the dim bulb of the porch light threw only a small circle of light to illuminate the steps to the ground. Erin could see the brilliant stars in the night sky, not washed out by light pollution. Erin could hear an owl hooting in the stand of trees between the house and the barn.

Della's attitude changed suddenly from irritation and impatience to alertness.

"Ma?" Salman moved forward, the shotgun still in his grasp. He lifted it slightly as he moved forward to stand next to his mother.

"Bruno and Chase," Della said in a barely audible whisper. "Where are they?"

The dogs that had barked and threatened when Erin and Vic had arrived. Erin assumed that the reason they weren't barking was that their owners were there. They were only trained to bark at strangers, to guard the house. There wasn't any point in their barking if Della, Salman, and Harold were right there.

But maybe their training extended beyond that; they should have been at the door, poised to assist at any sign of trouble.

Della had said that Tara had been showing up at the farm, exploring the outbuildings. How could she do that with the dogs present? Was that part of the story made up? Or did Tara only show up during the day when the dogs were shut in their kennels? It was so difficult to figure out what was true and what had been said to mislead them.

Salman raised the shotgun the rest of the way and, looking down the barrel, scanned right to left for any threats. He whistled for the dogs. "Bruno! Chase! Where are you, you stupid mutts?"

Harold stepped forward to look outside or call for them, and Della put her hand on his chest and pressed him back.

Erin strained her ears for any movement in the dark. All she could hear were the hooting of the owl and the rustling of the leaves in the trees.

"I know you're out there," Salman called. "Yeh better show your face if you don't want a belly full of Brenneke."

Erin held her breath, straining for an answer or a movement in the darkness. She remembered the floodlights at Theresa's farm, and wished that Della had thought to improve the lighting outside the farmhouse, especially in light of the recent intruders. Theresa's stadium lighting had illuminated the entire clearing around her house like noonday.

Salman moved the gun back and forth, watching for any movement.

"Kid, go get Anton."

"I can help," Harold told him in a flat voice. There was no quaver, no emotion or hesitance. Erin had always seen him as a young, somewhat awkward and naive teen. But she was seeing a different side of him now.

"You can help by getting Anton. Put him at the back door. Get your rifle."

Erin swallowed and looked around. She realized that Vic, standing too close to her, nearly touching her, also had her gun in her hand. A small twenty-two that was normally in her bra holster. But with Vic's form-fitting dress, Erin wasn't sure where it had been concealed. There didn't seem to be any space for it against her body.

"You should get back, Erin," Vic said, making a slight motion with her gun hand. "Stay behind and out of the view-line from the door."

"But I don't… you're not…"

"Probably nothing will happen. But you need protection, and you're the only one unarmed."

Erin heard again all of the suggestions from Vic, Terry, and Willie that she should get a gun and learn how to use it. Life as the baker in Bald Eagle Falls seemed to be a strangely treacherous occupation.

But she wasn't interested in arming herself or learning how to shoot people. She didn't ever want to shoot someone or take a life. She didn't blame Terry for using the gun that was required by his service to the community, or even Vic for protecting herself, but it wasn't for Erin.

"Show yerself now," Salman shouted. "You're not going to get another chance."

Vic shifted, stepping in front of Erin and elbowing her back. Erin moved slightly to the side so she could no longer see out the door. If she couldn't see out, no one outside could see her. Harold returned to the living room, his step as silent as cat's paws. He stayed well back from the door, but Erin thought that was more so that he could run to the back if needed there than because he was reluctant to get too close. He positioned himself to get to either door quickly.

Despite his claims of wanting no part in the clan's violence or illegal dealings, Harold had clearly been trained with firearms and tactics, and trained to obey instructions. He wasn't panicked and clumsy. He was as cool and calm as any trained soldier. His eyes flicked around the room, noting Erin's location and Vic's gun and looking satisfied with their positioning.

They were silent, waiting for something to happen. The seconds ticked by, seeming interminably long. Erin just wanted to get into her car and drive away with Vic. Back to their home, back to normalcy, to safety.

After a long time, Salman moved. He reached over to the light switch and shut off both the outside porch light and the living room lights. They were plunged into darkness, with just the moonlight outside to navigate by. Erin was disoriented for a moment, experiencing vertigo. She wanted to hold on to something, but the only thing within easy reach was Vic, and grabbing someone holding a gun did not seem like a good idea at all.

"Moving out," Salman said in a whisper.

Erin wanted to hold him back, to keep him inside, where it was safe. But they would not be safe inside forever.

If Tara were out there, she might decide to go out guns blazing, shooting as many rounds in through the open door and windows as she could before being taken down. After what she had just heard, Erin thought Tara might be crazy enough to do it.

CHAPTER 49

S alman slipped out the front door, out of Erin's sight. Della moved forward, standing to the side of the door and peeking out, showing as little of her body as possible.

The owl was no longer hooting. Had it been scared away by the activity outside? Or maybe it had never been a real owl in the first place, but just Tara, teasing them or trying to put them at ease.

There was a sudden crash of roaring thunder, though Erin knew it had not been thunder. She didn't manage to suppress a shriek of surprise and alarm and, weak at the knees, dropped into a crouch to make herself a smaller target.

Her breath came in quick, short gasps and rasped loudly in her ears. She couldn't hear anyone's breathing but her own.

Hooking around the door, Della fired off a blast, even closer and more alarming than the first shot.

Erin felt the heat radiating off the gun, though surely she was too far away and it was only her imagination. The smell of gunpowder almost overwhelmed her hypersensitive nose. She resisted the impulse to cover her face or poke her fingers in her ears, forcing herself to stay alert and use all of her senses to follow what was going on to keep herself safe and describe to the police later, when she was called on to give an account of what had happened.

Because she *would* survive and tell Terry about it later, when she was somewhere safe. At the police department offices or at home in bed when he returned home from a late shift.

Harold flitted into the back hallway. Erin's throat constricted. She wanted to call him back or go with him and keep him safe, but this was not the same Harold she had been picking up each day for his shift at the bakery to avoid any bullying or vigilantism from the citizens of Bald Eagle Falls.

There were twin blasts from the back of the house, overlapping each other. Erin thought she heard running footsteps, and then there was silence. She waited for word from any of the Melvilles that it was safe to proceed.

In the distance, she heard the distant whine of an approaching siren.

How could the police already know that there was shooting going on at the isolated Melville farm? And how had they gotten out there so quickly?

Erin tried to catch a glimpse of the vehicle through the window as it pulled up to the house, but she was at the wrong angle and didn't want to place herself in a position where she could be seen from outside if there were still a shooter outside. The flashing red and blue lights shone through the windows and reflected off the shiny surfaces in the room.

A bright light came on outside. The police car's spotlight. Then a familiar voice over the loudspeaker.

"Drop your weapon and raise your hands over your head."

It was Terry. Erin was intensely relieved. Also, she was a little anxious about how he would respond to her presence there.

But she knew everything would be okay now.

Provided Terry didn't get shot by Tara Waldon. Erin was sure Salman wouldn't shoot at him, but if Tara were still out there, there was no telling what she might do. She could make up a story to cover her afterward. Say that it had been an accident or that he hadn't identified himself as a police officer or some other excuse for her recklessness.

Erin moved closer to the door in the hope that Terry would be able to hear her. Della whirled, the long barrel of her gun pointing dead center on Erin's chest. Erin raised her empty hands, and the barrel lowered.

"Terry," Erin shouted out the doorway, "there is a second shooter!"

"Stay inside the house," Terry's amplified voice instructed. Erin had no intention of leaving until the scene had been cleared and she knew it was completely safe. "Salman, drop your weapon."

"Not until I know she's gone! Get your spotlight off'n me afore she drills me!"

The spotlight began to perform sweeps of the yard, woods, and outbuildings. There were no more shotgun blasts, and Erin's heartbeat began to slow.

Another siren sounded in the distance. This time, Erin dared to peek out the window to watch the marked squad car approach. It pulled up beside Terry's truck, and Tom got out, and keeping low, approached Terry to be briefed on what was going on.

A third car approached. That was all of the Bald Eagle Falls active law enforcement officers. They might get the state cops involved, or get help from one of the other nearby towns if they felt they needed more. Beaver, a federal agent who lived in Bald Eagle Falls part of the time, might show up, even if she were not invited.

One of the spotlights was again focused on Salman, against the house, and this time, he obeyed Terry's instructions, putting his gun down and kicking it away, then raising his hands, interlacing them behind his head, and walking backward toward Terry. Terry patted him down and had him sit to the side without handcuffing him. K9 was alert at his side, sniffing the air, watching Salman and everything else going on around him.

"Occupants of the house, please toss out any weapons and come out one at a time, with your hands in the air, and follow my instructions."

Della, closest to the door, exited first, obediently tossing her shotgun to the side and allowing herself to be patted down as Salman had been. Then Erin, and then Vic. Erin could hear Sheriff Wilmot giving Harold and Anton similar instructions at the back of the house. Eventually, everyone was assembled in front of the house. Terry allowed Vic to sit in one of the patrol cars with her feet out the door, since her vintage dress and bare legs did not make it easy for her to sit or kneel on the ground.

"How did you get here so fast?" Erin asked Terry. The shooting had barely started, and he had been there. She knew it took half an hour to get from Bald Eagle Falls to the Melville farm. He could get there faster by breaking the speed limit, of course, but not *that* much faster.

"I was already on my way, almost here. When the dispatcher received reports of gunfire, I didn't have much farther to go."

"You were already on your way here?"

Did that mean that he knew about the problems between the Melvilles and Tara Weldon, and how Tara had escalated to murder?

"You told me where you were going. I was… I thought it would be a good idea to check on you and make sure everything was okay."

He could have just texted her back or called. But Erin was glad he had decided to make the drive.

There was no sign of Tara or any other shooter. But there were outbuildings and the woods, and it was dark. Difficult circumstances under which to perform a thorough search, especially with only a few law enforcement officers.

"Are you sure there actually *was* anyone out here?" Terry asked skeptically.

"You tell me where my dogs are!" Salman said explosively, "And if that stupid cow has killed them, I won't be responsible for what happens to her."

"Who exactly are you talking about?"

"Tara Waldon. Can I get up and look for my dogs?"

Terry's brows went up in surprise. "And did you see her out here?"

"I saw her muzzle flash, but I wasn't quick enough to do any damage. Moves fast for an old lady."

"But you didn't see her face. So you can't be sure it was actually her."

"I didn't need to see her face to know she'd done something to my dogs and was shootin' at me."

"No, you knew those things had happened, but you didn't identify her by sight; you just defended yourself."

Erin thought Terry referred to self-defense to de-escalate Salman and suggest that the police were not his adversaries. She didn't know if Terry really saw it that way or not. He wasn't likely to consider citizens blasting away at each other in the dark as "the good guys," no matter the provocation.

"Yeah, exactly," Salman agreed. "I'm not askin' for ID."

Terry nodded. "And you're sure it wasn't one of the others you saw... your brother, for example."

"Anton and Harold were in the house. Dad's outta town. Everyone 'cept me was inside the house. And that witch."

Terry looked at the others. "Did anyone else actually see Ms. Waldon?"

CHAPTER 50

*N*one of them volunteered an answer, shaking their heads.

"So you all just decided that Ms. Waldon was a threat? Did she say or do something that suggested she might attack?"

"She's been trespassing on our property for months," Della snapped. "She's been told plenty of times to stay off. She's been harassing Harold in town. She's got a big ol' grudge against our family from way back when."

"So, no, she didn't tell you she was coming here, and you didn't see her. She didn't make a threat against your family."

Della's chin lifted and she didn't answer any further. Her eyes went to Erin, and Erin knew she was pointing out just what she had said before, that the police wouldn't believe anything they had to say about Tara Waldon and her grievances against the Dysons, and particularly the Dysons living in her former home.

"Erin?" Terry challenged. "Just what do you have to indicate that Tara Waldon has anything to do with the business out here or what's been going on in town?"

"Well… I know what she has been saying about Harold. And I know that she tried to sell me a big song and dance about her family and what happened out here decades ago."

"And how do you know that?"

"Susan Brown was telling me. And she said if I wanted the real story, I should come and talk to Della. To Mrs. Melville. I think the reason for poisoning the Historical Club was so that they couldn't tell us about Tara's history and that she makes things up."

Terry considered this, but he obviously wasn't convinced that any of it was more than speculation and theory.

"And Frank," Erin pressed. "He was part of the Historical Club, and he would know something about Tara's handwriting and whether those letters matched other correspondence she sent out."

"So you *also* think that she attacked Frank in his home."

Erin nodded, but she could see the doubt in his eyes.

"And just what do you think caused this... rampage?"

"Did you look into her history?" Erin asked. "She was arrested for trying to kill her sister Ashley. And then Jason and Ashley disappeared." She gave Terry a stern look. "You remember how Theresa's parents disappeared?"

"Jason and Ashley's disappearance was before my time."

"But it would still be on your records, wouldn't it? Or Sheriff Wilmot might know something about it?"

There was a shout from Tom Banks, who came around the house a minute later. "We found the dogs."

Salman shot to his feet. "Are they dead? Did she kill them?"

"Not dead," Tom said, holding up his hands. "I think they've been shot—"

"No! I'll kill—"

"With tranquilizer darts," Tom finished calmly. "They're uninjured. Just down for the count."

Salman nearly collapsed.

Harold went to him, clasping his big brother around the shoulders and patting him soothingly. "It's okay, Sal. They're not hurt." He looked at Tom. "Can we go see them now?"

Tom looked at Terry, then nodded. "Yeah, sure. Come with me." He led them back around the house.

Anton shook his head. "Those big brutes are his babies," he told

Terry with amusement. "Pity the woman who gets between him and his dogs."

Terry chuckled. He dropped his hand down to K-9, who sat alertly at his side, waiting for any instructions or threats. He scratched the dog's ears.

"I hear you," he admitted. "If anything happened to my partner... look out."

"So that's proof that there was someone here," Erin pointed out to Terry. "It wasn't just imagination or a couple of guys who had been drinking taking shots at each other. Someone took the dogs out of commission. The only reason to do that would be so she could approach the house without anyone inside being aware of it."

Terry considered this, nodding slowly. "Okay," he agreed. "It is proof that someone was here, and that person had reason to get past the dogs undetected. But it doesn't prove who that person was."

"But now you'll look for evidence of who it was. You'll look for... bullet casings and cigarettes with her DNA on them and that kind of thing."

"Was Tara a smoker?"

"No. I'm just saying... there might be something that will lead back to Tara, to prove that she was here."

"Or to prove that it was someone else."

Erin shrugged. It was always a possibility. Everything fit with the theory that the writer, poisoner, and shooter was Tara Waldon, but it had not been proven beyond a reasonable doubt. The police would need to gather whatever evidence they could.

"Did you get anything back from the lab on the third letter? Fingerprints or DNA?"

"Nothing back yet. You forget they don't generally do anything over the weekend."

"Oh, right. But you have someone to compare it to now, if he gets fingerprints or DNA. You don't hit a dead end when it doesn't appear in the criminal database. You can get her to submit a sample."

"And if she refuses?" Terry gave her a tolerant smile.

"Then you follow her around and pick up her discarded cup or cigarette when she throws them out."

"I thought you said she didn't smoke."

"Well, maybe she'll be stressed and she'll start." Erin teased back.

"All right, well, I think it is time for you ladies to head home. You don't want to be asleep on your feet at the bakery tomorrow."

"I need my gun," Vic told him.

Terry looked at the house and apparently decided he had no reason to prevent her. "You didn't fire?"

Vic shook her head, "Not a single shot, officer."

"Multiple shots?"

Vic grinned. "No. You can check it if you like. I didn't fire *any* shots."

"You can get it."

As Vic walked toward the house, she walked by Terry. "Thank you for looking after Erin," Terry told her quietly.

"Always."

Erin stood up and walked over to Terry to tell him goodbye. He gave her a quick squeeze around the shoulder, not too demonstrative in front of others.

"It *was* Tara Waldon," she told him.

"We will investigate."

Erin shrugged. It was frustrating to be slowed down by police procedure, but she knew they had to do things the right way if they wanted charges to stick. If they wanted Tara to be behind bars for more than a couple of weeks—or days—they needed to build up enough evidence for an arrest and the ensuing trial.

"Sorry I didn't bring anything for you," she told Della. "I would have brought some eclairs, but Harold has been bringing so many home that I was afraid your freezer was already overflowing."

Della gave a little laugh. "It is nice to have a kid working at the bakery. I would never have guessed that we would all like gluten-free baking, but it is so much better than the prepackaged stuff we got in Nashville."

Erin nodded. "It's a lot easier when you can experiment with small batches, and it doesn't have to be something that can survive shipping and sitting on a shelf for a few weeks."

"I imagine so."

"Don't let her fool you, Mom," Harold warned. "It's not just because it's fresh and not full of preservatives. Erin has a real gift."

"*Miss* Erin," Della corrected.

Harold reddened. "Miss Erin is really talented. I've learned a lot from her."

Della looked at her son coolly. "It's been good for you to get some real-world experience. But you are not destined to become a baker."

He ducked his head, getting still redder. He glanced at Erin, begging with his eyes that she not say anything about the Dyson clan and their plans for him. Anton scowled and shook his head. Disappointed that he had not been the one to make the cut with Uncle Nelson, she imagined. The two older boys had been passed over for the youngest. But they did not seem to resent him.

"I'm sure that whatever Harold gets into, he will be good at it," Erin said neutrally. "He's very smart and hard-working."

Della nodded in agreement. "He'll be there for his next shift. But he won't be working there forever."

CHAPTER 51

"*J*'m going to stay over tonight," Vic informed Erin as they turned down the back alley.

Erin looked at her, surprised, but didn't argue. "Of course, you're welcome any time you want to come over," she agreed. "You know where everything is. Help yourself to the guest room."

"We don't know what happened to Tara or if she'll try anything tonight."

Erin pulled into the garage. She turned off the engine and waited for the garage door to close before leaving the car.

"You think... that she could come here to make trouble?"

Vic shrugged. "I don't know. She could."

"You think she would come after me or you? She's had the opportunity before. She's been all buddy-buddy. Helpful. Confiding about her life. Or about what she said was her life, even if it wasn't."

"But she's been trying to keep anyone from finding out the truth, and she knows that you know the truth now."

"There's no way for her to know. The only person I told I was going to the Melville farm was Terry."

"Erin, she was out there tonight."

"Yes, but she didn't see you and me..."

She realized just before Vic put it into words. "Erin, a blind man could find that yellow bug in the dark. There's no way Tara missed it. You're the only one who drives one and it stands out like a sore thumb." She smiled to take the sting out of the expression. "Like a *classic* sore thumb."

Erin shook her head. "Yeah, I guess you're right."

Vic's gun was in her hand again as she slowly opened the door to exit the garage and looked around. She motioned for Erin to wait until the automatic light on the garage door opener went off before exiting so that they would not be silhouetted by the light and their eyes would be used to the dark.

"Where exactly do you put that gun?" Erin asked.

"Concealed carry holster."

"But *where?*"

Vic grinned back at her and proceeded carefully, watching for any movement. The night was quiet, and Erin saw no sign that anyone had been around.

"I wish all the cops weren't still out at the Melville's," Vic whispered. She had never been one to rely on or even trust the police, so Erin knew she was really concerned.

But they remained alone and unmolested in their walk up to the house. Vic stood guard while Erin unlocked the door.

"Keep the burglar alarm armed and the door locked," Vic instructed. "I'll just pop up and get Nilla. Don't open the door without making sure it is me first."

Erin hadn't been that worried until Vic had gotten paranoid about Tara coming after them at the house. Now she was worried, jumping even when Orange Blossom shot into the kitchen to inform her that he was hungry and she was late getting home.

"Shh," she told him, as she got out a little bit of food for him and dropped it into his food bowl, "take it easy. We don't want to wake the whole neighborhood."

He looked at her for a moment, clearly surprised that Erin hadn't gone through the usual routine of having him chase a few treats across the floor and giving him scratches and attention before finally rewarding him with food in his dish.

This was what it felt like to be stalked. Erin couldn't help peering into every corner as if Tara might be hiding there. Nothing seemed out of place, and none of her senses were picking anything up, but she couldn't help but be worried Tara might somehow have gotten past the locks and burglar alarm and was waiting somewhere in the house for her.

There was a soft knock at the back door that made Erin jump. She walked over to check the peephole, sure it would be Tara or someone Tara had sent to do her dirty work. But it was only Vic, her back turned to the door as she scanned the backyard and waited for Erin to open it. She usually just opened the door herself, but it was clear why she had not. She had her gun in one hand as she watched for threats. And Nilla tucked under the other arm, his tail whipping back and forth happily.

Nilla was often yappy and delighted in running around wildly, but he was quite happy to be in the arms of his owner and was not making noise or trying to escape. Vic entered, and they locked the locks and entered the verification code on the burglar alarm so the door opening would not set off the alarm but it would remain armed.

"You see anything out there?" Erin asked.

Of course, if Vic had seen any sign of Tara, she would have offered it immediately. Erin just wanted the reassurance.

"No, everything quiet," Vic advised. She put Nilla down with an admonishment to stay quiet, and Nilla obeyed for once, looking around to see if K9 was there to play with. He approached Orange Blossom, who hissed and growled a warning. He did not enjoy playing with the little dog. Or sharing his meal. Nilla just stood there looking at him, tail waving back and forth slowly.

"Just gonna take a look around," Vic advised, and without putting her gun away, stepped into the living room, and then down the hall to check each of the other rooms. She eventually returned, nodding at Erin. "Everything clear. We're snug as a bug tonight."

"Well… that's good." Despite her exhaustion, Erin wasn't sure how she would get to sleep. Not while thinking that Tara might show up at any time and threaten them. Or not threaten them, just kill them in their sleep and dispose of their bodies with no one the wiser. Was that what she had done with her sister and brother-in-law? Killed them in their sleep? Or had she had the audacity to kill them face-to-face?

Erin didn't have any evidence at all that Tara had killed them. It was just a gut feeling, but she was sure she was right. It didn't make sense that Jason and Ash had left the farm Dwight had purchased for them without warning to anyone and had never contacted anyone since.

"Some sleepy tea?" Vic suggested.

Erin agreed. It probably would not be enough to put her to sleep, but it might calm her pounding pulse.

"How long do you think the police will be at the farm?"

Vic shook her head as she added water to the kettle. "You probably have a better idea of that than I do, living with a cop. Firearms discharge with no one hurt? I doubt they stay too long."

"They might stay until morning so they can search for Tara."

"Not unless Salman thinks he injured her. She would be long gone. She wouldn't stick around the farm and knows the area well." She turned to look at Erin. "And the Melvilles will obviously not want them to stay any longer than necessary. They won't ask for police protection."

"No," Erin admitted. She couldn't suppress an amused smile at the thought of Della wanting the police to stay. She would have them out of there as soon as she could convince them to go. "But then they'll have a bunch of paperwork to document what happened. Maybe they'll go to Tara's house to see if she is there and can account for herself?"

Vic nodded. "It would make sense," she agreed. "If the Melvilles think she was out there, but she can show she was somewhere else…"

Erin didn't like where that thought led. Because if it wasn't Tara, who was it? Someone had been out there. Someone had tranquilized the dogs and taken a couple of shots at the Melvilles. Maybe someone who had been there looking for Erin. Maybe someone who had followed her to the farmhouse and knew that if she and Della put together what they each knew, the jig would be up.

She went to the freezer. "I need comfort food."

"Good idea. Get some carbs and sleepy tea in you, and you'll be nice and relaxed."

"There's beer in here too," Erin indicated the fridge. "If you want to snag one…"

"No. Want to stay alert."

Erin looked at the clothes Vic had changed into before coming to the house. Not her usual sleeping clothes. Instead of a lacy nightgown, she wore a loose t-shirt and yoga pants; much easier to move around in than the coral dress.

"I thought you were going to sleep here."

"Maybe once Terry is back. But for now… I'll just keep an eye on things."

"Do you want to stay up together and watch a movie?"

"You can put on whatever you want. A movie is fine. But you should try to get some sleep if you plan to work in the morning."

Erin had still been planning to open up Auntie Clem's as usual. She didn't like it being closed for more than a day. People needed to know they could rely on her, and she wouldn't just shut the bakery down without warning. People needed their baked goods.

They were quiet while Vic got the tea ready and Erin thawed some cookies in the microwave.

"So… what are we going to do if Terry doesn't find any evidence that Tara is the letter writer, the person who poisoned the Historical Club, rigged the microphone at the town hall meeting, and hit Frank over the head?" Erin asked after munching her way through a chocolate chocolate chip cookie.

Vic raised her brows. "I thought you were just going to let Terry and the others handle it?"

"Well, I am, but… that doesn't mean we can't do anything to help him along. Or make suggestions as to how he could approach it."

Vic chuckled. "That's the Erin I love. You want to do something to help things along?"

"I don't like feeling… helpless. Just sitting around here waiting to see if she shows up." Erin glanced at the back window, looking for any movement. "Sooner or later, she's going to find the right time and place…"

Vic sipped her tea. She gave a short nod to acknowledge Erin's statement.

"Okay, then, what are we going to do? They need evidence if they are going to arrest her and put her behind bars. So far… we've got nothing. Just that she's got a huge grudge against the Dysons, and against the Melvilles in particular for living on 'her' property."

"Maybe they'll still find fingerprints or DNA on the letter. But we won't know about that for a few weeks. I don't want to be on pins and needles, waiting for her to show up."

"That's a long time to wait," Vic agreed. "But people do."

"I don't know if I can."

"Well…" Vic leaned in. "Then we'd better come up with something."

The noise of a key in the back door lock made them both jump and turn toward it.

Terry always came in the front door, where he parked his truck.

Vic's gun was in her hand again, her teacup and cookie forgotten, and she slipped out of her seat and pivoted to face the door.

It wasn't Terry.

But the face they saw there was not unwelcome.

"Willie!" Vic threw her arms around him. "What are you doing here?"

He shrugged, smiling at her reaction. "Just thought I would check in on my girl. What are you guys doing up so late? And what's with the gun?"

Vic relocked the door. "Well… we've got a story for you. And we could use your help."

CHAPTER 52

*E*rin had been doing what she could all day to draw Tara out. That involved a lot of talking and speculating with customers on recent events in Bald Eagle Falls without naming Tara as a suspect or mentioning their trip out to the Melville farm to discuss what had really happened to Tara's family.

She couldn't bring herself to say anything that pointed to Harold, but she threw shade in other directions, wondering about the other members of the Historical Club, a recent move-in or stranger lurking in their midst, maybe a distant Melville family from England, or any other outrageous theory she could come up with.

It got the ladies talking, anyway, even if they were crazy notions. Maybe the crazier, the better. Erin even brought the clair-voyant predictions back into the discussion, mentioning her former foster sister Reg, who was a psychic and had, in Erin's imaginative retelling, solved all sorts of crimes using her paranormal powers.

There were frowns from some of the women who knew that Erin did not believe in such phenomena. But most were happy to join the conversation and add their theories.

Before long, the entire town was abuzz with new theories. Harold seemed to have been forgotten. Maybe Erin should have made up new theories right in the beginning, and they would have left Harold alone instead of continuing to focus on him because of the stationery.

Erin had many theories of how someone could have come into possession of the stationery, including the aforementioned cousin from England, an estate sale, or a deliberate frame-up with manufactured evidence.

It was no surprise that Tara showed up later in the afternoon to hear it for herself.

"What's all this you're spreading around about the letter writer?" she asked with a frown. "I thought you had said that no one here had anything to do with that, and you weren't going to get involved."

"I know," Erin agreed, "but it just keeps pulling me in. Every time I try to walk away, something else happens. The letters, and Harold's accident. The poisoning of the Historical Club, the town hall, and now Frank!"

"Frank?" Tara repeated.

"You didn't hear? About how he was hit over the head? He was left there unconscious, and whoever hit him probably thought that he was dead, but he wasn't. The ambulance took him to the hospital in the city. They said it was just a little knock on the head, and he would be fine. He's already back here, at the care center, until they decide he's fully recovered."

"He's back? I didn't hear that. I mean, I didn't even hear anything about him being hurt. Things are really developing quickly."

"No kidding! And I'll bet all of it is related. When we figure out who it is, it will all make sense. The pieces will all fall into place. I'm sure Frank is key. He was going to tell me something."

"What do you mean, he was going to tell you something?"

"About the letter writer. You know, he handles more letters and other mail than anyone else in town, so it makes sense that he might be able to recognize the sender's handwriting or style. Or maybe he knows something about the paper and where it came from."

"How would he know that?"

"Well, he's an expert on paper stock, you know. And he's with the Historical Club; he knows all about everything that has happened here in town over the last fifty years, and I'll bet he knows where it came from. Who had it made, how long they used it, and where it's been stored since then. He's really amazing in what he knows and can recall."

Tara pursed her lips but was careful not to say anything negative about Frank. "Well, I'm happy to hear that he recovered from his fall. And he's at the care center? Do you know what room? I'll have to give him a call."

She was playing right into Erin's hand. Erin gave her a cheerful smile. "I'm sure he'd love to see you. You guys must go way back. Were you in school together?"

"I don't remember," Tara said tersely.

"Oh, well, sorry, I thought you must be around the same age. He would have known you, your sister, and some other kids your age."

Tara shook her head. "What room did you say?"

"I was just over there this morning. Number 108."

"What did he tell you?" Tara asked suspiciously.

"Oh, nothing this morning; he was still asleep. I'll have to go over in the afternoon instead." Erin smiled. "I'm eager to find out what he has to say. If everyone puts their heads together, I'm sure we'll be able to figure out who the culprit is and get them off the streets. They're making things too dangerous for residents of Bald Eagle Falls right now."

"I think that's an exaggeration," Tara cautioned. "I don't think anyone is responsible for everything you've been talking about. You're just painting it all with the same brush, but not everything is related."

"You don't think so? I'll bet there's a bunch of other stuff we missed before because we didn't know it was all tied together. This person might have been doing things for years, but until they started writing the letters, we never knew anything about it."

"Things like what?" Tara didn't wait for Erin to respond. "I

don't think so. There isn't some secret stalker who's been committing crimes around Bald Eagle Falls without anyone knowing about
it for years."

"Well, Frank will be able to pull it together for us," Erin
pressed. "He's the one who's been watching and tracking these
occurrences all through the years. I bet he has a lot of stuff in his
logs that we'll finally be able to solve." Erin gave a little chuckle.
"Or that the police will be able to solve," she said mischievously.
"They haven't been able to until now, but once I get it from Frank
and give it to Terry all tied up with a bow... he won't be able to
ignore it."

"You shouldn't be gossiping and speculating," Tara repri-
manded. "There is no big conspiracy, and you just get people all
wound up and paranoid."

Erin just stared at her, thinking about how, for more than a
week, Tara had been one of several townspeople who had been stirring things up and trying to get people even more upset about the
predictions in the letter and who was sending them.

"Well... I'll try to tone it down," she told Tara slowly. "But I
don't think it's my fault that people are upset. I'm not the one
writing creepy letters and poisoning people."

Tara had been turning toward the door but turned back to give
Erin one more scowl. "You don't know that there is any connection
between the letters and the poisonings at the Historical Club."

Erin just smiled. Tara turned and marched out the door,
making the bells over the door ring stridently.

Vic entered from the kitchen. Erin turned to her. "Was that too
obvious? Did I say too much or push her too hard?"

Vic shook her head. "I don't think so. You definitely hooked
her, though."

"Well, I hope it was enough." Erin walked out from behind the
counter to the front of the store to watch Tara's departure. "Do you
think she goes straight over there? Or does she have to get herself
psyched up for it first?"

"Or go in the dark of night," Vic suggested.

"He could be home by then. And I said I was going to go over in the afternoon, so that would be too late."

"He would already have had a chance to tell you about all of his 'logs' and secrets he'd observed over the years but never bothered to tell anyone about." Vic grinned.

"Okay, I laid it on pretty thick. But I don't think I'm that far off. Frank has been delivering the mail for years, and he knows more about people's secrets than he lets on. Did you notice the Melville house in his model train layout?"

"No. What about it?"

"There was a young man and woman in front of it."

"So?"

"Not a family. And they didn't look like Della and her husband. With how true to life everything else on his layout was, even the loft over my garage, do you think he would just arbitrarily choose to put a young couple in front of the house rather than a family and maybe two dogs?"

"But that would be mixing the past and the present."

Erin considered this, then nodded. "Yeah, it would. But maybe that's what he sees as the most important thing."

She took off her apron and handed it to Vic. "I'm going to run over there. You'll hold things down here?"

"I don't really have much of a choice, do I?"

"Thanks!"

"Let me know what happens."

CHAPTER 53

$\mathcal{E}$rin nodded as she hurried out the door in the same direction Tara had gone. It was only a couple of blocks to the care center she had told Tara that Frank had been transferred to, and she wasn't going to make the same mistake this time and drive the yellow VW there so that everyone knew where she was.

Or so that one person in particular knew where she was.

As far as Tara was concerned, Erin was still at Auntie Clem's, right where Tara had left her.

Erin worked up a sweat on the walk to the facility, but for once, she didn't care. She entered through the side door that Willie had propped open for her rather than going to the front reception area, allowing her to arrive at her destination before Tara. She pushed open door 109 quietly and let it close behind her.

The privacy curtain was pulled closed so that anyone peeking in the door could not see Willie and his equipment set up in the room adjacent to the one she had directed Tara to.

The receptionist had been given the same information, so if Tara had stopped to ask which room Frank was in, she would have been sent to room 108 rather than told that there was no Frank Grayson checked in.

For the moment, room 108 was empty, and there was no movement on the screen Willie was watching. Erin slipped in and sat down next to him.

"The trap is baited?" Willie asked.

"Yeah. She's on her way. I could see her going around to the front as I snuck in."

"Good thing we anticipated that. You wouldn't want to miss all the action."

Erin nodded. They both waited, watching the screen intently. The ward was quiet. There was not a lot of staff, and they were keeping out of sight. A few patients sat or slept in their beds behind closed doors, unaware of anything unusual happening outside their rooms.

Tara's footsteps were quiet and stealthy but audible in the echoing tile hallway. Tara stopped at the doorway to room 108, perhaps contemplating the blank nameplate beside the door. But looking up and down the hall at the other rooms, she would see they were also blank.

Patient privacy was more important now than it ever had been before. To get any more private, they would have to be assigned code names or file numbers and never be referred to by their actual names.

On the video feed, the door started to open slowly and cautiously. Standing in the doorway with her gun drawn, Tara's view of the patient beds was blocked by the privacy curtains, both pulled shut. She went first to the bed closest to the door, stuck her head and gun arm around the curtain, and saw that the bed was empty. She went to the second bed and, after thinking about it for a moment, repeated the action and again found an empty bed.

The door opened behind her.

"Looking for something?"

Tara jumped and whirled around to face Della and Harold, standing in the doorway. Both held handguns. Erin swore. "She wasn't supposed to bring Harold," she whispered. "And they aren't supposed to be armed!"

Willie just shook his head. Erin supposed she should have expected that. She was dealing with family and clan members with grudges, not trained police officers.

There had been much discussion among Vic, Erin, and Willie about whether to involve the police in their little sting. Or at what point to involve them. Erin figured that involving them right at the beginning would be counterproductive. They would argue that there was not enough evidence against Tara to commence any kind of action against her, even for information-gathering purposes.

Get them involved too soon and they would just break everything up before they had anything they could act on. They wanted to get Tara confessing on tape. Then, the police could move in and arrest her based on the recorded evidence. A confession wasn't always enough to prove guilt, but it was a start, and would allow them to get the warrants they would need to search for more.

But Erin had not anticipated Della bringing Harold with her and had believed her when she said she would follow their request in the letter.

"What are you doing here?" Tara demanded.

Della smiled. "Looking for Frank Grayson?"

"Yes. What happened to him? He's not dead, is he?"

"You'd like that, wouldn't you? Another witness out of the way, so no one could tell the police what you have been up to."

"Where is he? And what are you doing here?"

"I'm here to talk to you about your sister and my brother and what happened to them all those years ago."

Tara sneered. "I don't know what you're talking about. They ran away. Decided they wanted to start a new life for themselves away from Bald Eagle Falls and the clans. Something maybe you should have done, too. What made you come back here? Why didn't you just stay in Nashville?"

"Nashville wasn't what we wanted. We gave it a go, but being away did not solve our problems. And we wanted to be close to family. It was time for Harold to be closer to his family and to understand his place in it."

Erin felt sick to think how they were grooming Harold to become Nelson's heir or successor. And to see him there on the screen with a gun in his hand. Not protecting his home and family from attack, but here with his mother to confront an old enemy.

CHAPTER 54

*H*arold's hand and eyes were steady, not glancing at his
mother as she spoke.

"I just thought I would visit an old friend," Tara said. "But it
looks like he isn't here anymore."

"We know what you did. You thought you could turn everyone
against my son with your letters. You thought you could destroy
him and everything we have worked so hard to build, but you are
wrong. Your little game will just be a tiny blip in his life. It will
have no effect at all. He will go on to claim his place and fulfill his
destiny."

"His destiny?" Tara took a step toward them, her voice rising in
volume. "Like your destiny? You thought you could step into that
position, didn't you? You thought it was your destiny to lead the
Dysons, or at least be in the upper ranks. It never occurred to you
that you couldn't get there by birth. You had to actually *be good at
something* too."

"You don't know anything about me. Or about my family."

"I know a lot more than you think. I've had years to research
and learn all about you."

Della shrugged. "You aren't going to find out about me and
who I am from books or internet searches. You are just... chasing

shadows. But we know all about you. All of your pitiful failures. How you chased my brother and could never even get his interest. The clan could have wiped you off the board years ago. There's only one reason they didn't."

Tara snorted. "Yeah? What reason did they have to spare my life?"

"Ashley. She knew the things you had done. Even knew that you had tried to kill her. But she didn't want anyone to hurt you. She still had love for her sister. Not like you."

"She loved me? She hated me because Jason was attracted to me. He wanted to leave her, but he was afraid to do it. A cowardly Dyson." Tara chuckled. "I'm sure you would have been so impressed with his loyalty to his wife. How he wouldn't leave her because he was afraid to tell her he loved me. Afraid to get rid of her. He was so *weak* and *pathetic.*"

"He wasn't," Della snapped. "He was loyal and loved his wife. He knew you were nothing but a lying little worm. He had no interest in you."

"What would you know? You were what, eight? Don't act like you know anything about my relationship with Jason. You don't know anything about it. You weren't there."

Tara switched her gaze to Harold.

"And you. You think that you're the next great Dyson? Let me tell you, you got nothing. You don't know what it takes to be great. You're a stammering little whippoorwill. Your mother fills your head full of tales, and you think you have a chance to make it big someday. But you don't have it. You'll never have it."

Harold didn't move or show any emotion at the words. Maybe because he already knew he didn't want to be the leader of the Dysons. The comments rolled right off his back. He was not popular at school, but considered an outsider, awkward, and a wimp. It wasn't the first time he'd been mocked and insulted.

"Leave my son alone," Della ordered. "You've made his life hard enough with your letters and innuendo."

"My letters? They aren't my letters."

"Do you really think you can hide behind anonymous words

anymore? Frank had other samples of your handwriting. The police lab has found your DNA on the evidence Officer Piper took to the city. I'm sure they'll find your prints on the electrical wiring at the school. You can't keep doing this stuff without anyone figuring it out. Sooner or later, people were bound to start putting it together, and that Erin Price is as sharp as a tack. She has you dead to rights. It's just a matter of time before the police close in."

"How would you know what the police lab found? My DNA wasn't on any of those letters. I never touched one of them."

"You think the family wouldn't have eyes inside the police lab? A little heads-up every now and then when we need it? Of course we do. In a case like this, we get the word before the cops. It might be another day or two before Officer Piper gets it in his email. If I was you, I wouldn't still be in town when it arrives."

"You're making it all up. You're not smarter than I am, Della."

"And then there's the surveillance cameras putting you at the scene of Frank's attack."

"He didn't have a surveillance camera."

Della smiled, a fierce, predatory grin, triumphant at conquering her enemy. "You need to keep up with the times, Tara. There are so many doorbell cameras around these days. You can't go anywhere without being caught on camera. They're in every neighborhood. There's a lot of footage of you coming and going. And inside Frank's house…"

Tara shrugged and shook her head. "I've been in his house before. He doesn't have any surveillance cameras inside."

"Do you know how tiny cameras can be these days? Maybe if you knew anything about Frank's little hobby—" Della chuckled, "—his miniature hobby—you would know that he has cameras in all those little trains. He records video of them driving their routes around little Bald Eagle Falls and posts them online. People love it. Every one of those trains, Tara, think about that."

"If the police had video of me attacking Frank, I would be arrested."

"I'm sure they're on their way," Della said comfortably. "By the time you and I finish talking, they'll be here to arrest you. I just had to see your face. I want to know that my brother is avenged and my son is safe from your smear campaign."

Tara's hand tightened on her gun, and she took a step toward them and the only way to exit the room. Even if she didn't believe what Della was telling her, she was obviously getting anxious about getting herself out of the situation. She'd been trapped, and she didn't like it. Even if she didn't think the police were on the way, it was still best to get out of there, and she was outgunned two to one.

"Get out of my way. Unless you want your kid to find out what it feels like to be shot through the heart. Or should I go for a head-shot? The cops can't arrest me for it; they'll see I was just trying to defend myself." Tara pointed her gun directly at Harold's face.

Another shadow fell into the room, and a lean, blond man stepped in the door. He looked more like a geek than a mob boss, even now that he had been installed as the leader of the clan. The last time Erin had seen him face-to-face, he had denied wanting to lead the Dysons, preferring to "play with his toys." He was a big computer and tech guy, preferring machines to the running of a crime family. But he probably hadn't had much more choice than Willie.

Despite her bravery in the face of Della and her son, Tara blanched when she saw Nelson. She swallowed hard and looked around the room for some other exit.

"What are you doing here?" she muttered. "I'm leaving. Get out of my way."

Unlike Della, Nelson hadn't bothered to pull a gun on Tara. His mere presence was enough to terrify her.

"What I want to know," he said, "Is why you felt the need to kill my brother. I realize it was many years ago now, but there is no statute of limitations on murder. Or on my vengeance."

Tara shifted her stance, still looking for an escape from a room where there was none. There was a bathroom door. She could dash for it and lock herself in. But that wouldn't protect her for long. If she made it that far.

"I didn't kill your brother," she whined. "And he wasn't even your full brother. He was a horrible person, always bullying and belittling me. But I didn't do anything to him. He and Ash ran away. That's not my fault. If they didn't want to have any contact with the clan, then I guess that's your problem, not mine."

"I liked Jason. I was too young to do anything about it when he disappeared. But I always knew it was you. Ash was like an aunt to me. And she knew how disturbed you were. She knew that if they wouldn't keep you in that place, you would end up hurting her sooner or later. And then... they were gone."

Nelson studied Tara, nodding slowly.

"I've always left you alone because Ash felt sorry for you and said it wasn't all your fault. Jason *had* been horrible to you and you had a *history*."

Nelson looked at Della and Harold.

"But things have gone too far. You have been terrorizing my sister and nephews. Trespassing on their property. Shooting at them in their own home. And all of this *craziness* in town. I cannot allow it to continue."

"No!" Tara tossed her gun onto one of the beds and raised her hands. "I'm unarmed. Are you going to shoot an unarmed woman?"

He considered. "There's only one thing you can do, and if you do, I will let you leave town unharmed. But you must leave."

She gazed at him wide-eyed, wondering what that one thing would be.

"I want you to tell me where my brother's body is. He deserves a proper burial. We will move him to a plot with the rest of the family."

"And Ashley?"

He raised his brows. "What would you have me do with her? Bury her with Jason or leave her there?"

"I don't want her anywhere near that jerk. It has always bothered me that they are together." Tara's grief—real or imagined—was plain. "Why would she want to be with someone who hurt me so much? Why would she marry him?"

"From what I understand, *you* wanted to be with him. How is that not worse?"

"I didn't. Whoever told you that was lying."

Nelson glanced at Della and then back at Tara. "So? Are you taking my offer, or will you be sleeping somewhere far away from either of them?"

Tara licked her lips and swallowed several times, trying to keep herself under control. Her eyes went to Nelson several times as if trying to figure out whether he was telling the truth and would really let her go if she did what he asked.

Finally, she cleared her throat. "There's an old cistern on the property. Abandoned a hundred years ago. Past the back field, where the original homestead was. It's... not easy to find, even if you know it's there."

Harold showed emotion for the first time. "I know where that is! Yeah, I can show you."

Tara nodded, bowing her head. "I *knew* you were spending too much time there. I knew you would find it."

CHAPTER 55

*N*elson nodded. He stepped to the side to show that he was a man of his word and Tara could pass. Della stood there for a moment longer, making sure they understood that it was her own choice.

Tara looked at the gun where she had tossed it on the bed, deciding whether to go back for it or not. Nelson shook his head. She sighed and walked through the door.

Once out of the room, she was out of view of the camera Willie had set up, but she was right outside the door of room 109, and they could clearly hear the action.

"Tara Waldon, you're under arrest for attempted murder," a familiar voice stated clearly.

Tara's voice was flustered at first, but then she tried, as always, to talk her way out of it. "What? What are you doing here? How…? This is entrapment! You had your girlfriend send me over here and then ambushed me. I didn't admit to anything. Anything I said in that room is… the fruit of the poisoned tree. Besides, I only said what I did to get out of there! They were holding me at gunpoint, what did you expect me to do?"

Terry read Tara her rights despite her protests. Erin went to the door and peeked out. Terry spotted her and scowled.

"*There* you are. You want to tell me exactly what you were doing here? Exactly how did everyone happen to get here, and you just happened to witness an encounter between Della and Tara that might turn messy?"

"I just…" Erin thought about what to tell Terry. If they wanted him to see the video, he would have to know that Willie was involved and that they had set up a private sting. And that meant that Erin had been investigating and interfering with the police investigation, despite the number of times she had said she wasn't sticking her nose where it did not belong.

Terry pushed the door open farther, but could not see their set-up from there. Under his stern gaze, Erin pulled the privacy curtain back so Terry could see Willie and the monitoring equipment.

"You've got to be kidding."

"You can watch the video," Erin told Terry, "you can see on the recording that the police were not involved. No one can accuse you of having anything to do with it…"

Nelson exited room 108 into the hallway and followed Terry's gaze into room 109. His jaw dropped, and he stared at the ghost before him.

Willie stood up as though he could pull the curtain closed and Nelson would unsee what he had seen.

Nelson put his hand on the doorframe to steady himself, swearing.

"How could…? You're not…"

Terry looked at him. "Well, I guess the cat is out of the bag now."

"This is not possible," Nelson murmured. "It was fake? I saw the video. Everybody knows…"

"It was faked," Willie admitted, standing up and walking toward Nelson. "I'm sorry I couldn't let you know, give you a heads-up. Your reactions had to be genuine. No one in the clan could know, including you."

Nelson swore again, admiringly this time. "We read your will. I guess you already figured that. It was all planned out ahead of time. You planned to get me into position. And then… what?

What are you doing here? Why aren't you in Mexico or something?"

Willie looked uncomfortable. "Well, you were not supposed to see me yet. I didn't anticipate you coming here, or…" Willie motioned to the curtain Erin had pulled back. He shook his head. "I've just been keeping my head down, waiting until you were firmly entrenched."

"You cunning fox. But you couldn't resist coming out to play and seeing what was going on with these… ladies." Nelson looked at Tara and at Della and Harold standing in the doorway of room 108, "and Harold."

"Harold wasn't supposed to be here," Erin said, staring at Della. "Why would you put him into a situation like this?"

Della met her gaze calmly. "He was armed and protected. This was about him too; she was trying to destroy him," Della glared at Tara with disgust. "Of course he had the right to be here when this happened."

"Speaking of which…" Terry held his hands out. "Your weapons."

"The Tennessee Code allows us to carry," Della said, not making any move to hand her gun over. "It's our constitutional right."

"And there was a notice as you entered the building telling you that firearms are prohibited in the building except by security or police. And Harold is not old enough to carry."

Della scowled. "We will take them out ourselves. There is no need for us to stay here."

"You're going to need to answer some questions."

"She is the one you want," Della indicated Tara. "She is the one who has been causing all of the trouble and trying to kill people. It has nothing to do with me. You can see and hear everything that was heard on the video."

"I didn't consent to being recorded," Tara protested. "You can't do that!"

"Tennessee is a one-party-consent state," Terry advised. "If Mrs. Melville consented to the recording, it is legal."

"You can't do that!"

"We would like you to be available to answer questions—" Terry turned back to Della to continue the conversation.

"Watch the tape," Della snapped. "We have other things to do. Inspecting that cistern, for one thing."

"Uh, that will be a police matter. We will be the ones responsible for the removal of any human remains."

Della rolled her eyes and looked like she would protest it further, but Nelson shook his head. "Of course the police will handle any human remains," he confirmed. "Would you really want to do that yourself? It's not going to be pretty. They'll turn the bones over once they have been identified, and we can see that Jason is properly buried with the family."

Della folded her arms and did not object further to Terry's suggestion. "Fine. We are leaving. You don't have any reason to detain us. You got the person you were looking for."

Terry didn't look happy about it, but allowed Della and Harold to leave without any further objection. Erin wanted to talk to Harold, but didn't have any privacy there, so she resolved to talk to him later about everything that had happened.

Nelson lingered. He looked at Erin, who was blocking the doorway into room 109. "If I could have a private moment with Willie…?"

Erin moved into the corridor and let Nelson pass. He entered the room and shut the door. Erin heard the bolt slide, locking it securely.

That left her with Terry and Tara in the hallway.

"Attempted murder?" Erin asked, frowning. Tara had confessed to concealing the bodies of Jason and Ashley and, by extension, to murder, but that was not what Terry had arrested her for. They would have to investigate before they could charge her with anything on that matter.

"Frank Grayson," Terry advised. "He has woken up and given a statement about being attacked in his home by Miss Waldon."

"Where is he?" Tara demanded. "I thought he was supposed to be here!" She gestured to the room.

"No..." Terry looked puzzled. "He is still in the hospital in the city."

Erin shrugged. "I might have told her that he had recovered and was here and had some evidence he wanted to share with me later today."

"Oh, I see. Is that so? Well, sadly, Miss Waldon, you were misled. Frank is still in the city, and he is talking to the police, not Miss Price. That's how things are done around here."

Terry gave Tara a little tug. "We're going to have a little talk at the police department now, Miss Waldon."

"This is all a big misunderstanding. I don't know why everyone is ganging up on me. There's nothing to link me to these letters, the poisoning, or anything else!"

"We'll just see about that. It takes a while for forensic evidence to be processed, but we are starting to get our reports back."

Tara continued to protest, but he ignored her complaints.

"And you," Terry looked at Erin and then at the locked door behind which Willie and Nelson were having a long discussion. "I guess we have some talking to do too."

Erin shrugged evasively. "I think we've already discussed everything I was able to find out. Willie will give you the recording for everything you couldn't hear."

Terry tried to look stern, but the dimple in his cheek gave him away. He just shook his head and escorted Tara down the hallway toward the main doors.

CHAPTER 56

$\mathcal{E}$rin set the trays of eclairs down on the counter in the community center kitchen. She looked around, monitoring the rest of the activity. People were bringing food for the potluck, lining up the various pots and dishes along the buffet tables that lined one side of the meeting room.

"Do you think people will eat the eclairs?" she asked Vic softly to avoid being overheard. "After what happened at the Historical Club meeting? People might feel... anxious about it."

"If you stay here and keep an eye on them, everyone will know they are safe."

Erin nodded. It wouldn't hurt her to hang out in the kitchen and supervise rather than running back and forth to the vehicles helping get everything set up.

Vic put down the box she had carried in and rested for a moment.

"Did they find out what she put in the eclairs?"

"When they searched her house, she had a lot of boiled rhubarb leaves in her compost. They'll do testing, but they think that's probably what it was."

"Rhubarb leaves?" Vic shook her head. "Mercy. Whoever would have thought?"

"Tara, apparently. And you heard that they found the stationery at her house?"

"Thus proving she was the letter writer," Vic agreed. "I heard it from Melissa while you were out."

"And Melissa!" Erin remembered. "What about proving that Tara tampered with the microphone to try to electrocute someone?"

"Melissa didn't say anything about it. And I assume she would, if she knew. But they're still investigating. If they find Tara's fingerprints on any of the wiring or equipment, that will be proof, right?"

Erin shrugged. "As long as she wasn't involved in setting up the sound system for something legitimate. I don't know. Terry says she is still acting like she is the victim in all of this."

Vic rolled her eyes and shook her head.

"Speaking of wiring…" Erin paused while people brought in more boxes, set them down, and departed. "How is you-know-who getting along with his old partner? Does he think he can be resurrected soon?"

Vic nodded, her cheeks flushing a little. "Yeah, they're getting it worked out. He should be able to show his face again before too long."

"Good."

Erin stayed with the eclairs as everything else was set up, and people started to quiet down as they anticipated being fed. The array of food on the tables for the potluck was incredible, and the air was laden with the delicious smells released from each dish as it was uncovered.

Mary Lou was the unofficial woman in charge of the community gathering. She stood at the front of the room and waved away the microphone that was offered to her. It might be a while before anyone took hold of a mic without thinking about it.

Mary Lou smoothed her pantsuit and smiled briefly at the neighbors gathered before her. "Well… this is lovely. Thank you, everyone, for your contributions to Erin at Auntie Clem's Bakery for our desserts this evening and to everyone who helped to coordinate and get the invitations out. Our community has been through some difficult times the last few weeks, and we wanted to come together to support each other and break bread… so here we are."

There was a murmur of laughter from the waiting neighbors. "Bella Prost will offer grace, and then—dig in!"

There was a whoop, then quiet as Bella gave the called-for prayer, and then people lined up with plates in hand to dish up.

Erin saw a few people lingering at the door, hesitating about coming in. She approached them.

"Come on. You don't want to miss out on the grub," she invited.

Harold looked at the long line of tables. "It sure smells good," he offered.

"I'm sure it will all be delicious. Go on, get in line."

He still hesitated. "I don't know if people will want us here."

"They know now that you did not write the letters. That you were just a victim."

"Yeah, but it's more than that. We're outsiders and Dysons."

"Come in. You're my special guests. And if anyone says anything, they will have to deal with me."

Harold gave a little laugh. "Okay," he agreed finally, and headed over to join the line.

Della looked at Erin. "Getting a head start on being a mama bear?"

"Nobody harasses my employees. And Harold was an ally before he ever came to ask for a job at Auntie Clem's. He's a…" She didn't think 'sweet boy' would fly with Della when she wanted him to be the leader of the Dyson Clan. "He's a fine young man, and I'm proud to have him working for me."

"Thank you." Della nodded. "I appreciate you standing up for him when others were attacking."

She motioned for Salman and Anton, hanging around listening to the conversation, to help themselves to the food. They eagerly went on ahead.

"How are *you*?" Erin asked. "Having to deal with your brother's and Ashley's remains being found on your property…"

"It was always a sore spot with the clan. Some people may have thought they just ran away one day, but those of us who were close knew that wasn't what had happened." She sighed. "But you have to keep some things under the radar when you're in our position. If there had been a big investigation into what had happened, it would not be good for the clan. And as much as we might have wanted to retaliate, Dwight wanted to honor Ashley's wishes that we not do anything to hurt Tara."

"Now that you know what happened to them… does that bring you some satisfaction?"

Della considered for a moment and then shook her head. "No. I can't say I'm any happier having found them and knowing that their killer is behind bars. My brother is still dead, and not over something important, but because some crazy… old bat, as Anton likes to say, decided he had done her wrong."

Erin nodded. Jason had definitely done Tara wrong, but for Tara to retaliate by killing both him and her own sister was incomprehensible.

"Well, have something to eat. I'm glad you guys came. And save some room for chocolate eclairs for dessert."

Did you enjoy this book? Reviews and recommendations are vital to making a book successful.

Please leave a review at your favorite book store or review site and share it with your friends.

Don't miss the following bonus material:
Sign up for mailing list to get a free ebook
Read a sneak preview chapter
Other books by P.D. Workman
Learn more about the author

Your First Bite – Cozy Mystery Starter Pack

Get Your First Taste of Murder and Muffins at pdworkman.com!
Start your cozy escape with a free ebook + audiobook, printable
recipe cards, and more.

PREVIEW OF QUICHE
ME GOODBYE

PREVIEW CHAPTER 1

*S*tanding on the grass in the backyard, looking into the woods behind the house, Erin moved through her tai chi forms slowly, stretching and flexing her muscles as she moved through each of the familiar movements. The sky turned from blue to orange, and the sun dipped behind the trees. Cicadas buzzed in the trees.

It had been a long day, at the end of a long week, and she was sure the upcoming week would not be any more restful. Though she had to admit that she was eager for the festival to get under way after the weeks of anticipation. Who knew that a food festival took so much preparation? She wasn't even the organizer, but she felt like she had been swept into someone else's life, no longer just a humble gluten-free baker, but a foodie, a participant in The World's Largest Festival Celebrating the Humble Chickpea. She didn't even care about the contests and awards; she had just wanted to participate in what had seemed like a fun local tradition. A lighthearted way to kick off the summer with food, fun, and festivities.

Maybe it was not such a good thing that the festival organizers had decided that Bald Eagle Falls was just the place to hold the festival when the previously selected host town had been struck with a large water main break that might take the entire summer to fix.

Bald Eagle Falls had been familiar to the organizers of the festival because of the tragedy that had occurred there some months earlier, when Gerald Montgomery, a celebrated food critic, had died suddenly after eating Erin's debut Morning Sunrise muffin. Rather than being disastrous for business at Auntie Clem's Bakery, as Erin had feared, Montgomery's death had spurred tourism to the tiny Tennessee town as Montgomery's fans and followers took their pilgrimage to Bald Eagle Falls to get a taste of the gluten-free strawberry compote muffins that had been the cause of the icon's death. Though the idea seemed morbid, Erin welcomed the Instagrammers and influencers, giving them a selfie-worthy experience and accepting their generous tips.

The rest of the town couldn't complain about the extra business the pilgrims brought to Bald Eagle Falls buying mementos at the General Store, staying at the new B&Bs that had sprung up, and spending their money at the grocery store or restaurants. And now, bringing the chickpea festival to town at the last moment when Moose River had found themselves unexpectedly underwater.

Erin heard Vic open the door from within the loft apartment over the garage and come most of the way down the stairs attached to the outside of the building. She knew without having to turn to look that Vic had taken up her customary seat on the stairs to watch the sunset and wait for Erin to finish her tai chi before going inside for a cup of sleepy tea and conversation before bed.

After Erin had moved to Bald Eagle Falls to claim her legacy following Clementine's demise, Vic had quickly become her best friend. Erin had taken in the young, homeless, and recently outed trans woman who had been sleeping in the basement of Clementine's old tea shop, which Erin had transformed into Auntie Clem's Bakery. Neither Erin nor Vic had been particularly popular in Bald Eagle Falls in the early days, and they had relied upon each other for company and support.

Erin drew her practice to a close, standing and holding the final position for a few extra breaths. Then she relaxed her muscles and sighed.

"How has your evening been?" she asked her young employee, turning her gaze to the willowy blond sitting on the stairs. Erin swiped a few dark, stray hairs away from her own face in irritation. She didn't spend much time fussing over her looks, but did sometimes feel like an ugly duckling; or a duckling who had never managed to figure out how to do her hair and makeup properly, when comparing herself with Vic.

It wasn't like they had been apart for long. They had closed Auntie Clem's Bakery together only a few hours earlier. But Erin never tired of Vic's company. They always found things to talk about. Or they just worked or sat in companionable silence while Erin rewrote lists in her planner and tried to think of what else needed to be done before the festival kicked off in a few days.

"Quieter than a whisper," Vic advised. "I'm telling you... I thought I would be happy when people found out that Willie's death had been faked and people stopped bringing me flowers and casseroles... but the silence has been... unsettling."

People had been rather chilly toward Vic and Erin since they learned about the deception. But Erin didn't know what people expected them to have done. They'd had to keep Willie's secret until it was safe for him to make it known that he was still alive. And they'd never *told* anyone he was dead; that news had been spread by those of the Dyson clan who were loyal to Willie and helped with the plot to get him out of the criminal syndicate.

"Folks don't really care what we said," Vic said, as though she could read Erin's mind. "We definitely let them believe that Willie was dead, and I accepted their gifts and condolences as if he was." She let out a heavy sigh. "It's going to be a long time before they forgive me for that."

Erin nodded. She couldn't disagree with Vic's sentiment. It looked like it would be a long time before the townspeople forgave them. But Terry assured her that they wouldn't hold a grudge forever.

She wasn't sure she believed it, after learning about some of the grudges and feuds that had been going on in Bald Eagle Falls for generations. Maybe her great-grandchildren would be forgiven for Erin's deception. But she wasn't sure *she* ever would be.

"Let's go in for tea," Vic suggested.

Erin nodded, and they walked together into her kitchen. She put on the kettle and puttered around while she waited for it to boil.

They had just barely sat down at the table when there was a sharp knock on the front door. Erin looked at the clock on the wall. Bakers kept very early hours, needing the time to get the bread, muffins, and other goodies baked before opening the door for the before-work crowd, so they also headed to bed early. But although it was getting close to their bedtime, it was still early enough in the evening not to be considered rude to pop in for a visit.

Erin shrugged and stood. "I'll be right back," she promised.

PREVIEW CHAPTER 2

*E*rin was never sure who to expect at the door. She had been targeted by some nasty characters since she had moved to Bald Eagle Falls. But the slim figure on the other side of the fisheye peephole was familiar and not someone she was afraid to open the door to.

"Joshua!" Erin greeted the teen with a smile and motioned for him to enter. "Come on in, how are you?"

Joshua smiled and entered. He made his way to the kitchen when he saw Vic at the table there. He pushed dark, wavy hair back from his eyes.

"I don't suppose you want tea," Erin said, "but how about a cookie?"

Joshua grinned. "Well, you know I'm always up for a treat," he admitted.

Erin smiled and opened the freezer to see what she had for him. Joshua was a growing boy, and his family was on a tight budget, so he didn't get a lot of treats. His lanky form was just starting to fill out. He would be a handsome man, in Erin's opinion. He had the same dark, wavy hair as Campbell, his older brother, but didn't have the same hardness in his face, even after being kidnapped and after all the tragedies his family had suffered.

Erin thawed a few cookies in the microwave and put them in the center of the table, distributing smaller plates to the rest of them. Erin didn't allow herself a lot of treats. She did not have Vic's height, and every pound she gained showed at her waist. But she decided to indulge in one cookie with her friends tonight.

She sipped her tea and nibbled a ginger cookie. "How is your family?" she asked Joshua.

"Everyone is okay," Joshua said with a shrug.

His bar for "okay" was probably lower than most people's. They were not financially secure. His father suffered from cognitive and emotional problems, was heavily medicated to prevent violent outbursts, and required a lot of work on Joshua and Mary Lou's parts. Cam had dropped out of school and moved to the city. Joshua had dealt with a lot of challenges personally, most recently the disappearance of Mary Lou, his mother. But she was back now, so he didn't have to handle everything alone.

"How is Mary Lou?" Vic asked.

"She's fine," Joshua said automatically. But his lips thinned and turned down, and worry lines deepened between his eyes. "She hasn't been the same since she came back."

"Is there anything we can do?" Erin offered. Her first thought was for what they could take to Mary Lou. A box of baking to lighten the financial load and the amount of work she had to do to prepare meals. But food probably wasn't what she needed. Their financial circumstances had not changed so much as Mary Lou's outlook and her worries that people would recall her relationship with Willie when they had both been young, a past she had been able to bury, but was too close to the surface now.

Josh shook his head. "No. She's doing the best she can, and... there's nothing anyone can do about what people think about her disappearing or... anything." Joshua took a big bite of a cookie, which he chewed in silence for a while.

When he swallowed that mouthful, he forced a smile and changed the subject.

"I wondered how things were going with your preparations for the 'Bald Eagle Falls Chickpea Palooza, a Taste of Togetherness and Festival of Friendship.'" He grinned.

"What a name!" Erin laughed. "Let's just stick with Chickpea Palooza."

"That rolls off the tongue a little more easily," Vic admitted. "What a grand name for a little food festival."

Erin nodded her agreement. "I don't know what possessed them to make it so long. It's crazy."

"I guess they really want it to be about getting together, not just about chickpeas," Joshua said. "That seems to be where the marketing is focused. I guess they figured chickpeas themselves wouldn't be enough to get people out."

"Well... they might be right," Erin allowed. "Most people I know rarely even eat chickpeas. Unless they are vegetarian or from some other country. The chickpeas on the grocery shelves here had been sitting on the shelf for quite a while."

"But..." Vic said, her voice encouraging Erin to expound further, and Erin knew she had spent way too much time extolling the humble chickpea over the past few weeks.

She grinned at Vic. "But they are a great source of protein and extremely versatile," she told Joshua. "You can use them in all kinds of foods, savory and sweet. You can use the chickpeas whole or mashed, use the brine or cooking water as an egg substitute, or grind chickpeas into flour for baking."

"Gluten-free?" Josh guessed.

"How did you know? Chickpeas—or garbanzo beans, they are the same thing—are entirely gluten-free and the flour is light and sweet and works in all kinds of applications."

Josh laughed. "So I've heard," he said. "I've been trying to get interviews with all of the contestants, and they've been talking my ear off about the humble legume."

"So... do you know what everyone is planning to make?" Erin asked with interest.

"People are pretty closed mouthed about their planned dishes. But I can guess what a few of them will be."

Erin leaned forward. She took another sip of her tea, waiting to hear what Josh could tell her. The more she knew about her rivals and their entries in the festivity's contests, the better. She might need to adjust her own repertoire, and while she had been baking all kinds of test products, she hadn't yet made the final decision as to what she was going to enter. It would help her to know what everyone else had in mind.

"What did you mean about cooking with the brine?" Josh asked. "Wouldn't that be... salty and gross?"

"Well, it's not brine like you use to make pickles," Erin assured him, letting herself get distracted momentarily. "There is some salt, if you're using canned chickpeas. But not if you're cooking your own. But you can whip it up like egg whites to make a meringue. You wouldn't believe it, but the proteins in the aquafaba—"

"Here we go..." Vic intoned.

Erin rolled her eyes and sat back. "You can use it as an egg whites substitute in some baking," Erin said flatly. "Now, don't think I'm going to let you get away with distracting me. What do you know about what the other contestants are making?"

"Well, I don't know if I should," Josh teased. "You know, I have professional ethics..."

"If you want to get anything out of me, you have to dish," Erin told him sternly. "You can't just use me as a source."

"Well..." Josh's hand hovered over the plate of cookies as he considered his next choice. "I wouldn't want to give away any trade secrets..."

"You know you're going to tell me. So get on with it."

Josh shrugged. "Well, who do you know out of the competitors?"

"I don't know anyone really well. Marty Lawson and I have run into each other a few times at other events. She specializes in Mediterranean foods, so I guess she knows lots of traditional dishes that use chickpeas."

Josh nodded. "I don't know what she's making, but she seems to know her stuff."

That wasn't news to Erin. She knew Marty's reputation and how much Marty bragged about her own knowledge and skills.

"You didn't find *anything* out about her?" Erin prodded, appealing to his investigative reporter's mind.

"Sure, I found out plenty about her. She comes from a family of restauranteurs. She's toured all over the Mediterranean, learning about the cultures and how to make their traditional dishes."

Erin didn't know how she, who had never been out of the country except for a quick trip through Vancouver on the way to their Alaskan tour, could compete with Marty's experience. She had certainly never been to Europe.

"So you figure she'll do some kind of traditional chickpea dish."

Josh shrugged. "That would be a good guess. But I'm sure she wouldn't confirm or deny it if I suggested it."

Erin agreed. Marty was a force to be reckoned with. A brusque older woman who didn't have much tolerance for other people's opinions. Someone who knew it all and wasn't afraid to tell anyone so.

"So, who else?" Erin asked. "Do you actually have any information, or are you just going to keep teasing me and hoping that I tell you something you don't already know?"

Josh put his hand on his chest in mock hurt. "Would I do that?"

Vic and Erin both nodded. "We know how good you are at getting the scoop," Vic encouraged. "So…?"

"Well… how about Frankie Delaney?"

"The food truck guy?" Erin asked. "I've seen him. Well, he's pretty hard to miss, isn't he?" She giggled. The food truck owner was a gawky-looking man with bright pink hair done up in a bun, held in place with a pair of chopsticks or other kitchen implements.

Josh chuckled. "He does stand out a little, doesn't he?"

"Like a sore thumb," Vic agreed. "I think he might be a few fries short of a Happy Meal." She giggled.

"Have you eaten at his food truck?"

Erin shook her head. "I suppose I should take the opportunity to check out the competition and what he can do."

"He makes grilled cheese sandwiches," Joshua offered.

Erin nodded slowly. "Seems like sort of a limited repertoire."

"But he doesn't just make your average grilled cheese sandwich. He has all kinds of different breads and cheeses, and he adds different condiments and additional ingredients. And serves them with fries or other sides. It ends up being quite a varied menu."

"But it's still just grilled cheese sandwiches."

Josh shrugged. "Just grilled cheese sandwiches," he agreed. "So what do you think he's making for the competitions?"

"Grilled cheese sandwiches," Vic filled in.

Josh grinned and pointed at her. "Exactly."

"But what kind of grilled cheese sandwiches?" Erin demanded. "Is he going for a chickpea filling with the cheese? Like a vegetarian tuna melt? Or is he going to make a chickpea flour bread? Soca or Cecina? Or an actual yeast-raised loaf that is gluten-free or wheat flour enriched with chickpea four?"

"I don't know," the young reporter admitted. "I thought it was pretty weird to put chickpeas in grilled cheese sandwiches, so I didn't have a lot of follow-up questions."

"So your startling revelation to me is that the grilled cheese guy is going to make grilled cheese?"

Josh nodded, grinning.

"You're not very much help," Erin told him. "Next, you're going to tell me that the Mexican food truck lady will make chickpea tacos."

"Something like that," Joshua agreed. "I mean... it could be burritos or tostadas. But you can bet it will be some Mexican dish with other beans swapped out for chickpeas. Or chickpeas added."

Erin shook her head.

"Or use socca or another flatbread for the wrap," Vic suggested.

"So you don't really know what anyone is planning," Erin accused.

"I know Frankie is going to make grilled cheese sandwiches," Joshua laughed.

"How about Nina Chu or Liam Harper? Do you know what either of them is planning to do?"

"No," Joshua admitted. "Everyone is playing it pretty close to the vest. Maybe we'll find out more as we get closer to the competitions."

"Not likely."

"What about you? What are you planning to make?" Josh asked. "I'll bet you've got something delicious planned."

Erin and Vic exchanged glances. "Of course I do," Erin agreed. But she didn't tell him what any of the dishes she was experimenting with were. She certainly didn't want to be the only one whose plans were known ahead of time. She wanted her offerings to be a surprise, just like everyone else. "I think the contestant I'm most worried about is Nina, because she's a pastry chef. Chances are, she's going to pick some sweet dessert, which will compete directly with any dessert I make."

"But there's such a wide variety of options," Vic said. "She's not going to pick the same thing."

"But some of them are really trendy right now. The aquafaba meringues, blondie flourless brownies, truffles…"

"Exactly how popular are they?" Josh asked. "I've never heard of any of them."

"But in healthy eating and vegan circles, they are well known. So I don't want to pick anything that is trending right now…"

"And then there's that Liam Harper," Vic pointed out. "He's really into the trendy vegan foods, so he could pick one of them too."

Josh wrinkled his nose. "Liam Harper…"

Erin couldn't help laughing at his expression. Especially after meeting the vegan chef in passing. He had rubbed her the wrong way, and apparently, Joshua had reacted the same way.

"He's a bit much, isn't he?" she laughed. "Maybe I'm mistaking his body language and tone of voice, but… he seems very superior and condescending."

"It's more than that, but yeah!" Joshua shook his head. "The guy is very… abrasive."

"His restaurant is called 'Chickpea Charm,'" Erin said. "You would think that with a name like that, he would be barred from entering the competition. I mean… it's his specialty. He's a professional chickpea cook!"

"Maybe someone should tell him that," Vic said with a chuckle. "I'm sure it would go over really well."

"Yeah," Josh agreed. "I'm sure he would take it with good grace."

They all laughed at the thought.

There was only one way Liam Harper could be eliminated from the competition.

~

Quiche Me Goodbye, Book #27 of the *Auntie Clem's Bakery*
culinary cozy mystery series by P.D. Workman
can be purchased at pdworkman.com

~

ABOUT THE AUTHOR

P.D. Workman is a USA Today Bestselling author and multi-award winner, renowned for her prolific output of over 100 published works that span various genres. With a knack for crafting page-turners, Workman captivates readers with everything from cozy mysteries like the Auntie Clem's Bakery series to gripping young adult and suspense novels.

A prolific reader and writer since childhood, P.D. Workman crafts emotionally powerful stories that don't shy away from hard topics. Her books tackle mental illness, addiction, abuse, and trauma with raw honesty and compassion, giving voice to the often unheard. If you crave authentic, character-driven page-turners that hit deep and stay with you long after the final page, you're in the right place.

With each new release, fans eagerly anticipate another thrilling blend of thought-provoking storytelling and relatable characters that define P.D. Workman's brand as an author of unforgettable page-turners—gripping tales that leave a lasting impact long after the last page is turned.

> P. D. Workman, does not shy from probing the deep psychological scars of childhood trauma, mental illness, and addiction. Also characteristic of this author, these extremely sensitive issues are explored with extensive empathy, described with incredible clarity, and portrayed with profound insight.
>
> — —KIM, GOODREADS REVIEWER

Some of Workman's titles have been translated into Spanish, French, Portuguese, German, and Italian.

Workman began writing at an early age and is a prolific reader as well as writer. She is also passionate about teaching and learning, expresses her creativity through art and cooking, and loves exploring the Calgary parks and green spaces where the Parks Pat Mysteries are set. She was a legal assistant for many years and has done extensive charitable work.

Workman was born and raised in Alberta, Canada, and is married with one adult son.

~

Please visit P.D. Workman at pdworkman.com to see what else she is working on, to join her mailing list, and to link to her social networks.

~

If you enjoyed this book, please take the time to recommend it to other purchasers with a review or star rating and share it with your friends!

tiktok.com/@pdworkmanauthor

facebook.com/pdworkmanauthor

x.com/pdworkmanauthor

instagram.com/pdworkmanauthor

amazon.com/author/pdworkman

bookbub.com/authors/p-d-workman

goodreads.com/pdworkman

linkedin.com/in/pdworkman

pinterest.com/pdworkmanauthor

youtube.com/pdworkman